YOU DO
SOMETHING TO ME

~ New York Sullivans, Book 3 ~

Bella Andre

YOU DO SOMETHING TO ME

~ New York Sullivans, Book 3 ~

© 2017 Bella Andre

Sign up for Bella's New Release Newsletter

www.BellaAndre.com/newsletter

bella@bellaandre.com

www.BellaAndre.com

Bella on Twitter: @bellaandre

Bella on Facebook: facebook.com/bellaandrefans

Alec Sullivan has always believed he has it all. A billion-dollar private aviation business. A penthouse apartment in New York City. Beautiful women who know better than to expect him ever to fall in love. And great siblings for whom he'd do anything. But when Alec's business partner passes away and leaves everything to a daughter Alec never knew about, in an instant everything in his life turns upside down. All because of Cordelia.

Cordelia Langley always thought she was perfectly happy with her life. She owns a garden store she loves, lives in a pretty little cottage in the same town as her adoptive parents, and figures there's plenty of time to meet Mr. Right. But she never counted on becoming the surprise heir to a fortune—or on meeting a man like Alec Sullivan. A shockingly sexy billionaire who makes her heart race and melt all at the same time.

Neither Alec nor Cordelia plans on getting any closer than they have to. Only, how can either of them fight this kind of heat, this depth of desire? And when Cordelia needs Alec's support, it's pure instinct for him to be there for her. But when it's her turn to help him confront his deepest pain, will Alec let her in? Or will he push her away, just as he's pushed away everyone who's loved him for the past thirty years…

A note from Bella

Nothing makes me happier than writing about a Sullivan falling in love! Especially a hero like Alec Sullivan, who is absolutely positive that he'll never be touched by love. I simply couldn't wait to prove him wrong and I thought I knew exactly how it was all going to go down.

I should know by now that whenever I think I know how a story is going to unfold, it will go in a completely different direction! From the very first day that I sat down to write *You Do Something To Me*, I was shocked. Because as soon as I gave Alec his own story, he turned out to be one of the most breathtakingly romantic, loving, *wonderful* Sullivan heroes of all time.

Can you tell how much I adore him?

So. Very. Much.

I absolutely cannot wait for you to read Alec and Cordelia's story. I wrote it while sitting outside in my own garden and I hope you can find a bloom-filled spot of your own to enjoy it.

Please be sure to sign up for my newsletter (bellaandre.com/newsletter) so you don't miss out on any new book release announcements.

Happy reading!
Bella Andre

CHAPTER ONE

Alec Sullivan hated surprises.

When he turned thirty, his sister, Suzanne, threw him a surprise birthday party. He'd had a hell of a day at the office dealing with a new aviation engine company that had promised him the best and had delivered anything but. Finding fifty people in his apartment expecting smiles and laughter and small talk over birthday cake was the very last thing he'd wanted. Five years later, Suzanne was still apologizing for that night, even though they both knew she'd just been trying to make him happy.

Alec would do anything for his sister and his brothers, Harry and Drake. He'd been taking care of the three of them since he was five and their mother had taken her own life, leaving his father as wrecked as a man could be—and unable to be a father anymore.

Which was where Gordon Whitley had come into the picture. He'd been Alec's boss out of business school and then Alec's business partner. They'd built S&W Aviation together.

And Gordon had been the father figure Alec never had.

Yesterday, Alec had found Gordon on the floor by his desk. Alec had dropped to Gordon's side, pleading with his friend to wake up, yelling for his executive assistant to call 911. But he'd been too late. The heart attack had been massive, all Gordon's years of joking that he should drink less and exercise more suddenly coming to an end in the middle of the workday.

Gordon's eyes had opened for only a moment, his lips forming one word: *"Cordelia."*

And then he was gone.

The blow of losing Gordon was bad enough. Twenty-four hours later, Alec still felt cold, and his gut hadn't stopped churning. But as Alec worked to process what Gordon's trust attorney had just told him, he felt as though he'd been hit by a second blow.

A blow so big he was still having trouble believing what he'd just been told was true.

"Gordon had a daughter." Alec's lawyer, Ezra, and Gordon's lawyer, Caleb, remained silent while Alec processed the shocking information aloud. "She's twenty-five, lives in Yorktown...and apart from the 1934 Packard convertible he wants me to have, he's willed her all of his worldly possessions. Including his half of our company."

Gordon Whitley was the kind of guy you expected

to live forever. But Alec had always assumed that if something did happen to his friend and partner, he'd end up with Gordon's share of the company. At the very least, that extra one percent that meant no one could tell him what to do with S&W Aviation.

"Has she been informed of her inheritance yet?" Alec asked.

"I've spoken with her briefly on the phone, but will be meeting with her directly after leaving your office," Caleb replied.

Had she and Gordon been close? Had this wind-fall—making her a seriously rich woman who now owned half of the most successful private aviation company in the world—been one she'd known would come one day?

Or would she be as surprised as Alec by this news?

Alec had trusted Gordon implicitly. He'd believed there were no secrets between them. How could there be when they'd worked side by side every day for nearly twenty years?

Cordelia Langley was one hell of a secret.

He bit back a curse as he rubbed his chest, where everything felt tight. He was in perfect health, but it still hurt like the devil to lose his closest friend. A friend who had kept something *huge* from him.

"Set up a meeting with her here," he told Caleb. "Tomorrow. She and I need to talk."

Alec had known about Cordelia for only five minutes, but he'd already begun to put together a plan. His brain had always worked like that, even back when he was five and his father had told him that his mother was gone. Alec had immediately started making plans for how he was going to take care of Harry, Suzanne, and Drake. Because he'd known his father couldn't do it. And now that his siblings were fully grown and totally capable adults, Alec still watched over them. He always would.

After Gordon's attorney had gone, Alec turned to his lawyer. "I'll have the details of my buyout plan to you before I turn in tonight, so that you can draft it in ironclad legal terms."

Ezra didn't seem surprised by Alec's intention to buy Cordelia out of the company. It was, after all, the only part of this that made any sense.

"I'm sorry, Alec. Sorry we lost him." Ezra looked morose as he pushed out of his seat, gathered his files, and headed for the elevator. "Gordon was a good man."

Closing the door, Alec was tempted to pour himself a glass of the Irish whiskey that he and Gordon had often shared at the end of a long day, whether to celebrate a big win or commiserate a rare loss. No business loss had ever stung this badly, though. Or made Alec feel so empty inside.

But Alec's phone was ringing—a royal from a small country in Europe was waiting for a tour of S&W's best jets.

His silent toast in honor of the best friend he'd ever had would have to wait.

* * *

The following day, as Cordelia stared up at the shiny office building in Scarsdale, New York, one of the wealthiest cities in America, her heart was pounding out an uneven rhythm inside her chest.

Half of this building was hers now, as was half of the massive list of private planes that Gordon Whitley's trust attorney had given her. Along with a staggering list of customers that included some of the wealthiest, most-well-known people on the planet. Actors and actresses she'd watched at the movies. Billionaire tech founders. Even royalty.

Cordelia had spent the past twenty-four hours trying to come to grips with this shocking information. But she was still having trouble with it.

A *lot* of trouble.

Of course she'd wondered who her birth parents were. What adopted kid didn't? Her mom and dad were great—warm, loving, completely supportive of her in every way. They'd never pushed her into situations that made her uncomfortable. They had always understood that she was happier with plants—she'd planted her own vegetable garden when she was five, her first rose garden a year later—than she was with big groups of people. Or ever would have been inside an office.

Her group of friends was small and loyal. Her life running an organic vegetable and flower garden center in a sleepy suburban town was a good one. She was right where she wanted to be—working in the sun and the rain with soil and seeds all day. Then settling down at night with a cup of tea in her small, cute cottage at the back of her property.

The lawyer beside her cleared his throat. "Ms. Langley, are you ready to go inside now?"

She nearly snorted aloud. *Ready?* She was anything but ready for any of this.

Because for all that she'd wondered about her birth father, she'd never imagined he'd owned something this massive, this impressive.

Once she was old enough to understand, her parents had told her everything they knew. Her birth mother had passed away having her, and her birth father had put her up for adoption immediately. He'd chosen her parents personally, though they'd never met him. Her birth father had opted to remain anonymous, rather than put his name on file to be opened when she came of age, leaving only a short letter for her parents.

Please give my daughter everything I can't.
I'm trusting you both with her life, with
her happiness.

Her parents had given her the letter when she graduated from college with a degree in botany, the same day they'd surprised her with the greatest graduation gift in the world—one acre of land to grow her future on. It was a major extravagance for two schoolteachers and she'd vowed never to let them down—to do whatever it took to live up to the promise they saw in her.

Three years later, she had a small, thriving nursery business…and now, shockingly, a billion-dollar stake in a private aviation company. Courtesy of the man who had given her up the day she was born.

Cordelia wanted nothing more than to be in her garden now—the private one in front of her cottage, where she'd planted alyssum for the butterflies, dahlias for the hummingbirds, and cosmos for the bees. But all the wishing in the world wouldn't change the facts.

Gordon Whitley was her birth father…and he'd given her the keys to his kingdom.

She understood that most people would call this the lottery win of the century. But Cordelia knew without a shadow of doubt that this life—fancy airplanes and celebrity clients and more money than she could wrap her head around—wasn't for her.

Today, she was here for only one reason. To sell her share of the company to Gordon Whitley's business partner. She'd take a small amount of her unexpected inheritance to make her parents' lives better, give the rest to charity, then return to her normal, quiet life among the blooms and the birds. As if none of this had ever happened. As if it hadn't turned out that her birth father had been less than thirty minutes away all along, but had never reached out, never tried to contact her, never tried to get to know her, even as an adult.

Working hard to push away the sting in her chest, she took a deep breath, straightened her shoulders, and lifted her chin. "I'm ready."

CHAPTER TWO

From his office window, Alec watched Cordelia standing out on the sidewalk. She was pretty, dark haired, and slim, with a definite resemblance to Gordon. She wasn't the kind of woman Alec would notice in a bar, nor was she the type of woman with whom he'd roll around in the sheets. He dated only women who understood that he was in for a good time, for pleasure—not *forever*.

Cordelia had paused in front of his building—her building too, until she accepted his buyout offer—for several minutes. She hadn't looked impressed. Hadn't looked scared either. She'd looked more confused than anything. As though she hadn't yet been able to wrap her head around her enormous inheritance.

That made two of them.

Alec had barely slept since learning of her existence. He'd wanted to do his research on Cordelia thoroughly, because the kind of offer that would work for a ball-buster with visions of taking over the corporate world was completely different from the proposition he'd make for a small-town girl who had been tossed completely out of her league.

Cordelia Langley was in her mid-twenties and unmarried. She'd grown up in suburban Yorktown with her adoptive parents, Amy and Walter Langley, who were both teachers. She hadn't played on any sports teams or been a member of school clubs growing up, apart from the garden club. She'd graduated from Pace University, just up the road from where she'd grown up, then opened her own garden center at twenty-two. She lived alone in a small cottage on site.

The picture his research painted was clear: Cordelia was a quiet, simple woman. One who must feel *way* in over her head with all of this. Odds were definitely in his favor that she was dying to unload it all.

Alec had to marvel yet again at the fact that his often ruthless business partner, a man who had dreamed big and achieved even more, was in any way related to a woman who grew flowers for a living. Alec had a heck of a lot of issues with his own father, but in truth, the apple hadn't fallen all that far from the tree. At one time, William Sullivan had been the most successful painter in the world. Giving it up to build homes on a lake in the Adirondacks hadn't changed who he really was at his core: driven to be the best. Just as Alec had always been driven to succeed. To win. To triumph.

Which was why he was prepared to make this transition as easy as possible for Cordelia with an extremely generous buyout offer. Honestly, he couldn't imagine a scenario in which she'd want to keep her half of S&W Aviation. She was likely counting the minutes until she could be back in her garden, knees in the soil, trowel in hand.

Hearing footsteps outside his office, Alec put on a smile and moved to greet Cordelia. But his step—and his smile—both faltered when he came face to face with her.

Alec had never seen eyes so green. Or a mouth so soft, so sweet-looking. And his palms had never gone sweaty in front of a beautiful woman before.

From the window, he'd thought she was merely pretty. But now he knew that had been a dire miscalculation. Because the undeniable truth was that she looked like a breath of fresh air on a perfect blue-sky day.

Damn it, sweaty palms were one thing. Spouting poetry was another. He was obviously more thrown off his game than he'd thought by his partner's sudden death and the news that Gordon had a daughter.

"Cordelia." As Alec offered her his hand, it struck him how perfectly her name suited her. Elegant and slightly old-fashioned, but beautiful nonetheless. "Thank you for coming to meet with me today. I'm Alec Sullivan, your father's business partner."

She hesitated for a moment before putting her hand in his. A moment that somehow felt longer than it really was—thereby affording him an even better glimpse into her stunning eyes, which were not just green, but flecked with gold all around the iris. Her breathing seemed slightly uneven as she faced him and he could see the pulse point at her neck jumping beneath her skin. Her hand was small, but strong, likely a byproduct of working all day in a garden. At the same time, her palm, her fingers, were surprisingly soft.

"He's not my father." Her unexpectedly fierce statement had Alec squeezing her fingers before he realized he had to let her go.

"I've been told in no uncertain terms that he was your father."

Her mouth set in a line as anger—and something that looked like grief—flashed across her face. "Biologically, yes. Any other way, no."

Alec found himself surprised yet again. Her grip and her personality were much stronger than he'd expected from his research.

Had he miscalculated his buyout offer?

No. It would be best just to get this done and over with. Not only because he had a business to run, but also because she clearly didn't want anything to do with her birth father.

"Come on into my office and make yourself comfortable." Their lawyers were already seated inside. He'd arranged for them all to sit on the couches rather than around the conference table, as the informality would help keep Cordelia from feeling too out of her depth. He didn't want to frighten her. He just wanted to close the buyout deal as painlessly and quickly as possible. "Can I get you anything to drink or eat?" His office was stocked with everything from the finest champagnes to Coke, from caviar to cheese puffs. Whatever his clients wanted, they got. It was how Alec and Gordon had built the most prestigious, and the most profitable, private aviation company in the world.

"No, thank you."

Her back was ramrod straight, her hands clasped tightly in her lap. In other words, she wasn't nearly comfortable enough yet to agree to a deal. Fortunately, putting women at ease was one of Alec's greatest skills. Young or old, quiet or loud, introverted or extroverted—he had never met a woman he couldn't charm. He was certain that Cordelia would be no exception.

Taking out a carafe of sparkling water and four glasses despite her refusal of his hospitality, he poured each of them a glass, then smiled and said, "I hope your drive was a good one, without too much late morning traffic?"

"The drive was fine."

Her terse answer didn't daunt him. "I've heard the heavy rain we had this winter made it an especially good year for blooms. Even the sides of the roads are thick with flowers, aren't they?"

Where he'd hoped for a smile, he got a frown instead. "You've obviously done your research and know what I do for a living."

Alec barely managed to hold on to his smile. "I have done some research," he admitted. "I felt I had to, given that I didn't know anything at all about you until yesterday."

She went perfectly still. "He never told you about me?"

"No. And if I didn't know about you, no one did." Alec hadn't wanted to dive into fraught emotional territory with her, but some questions needed to be asked. "Did you know who he was?"

Her face went pale a beat before she shook her head. "No." The word came out hoarsely enough that she reached for the water she hadn't wanted and took a sip before continuing. "I found out yesterday. Just like you."

For nearly twenty years, Alec had nothing but the utmost respect for Gordon. But now he had to wonder how his friend could have known about the woman sitting here today—a woman who clearly wouldn't hurt a fly, even if it was eating one of her plants—and not reach out to her.

If Alec had a daughter, he would want to know her, no matter the circumstances of her birth. He would never in a million years do what his mother had done when she'd decided to leave her children by taking her life. For three decades, Alec had lived with the knowledge that neither he nor his siblings had been important enough to keep Lynn Sullivan holding on, to keep trying. And now, he hated the thought that Cordelia might think she wasn't important enough for Gordon to acknowledge.

"I'm sorry," he said in a low voice. "Your biological father was a good man. A great one. But I don't understand the choices he made where you were concerned any more than you do."

"Leaving his half of the company to me, you mean?"

"Yes. But also why he kept you a secret. And why he didn't contact you." Alec realized she needed to know something else. "When I found Gordon in his office after the heart attack, he was still breathing. Just barely."

"I don't want to hear this." She might spend all day with plants, but again it struck him that she wasn't nearly as meek as his research had led him to believe. "He wasn't—isn't—anything to me."

"But you were something to him."

"How can you say that?" She burst out of her seat, knocking into the coffee table hard enough that the water sloshed over the rims of all four glasses. "He never once tried to contact me. He lived, worked, only thirty minutes away his entire life and never did one single thing to make himself known to me until after he was gone. I meant *nothing* to him!"

"Your name." Alec stood too, needing to look into her eyes. "It was the last word he spoke."

He was watching her so carefully that he knew the exact moment her knees began to give way. Quickly gripping her hands, he held her steady. "Ezra, Caleb," he said to the lawyers, "give us a few minutes alone."

The two men couldn't wait to get out of the room.

"We don't have to do this today, Cordelia." Alec spoke softly, soothingly, the way he would to a spooked animal about to bolt. "We can wait until you've had more time to process things."

"There's nothing to process." She slid her hands from his and walked over to the wall of windows that looked out over his empire, the hangars and runways that held his planes. "He might have been a great man to you, to your clients, to your employees, but to me he's nothing more than a total, complete, utter stranger." When she turned to face him, Alec was struck all over again by the mesmerizing beauty of her gaze, the lush fullness of her lips. "He left me half of a company that I know nothing about, in an industry I have no interest in whatsoever." She half laughed, though there was no humor in it. "I don't even like to fly. It gives me motion sickness."

Alec had to laugh as well, couldn't keep it in regardless of how heavy the moment might be. "Flying made him sick too. It was something he made sure no one knew—that he was an airplane mogul who could barely stand to even taxi down the runway."

"It's just genes," she shot back. "My mom, my dad—the people who actually raised me, the people who love me—are the ones who matter, not a stranger. Not even one who's just given me half of his bazillion-dollar company." She lifted her chin. "If he thought he could buy me, he's wrong. My heart, my love—they aren't for sale. I don't want half of S&W Aviation. No more than you want me to have it." She gestured toward his desk. "If you've got an offer for me, I'm ready to see it." She looked back out the window at the planes and hangars and practically shuddered. "More than ready."

This was exactly what Alec had wanted. For Cordelia to walk in and tell him to take what should have been his. He should have been leaping at the chance to get her to read through his offer—and sign it—as quickly as possible. It was the only thing that made sense in this crazy situation. She didn't know anything about planes or big business, and he sure as hell didn't have the time or inclination to train a greenhorn partner.

And yet...

Something was stopping him. In all the years they'd worked together, for all that he could be ruthless while playing the business game, Gordon had never deliberately hurt anyone—even their worst-behaved clients who deserved a little pain. But he'd hurt this woman. Badly.

And Alec couldn't escape the thought that it was now up to him to help Cordelia.

He knew how badly parents could mess you up— dead *and* alive, in his case. But he'd had his brothers, his sister, his cousins, his aunts and uncles to offer to help him deal with it all. Even if he'd never actually taken them up on their offers, they'd still been there in the wings. Who did Cordelia have apart from her adoptive parents? Would she be willing to admit any of this to her girlfriends? To a boyfriend, if she had one?

The thought of a boyfriend didn't sit right with him. Which didn't make any more sense than anything else had in the past fifteen minutes. All he knew was that they needed to hit the pause button before either of them made a decision they'd regret.

"I never thought about Gordon dying," Alec told her. "Never imagined a force of nature like him could go so quickly at fifty. And I sure as hell never thought that you would be standing here with me, holding the keys to half my kingdom."

"I already told you, I don't want your kingdom." She moved closer. "Make me an offer, Alec. If it's fair, I'll be out of your hair so quickly it will be as if I'd never been here at all."

His chest clenched at her words. Was that why he didn't want to present her with his buyout offer? Because it would be akin to erasing her? And regardless, had Gordon really thought his flower-loving daughter would actually *want* what he was trying to give her?

Beyond frustrated, Alec ran a hand through his hair, then spoke the four words he never thought he'd say to her. "I need more time."

She gaped at him. "You're kidding me. The lawyers are already here, and you were all shark-teeth smiles when I walked in."

"You think I smile like a shark?"

"You know what I mean—you looked hungry for a deal to be made. And I don't blame you. Why would anyone in his right mind want his business partner's secret daughter that he gave away within seconds of her being born to become his new co-captain in a really big business? I get that he might have been smart about some things—really, really smart, if the success of your business is anything to go by—but giving me half of his company is literally the dumbest idea in the world."

Alec knew laughter was completely out of bounds. But he couldn't hold it in.

Women rarely made him laugh, apart from his sisters and cousins, who didn't want anything from him. His female relations weren't like the women who clawed their way into his life looking for someone to buy them jewelry and tell them pretty lies. His sister and cousins simply accepted him for the cynical, blunt guy that he was—and in turn they knew that he would defend them with his life.

"This isn't funny," Cordelia said, looking irritated and also a little concerned by his behavior. As though he had transformed from a shark into an unhinged billionaire.

He ran a hand over his mouth in an effort to wipe away the grin. "I know it isn't. I just wish I could have seen Gordon's face when you said he'd had the dumbest idea in the world. People usually kowtowed to him."

Despite her professed disinterest, she looked intrigued by what he was telling her about her father. Still, she insisted, "Well, I'm definitely not going to kowtow now by taking a company I don't want. I'm ready to make a deal with you. Right here. Right now."

But instead of presenting her with the buyout offer

she so desperately wanted, he asked, "Do you like working in your garden store?"

The look she gave him made it beyond clear that she thought he was crazy not to grab with both hands at her offer to walk away from his company. "I love it. It's what I've always wanted to do. The *only* thing I've ever wanted to do. Just like I'm sure that this—" She gestured again to the planes. "—is all you've ever wanted."

He should have nodded, would have agreed had anyone else said it. But just as he couldn't make her the buyout offer he wanted, he also found he couldn't tell her that lie. "When I was a kid, I wanted to open a restaurant." He used to cook for his parents, his brothers and sister. He remembered writing up menus, putting out little tables and chairs. But then when his mom died and his father left the four of them to fend for themselves, it had been solely about keeping it together from that point forward, making sure his siblings didn't get lost in the cracks while their father was too busy grieving to take care of his kids, who were grieving too.

"Then why don't you?" Cordelia asked.

She made it sound so easy. This woman who knew next to nothing about him apart from the fact that he had built a business with her birth father that had made them both billionaires. "My sister says I'm enough of a workaholic already," he said. "She'd probably try to have me committed if I went from the office to cook in a restaurant every night."

"Or you could sell this company and just cook. I mean, if you think that would be more fun than what you're doing now, why not?"

Today had been perfectly linear in Alec's head. Cordelia was going to show up at his office, he was going to make her an offer she couldn't refuse, and then he would move forward with his life in the same way it had been before.

Were they really standing in his office discussing how he should sell *his* half of the company too—and cook for a living?

"There are so many reasons why not," he told her, "that I could keep you here until dark listing them."

In a heartbeat, the air between them changed. Maybe it was the idea of keeping her with him until night fell that suddenly sent sparks crackling. Or maybe it was that with Cordelia, nothing had gone as he'd planned. And everything *always* went the way Alec intended.

"I'd like to come by your garden," he said.

Her frown went deep, and she took a step back. "Why on earth would you want to do that?"

"I'd like to see where you work. Understand more about the business you've built."

"You can't possibly be trying to see if I'm a good fit

to work with you here, can you?" She held up a hand before he could answer. "Because I really, *really* don't want to help you sell rides on fancy planes to fancy people."

"I've got that covered, thanks."

"Then what could you possibly want with me and my garden?"

"Honestly?"

"God, yes, please be honest," she said. "That way I'll know what to say to change your mind if you're thinking something crazy."

It was something he could picture his sister saying, or his cousins Mia or Lori or Cassie. All of them would like Cordelia. And they'd be beside themselves with glee at the chance to sit in the corner with a box of popcorn to watch this conversation play out.

"I'm never crazy," was the first thing he needed her to know. And then, "I thought I knew exactly how to resolve this situation Gordon's sprung on us."

"So you *do* have an offer for me?" She looked hopefully at the papers on his desk.

"I did." She made a face at his use of the past tense. "But my gut is telling me that what I've got prepared might not be the right offer. And I always trust my gut."

"If you think I'm greedy for his money," she said, "I swear that's not why I'm in such a hurry to make a deal with you."

"I know you're not. I can spot a gold digger a mile away."

She stared at him a little longer than was comfortable. "I'll bet you can." Then she waved a hand in the air as if to clear the thought away. "I just don't want this. Don't want any part of *him*. You've got to understand that, don't you?"

"I do, Cordelia. But I also know he wanted you to have this. I'm not stalling because I want to make you miserable. I just need to make sure everything is straight in my head before we dot the *i*'s and cross the *t*'s."

"If I invite you to my garden tomorrow, will you bring the offer? One that makes your gut feel good?"

He knew the answer she wanted. Still, he had to tell her, "I don't make promises I can't keep, so I can't answer that yet. Will noon work?"

She was gritting her teeth so hard that he half expected to hear them crack. Finally, she nodded. "Noon will work. But it might rain tomorrow, so I can't guarantee you'll leave my garden looking as clean and polished as you do when you arrive." She headed for the door, then stopped with her hand on the doorknob. She turned to look back at him. "I expected you to be a ruthless businessman. It would have been much easier if you were."

And then she left.

CHAPTER THREE

Cordelia's knees ached from kneeling, her hands were sore from digging into a patch of hard soil with a shovel and trowel, and she was covered with smears of dirt. She'd gotten up with the sun and had taken only a short break to eat a quick bowl of granola. And she'd never been more pleased by the hard work she had to put in every single day to build her garden and her business.

Without all that work, she would have been left alone with too many thoughts, too many questions.

For the second night in a row, she'd barely slept, doubly plagued now by confusion about her birth father and why he'd done what he'd done—and by thoughts of Alec Sullivan.

He was a billionaire businessman. Her birth father's corporate partner.

And hands down the best-looking man she'd ever set eyes on.

Even now, just thinking of Alec made her hot in ways that had nothing to do with the sun shining down on her. He wasn't her type—she'd never gone for that king-of-the-world vibe. And yet, she'd reacted to him in a very feminine way.

Most of all, though, she'd been stunned by the empathy he'd shown her.

She'd expected him to make excuses for her birth father. But when Alec found out that she'd been kept in the dark about Gordon until yesterday, he hadn't made any excuses at all. And she appreciated that more than he'd ever know.

What she *didn't* appreciate, however, was the fact that he hadn't made her a buyout offer yesterday. S&W Aviation felt like a noose tightening around her neck. The longer it was there, the harder it got to breathe.

She definitely didn't want the business, and though she knew pretty much everyone would think she was nuts, she had extremely mixed feelings about the money as well. If she'd earned it herself, that would be one thing. But to inherit a shockingly huge sum from someone who hadn't even wanted her in his life? She couldn't shake the fact that it felt like dirty money.

Like an apology that had come twenty-five years too late.

Like a bid to buy her forgiveness.

She sighed as she took off her thick gloves to push back the hair that had sprung loose from her ponytail.

Again and again, she'd reminded herself that there was nothing to forgive. Plenty of babies were given up for adoption by their birth parents. Her story—an overwhelmed man giving up his baby after his wife died in childbirth—wasn't even particularly special. And Cordelia would never complain about her adoptive mom and dad, who were amazing.

All of which meant that there was no point in being angry, no point in being hurt that Gordon Whitley hadn't been able to find the time—or the desire—to drive thirty miles from his fancy office building to meet her.

Today, she promised herself, she'd sell her half of the company to Alec Sullivan, and then she'd promptly get over herself and her hurt feelings.

The antique clock she'd bought at a farmer's market chimed a quarter to noon. Standing, she tried to brush some dirt off her jeans, which only made a bigger mess. She was more tempted than she should be to run back to her cottage and take a quick shower, maybe put on a sundress while she was at it.

But she wasn't trying to impress Alec. Not that she could manage that in the best of circumstances, of course, given that men like him didn't so much as glance at women like her—for which she was profoundly grateful. She liked her quiet, simple life. Loved selling petunias and lavender plants to retirees and then spending her evenings weeding and watering her own cottage garden.

Still, that didn't mean she needed to be a sweaty, filthy mess when he got here. A new T-shirt wouldn't be too big a concession. Fortunately, she had a clean stack of LANGLEY GARDEN CENTER shirts in a storage room for when her part-time employees forgot to bring theirs to work.

She was just heading toward the main building, which held the registers and the gift items that couldn't be left out in the sun, when Brian came jogging up. He worked three half days a week and was working toward his own degree in botany.

"Cordelia, I just got a text from my professor. He said I can make up my test today, but only if I'm there in the next fifteen minutes. You know I hate to bail on you like this."

"It's been a slow morning at the register," she said with a smile. "Go ace your test and I'll see you on Thursday."

He grinned. "Just like I always say, you're the best boss a guy could have."

As she watched Brian lope off on legs that seemed too long for the rest of him, Cordelia felt far more than five years older. Funny how much could change in forty-eight hours. She didn't understand why Alec hadn't felt ready to make her a buyout offer yesterday, but surely after she'd made it clear to him in no uncertain terms that she didn't want half of his company, he'd seen the light.

She'd nearly reached the storeroom when her attention was suddenly caught by a bright flash of sunlight reflecting off something in the barn. She shielded her eyes against the shimmer of light, only to realize that Alec Sullivan was standing mere feet away.

"Hello, Cordelia."

Seriously, she should *not* have just gotten goose bumps from nothing more than hearing him say her name. And also, what kind of billionaire showed up early to meet with a garden shop owner? Early enough to catch her looking as sweaty and gross as she hadn't wanted to be in front of him. Didn't he have diamonds to buy or companies to take over? What's more, she'd expected him in a suit, not a pair of well-worn jeans and a T-shirt that did far too good a job of showing off the muscles in his arms and shoulders, along with abs that she could easily guess were rock hard too. He was even wearing scuffed work boots, as though he knew his way around hands-on work. Did he? And why did she even care when the plan was to simply resolve their temporary partnership and then go their separate ways, ASAP?

"Hi, Alec." Her mind blanked after that. She wasn't the chattiest person in the world—unless she was talking about her beloved plants—but this was extreme even for her. Then again, what did they have to say to each other apart from agreeing on a few really big financial figures? "I'm sure you're really busy," she finally got out, "and since I don't have any customers who need help right now, why don't we just get down to—"

"Cordelia, darling," an elegant gray-haired woman burst in. "I'm finally ready to redo my *entire* front yard. Lawn out, flowers in. I do so hope you have some time to sit down with me to discuss it."

Belinda Billingsworth was one of Cordelia's best, and most demanding, customers. She was constantly changing out garden beds, which was usually a very good thing.

"Belinda, that's great news," Cordelia said with a smile. "I'll be in a meeting for about the next hour, but as soon as that's done, I'm all you—"

"Excuse me, could someone help me put ten of the big bags of soil onto my cart?" An older woman Cordelia didn't recognize was waving at them from across the brick path.

"I'd be happy to help," Alec said.

Before Cordelia could tell Alec his offer was very nice, but not at all necessary because she could take care of it all, he was heading off toward the woman and her bags of soil, looking as comfortable in the garden center as he had in his swanky office, surrounded by his zillion-dollar planes.

"Where did you find your new help?" Belinda purred.

"He doesn't work for me," Cordelia said before she could think better of all the questions she'd just opened herself up to.

"A new boyfriend, then?" Belinda's eyebrows waggled up and down. "Much better-looking than your last one, that's for sure. And with big, strong hands that I'll bet he knows how to use, if you know what I mean."

Cordelia could feel her cheeks flaming and was struggling to find a way to explain Alec's presence...when she suddenly realized that Alec had come back into the barn from behind them and had surely caught the end of Belinda's sentence.

"Mrs. Angelo had a question about the best soil to use in a semi-shaded, wet area." His question was a simple one, but his eyes were sparking with what could only be described as *wickedness*.

Cordelia's heart was racing far too fast as she said, "The loam-sand mix."

"Great, thanks." Judging by his low drawl, he clearly hadn't missed her flaming cheeks or pounding pulse. "I'll let her know."

"Alec." She put her hand on his arm to stop him, then pulled it away as if scalded. Which she had been.

Because he was so warm. And his muscles were so hard. And everything about him was yummy in ways she shouldn't be noticing. "It's really nice of you to help, but if you'll just give me a few minutes to take care of things here, we can talk."

"I have a cousin in the retail business, so I know my way around a cash register. I'll take care of things with Mrs. Angelo and anyone else who needs help while you meet with—" He reached out a hand to Belinda. "I'm Alec."

"Belinda Billingsworth." She wasn't shy with her appreciation. "And aren't you just a dream to pitch in with your girl like this?"

"We aren't together!" Cordelia's protestation came out too loud, too strident, borderline desperate even. "Alec and I just have some business to resolve, that's all." Trying to pull herself together, she turned back to him and said, "That would be great if you could pitch in for a little while, thank you. I'll come find you as soon as I can."

With a nod, and another smile for Belinda, he headed back toward the customer he was helping. Belinda didn't look away from his denim-covered backside, and honestly, Cordelia barely managed it herself.

"He's perfect for you, you know," the other woman said as they headed into Cordelia's small office.

Cordelia didn't normally like to argue with her customers, but she had to say, "I only met Alec yesterday. And the circumstances are strange enough that I can promise you we're not going to start dating. Now or ever."

"All I know," Belinda said as she sat on one of the soft rose-colored seats in Cordelia's office, "is that the last time a man looked at me like *that*, I ended up married to him."

CHAPTER FOUR

That afternoon, the hours moved faster for Alec than they had in years. He couldn't think of the last time he'd been able to work outside with his hands in the company of pleasant, happy, relaxed people. His usual day at the S&W Aviation office was as far from this one as it could possibly be. His customers tended to be high-strung and demanding, rather than mellow. Every hour there were tens of thousands of dollars on the line, instead of hundreds. He wore bespoke suits and thousand-dollar handmade shoes, not jeans and work boots.

And he sure didn't get to catch glimpses of smiles as pretty as Cordelia's.

He hadn't shown up today expecting to pitch in at her garden center, but when customers appeared just as they were about to meet, he'd immediately had his executive assistant cancel his afternoon meetings, then got to work ringing up and loading cars with as many of Cordelia's plants as he could convince customers to buy.

He was damned good at up-selling the product, if he did say so himself. She made it easy, of course, having taken meticulous care of her broad inventory.

Cordelia made other things easy too. Like fantasizing about doing a hell of a lot more than using his "big, strong hands" to help out with her store. Even in baggy jeans and a shapeless T-shirt with streaks of dirt on her cheeks, she was beautiful. Almost more so in how effortless it was, as if it would never occur to her to waste time worrying about what she looked like, or to try to impress a man. That was the irony that the women in his circle rarely understood—the more you tried, the less impressed everyone was.

He couldn't imagine Cordelia at one of the glittering fundraisers where he'd spent so many nights during the past ten years. Now that her net worth was in the eleven figures, of course, she would be in high demand.

The urge to protect her from that see-and-be-seen world was as instinctive as the urge to step in to help at her store today.

If Gordon had known her at all—if he'd taken the time to have even one conversation with her, or to visit her store—he would have understood that leaving her half of S&W Aviation was, just as Cordelia had said, the dumbest idea in the world. Not because she couldn't handle the pressure, but because she'd go crazy if she had to give up her plants and flowers and friendly customers for meetings in airless boardrooms with demanding celebrities.

Alec rarely second-guessed himself. He made decisions with confidence, then stuck with them. Yet something had come over him in his office when he'd balked at presenting his buyout offer to Cordelia— something he didn't want to look at too closely.

But now that he'd seen Cordelia in her natural environment, he knew he had to do it. He had to set her free.

"The last happy customer is on her way." At 5:45 p.m., she closed the double front doors that led into the garden center from the parking lot and clicked the lock into place. Her expression was serious as she turned to face him. "I don't know how to thank you enough for your help today. I usually have someone here with me in the afternoon, but Brian had a test to make up at the university. I honestly don't know how I would have coped without you. Especially considering I don't think I've ever moved this many plants in one afternoon. You'll have to tell me your secrets before you go, although I'm not sure I'll be able to charm my customers anywhere near as effectively as you did."

Every word from her lips, every gesture, every glance was genuine. It was another thing Alec wasn't used to. The women he dealt with aimed to entice, to appeal, to reel in and hook. If they said thank you, it was only because they felt they'd earned whatever gift they'd been given.

"I enjoyed myself today." He was surprised to realize it was no more complicated than that.

"I'm sure you must have had a million more important things to take care of this afternoon. Or even tonight. I've got to be keeping you from something, aren't I?"

He'd been planning on a night at the opera with a leggy blonde he'd met through one of his customers. But he'd already arranged for Tiffany's to courier over a bracelet along with his apologies. "Nope, I'm all yours."

Cordelia's cheeks heated the same way they had earlier when he'd overheard her customer talking about what he could do with his hands. And just as he had then, he found himself wondering what it would take to make the rest of her skin turn that rosy, that warm. A touch? A kiss? Or more?

"Great," she said, but her voice sounded a little strange. Almost as though she was wondering the same naughty things. "Are you sure you're still up for talking business tonight?" When he nodded, she asked, "Can I at least feed you first? I'm the world's worst cook, but I have plenty growing in my kitchen garden for a salad."

Women rarely offered to cook for him. They were much more interested in being seen at the hottest new restaurant. But even more rare was his offer to cook for them. His prowess in the kitchen was something he rarely pulled out of his hat, and usually only for family. "I'll take care of making dinner."

Her eyebrows went up. "You're offering to cook for me? After running around my store all afternoon helping my customers?"

"One thing I learned from Gordon early on was never to negotiate on an empty stomach."

Again, he saw that spark of interest in finding out more about her birth father, before she shut it down. "Okay, if you don't mind cooking in the world's smallest kitchen, why don't we head over to my cottage?"

After an afternoon working on site, he was familiar with most of her acreage. The only part he hadn't explored yet was the back corner with her cottage and private garden. Her home was one story with a bright blue front door and flower boxes at the windows on either side.

"It's straight out of the illustrated fairy tales I read to my nieces." Her cottage could be in rural England and it would fit right in. Heck, he was expecting a couple of fluffy bunny rabbits to come hopping by any second now. His contemporary penthouse was the polar opposite of her cottage. Just, he reminded himself, as he was to her.

The gardener and the businessman—they were as different as people could be. Which, he decided, explained the attraction. What man didn't hanker for a taste of the new, the different? Especially when Cordelia came in such a pretty package *and* smelled like lavender?

"How many nieces do you have?" she asked.

"None of my siblings have kids yet," he clarified as she opened the gate and they headed through the vegetable garden that took up most of her front yard. "But I've got a ton of cousins with kids. Summer's ten. The twins, Jackie and Smith Jr., are three. So is Emma. Julia and Logan are both just starting to walk. Aaron isn't yet one. And a bunch more babies will be born soon, starting with Naughty's."

"Naughty?"

He had already pulled out a couple of thick carrots and was rooting around for some potatoes when he said, "Lori's nickname. She's a professional dancer in San Francisco, married to an organic farmer who provides produce, cheese, and milk to the local families. You'd like Grayson. And he'd really appreciate what you've set up here."

"Your family sounds huge."

He paused in his vegetable gathering to look at her. He'd assumed she knew all about him the way other women always did. Not only his net worth, but the fact that his siblings were a brilliant academic, a technology whiz, and a painter; that his father was one of the most famous men the art world had ever known; that his cousins comprised a movie star, a pro baseball player, a race car driver, and more.

He should have known that when it came to Cordelia, his assumptions would all turn out to be wrong, one after the other.

"There are Sullivans all over the world," he told her.

"Are you close to all of them?"

"Most of us, yeah, we're pretty tight."

She took the carrots and potatoes from him so that he could move on to foraging for onions and beets. "You're pretty much describing my dream life," she said in a slightly wistful tone. "I mean, my parents are amazing, but they were both only children, so there were never cousins or any extended family. Just the three of us."

"But you were happy, weren't you?" He needed to confirm that his friend, his business partner, hadn't screwed up twice over by passing his kid off to a couple who hadn't given her everything she deserved.

"I was. Really happy." As if she could read his mind, she added, "And I would have much rather grown up here than wherever your partner lived."

He noticed she never said Gordon's name. But

something told him she was still itching for details, no matter how she might deny it. "Gordon had a house in Scarsdale, a loft in Tribeca, and a vacation home in Florida on the beach. I used to think it was strange how he managed to fit in a vegetable garden at each place, even in the middle of New York City. But now I can see it must have been in his blood."

The same way it's in yours.

"The strawberries are super ripe right now." She didn't look at him as she spoke. "I'll take these vegetables inside and get a bowl for the fruit."

He understood not wanting to talk about the parents who had disappointed you. But if there were similarities between Cordelia and Gordon, he still thought she'd want to hear about them. If only to put to rest the questions she surely had.

Alec knew firsthand about how those questions could haunt you. If his mother were here right now, he'd flat-out ask her how she could have done it. How she could have left him and his siblings and his father without even saying good-bye. But just as Cordelia's father wasn't around to ask, neither was Alec's mother. All they'd ever have to go on were clues, hints from what other people told them.

It was frustrating as hell.

For the next few minutes, the two of them gathered fruit in silence. When the bowls were full of strawberries and plums and apples, they headed into the house.

Alec stopped just inside her front door. "It looks the same inside as it does out."

"I kind of have a thing for flowers."

That was the understatement of the century. Flowers were *everywhere*. Pouring over every windowsill, potted plants in corners, vases of cut flowers on every table. "Gordon would have loved your house, your garden. He would have been comfortable here in a way that he never was at any of his own homes." Alec felt comfortable here too, could easily see his siblings and their mates gathered around the old pine table in the kitchen playing a fierce game of cards. Could see himself there with them too, for once, instead of bowing out due to a business obligation.

Just as she'd ignored his comments about her birth father outside, she said, "Tell me what you need to make dinner and I'll get it out for you. I'm assuming a sharp knife and a cutting board, which is as far as my culinary skills extend."

"I'll also need a frying pan, a couple of mixing bowls, olive oil, salt, pepper, and whatever herbs you've got."

"Herbs are the easy part," she said, before disappearing to root around in her kitchen cupboards.

There was something oddly appealing about a

woman so gifted with a green thumb but who was utterly useless in the kitchen. Yet again, she turned his expectations on their ear.

How else would she surprise him? If he kissed her, would she be as soft, as sweet as she looked—or would she be all heat and desperate lust?

He had to work harder than ever to push the thought away. She'd attracted him from the first, but Alec knew better than to let an unexpected attraction hold sway over his common sense. Anyone who lived in a fairy-tale cottage like this, who surrounded herself with flowers of every color of the rainbow, would want the rest of the fairy tale too. She'd want a doting husband. She'd want little kids chasing butterflies and digging in the dirt outside. She'd want all the things Alec didn't. He was happy with his fast-paced life. Happy to do what he wanted, when he wanted, with no one to hold him down. There was no way he'd ever risk his happiness by falling into an obsessive relationship the way his father had with his mother.

Soon, Alec had everything he needed to begin their meal. He was chopping onions when Cordelia reached out to flip on the old-school radio on the ledge of the kitchen window. She immediately began to sway her hips and hum along with the music.

The knife stilled in his hand as he stared at her, mesmerized not only by her effortless beauty, but also by the sensuality that he was becoming less and less immune to by the second.

Her cheeks went pink when she noticed he was staring at her. "Was I singing out loud?" Before he could reply, she said, "I can't help myself. James Taylor is one of my favorite musicians."

Alec's arm felt as though it were moving through cement as he reached over to turn off the radio. His heart wasn't beating quite right anymore either.

"Alec? Is everything okay?" Cordelia was obviously surprised by his behavior.

But he couldn't speak, couldn't tell her that he'd finally realized what she'd been listening to. "Something in the Way She Moves." The song his father used to sing to his mother. When his mother teased his father about his off-key voice, Alec knew everything was okay for the time being. When she didn't seem to even hear the singing, that was a bad day.

"I'm just not in the mood for music right now."

"I should have asked."

"It's your kitchen—you didn't need to ask." But he didn't want to talk right now, didn't want to end up saying more than he should about his aversion to James Taylor's music. "If you want to take a shower, now's a good time."

"Are you sure? Because I'm happy to help with whatever I can."

"Go." He belatedly tried to soften the one hard word with a small smile. "I promise not to make your kitchen too big a disaster zone."

"I'm not worried about that." Her gaze seemed to add, *I'm worried about you.* But thankfully, instead of saying it out loud, she simply said, "I won't be long," then headed for the bathroom.

His chest tight, he turned his focus back to the onion on the chopping board and worked to block all thoughts, all memories, of his mother. But when the melody of the damned song kept playing on repeat inside his head, he turned the radio back on, found a heavy metal station, and blasted it loud enough that he couldn't think of anything at all.

CHAPTER FIVE

"I've never tasted anything this good." Alec had whipped up a glorious vegetable dish that made Cordelia's mouth water even as she shoveled it in like it was her last supper. "I'd ask you how you made this, but I'd only end up setting my kitchen on fire if I tried it." She pointed to the fire extinguisher in the corner of the room. "It's happened before."

Even the green salad he'd made was amazing. Though she loved the greens she grew, she'd never known they could taste like *this*. Not wanting to get in his way in the kitchen, especially after he'd abruptly shut off the music—looking almost as if he'd seen a ghost, though she couldn't understand why—she'd disappeared to wash up and change out of her dirt-stained clothes. When she'd returned a short while later, he was blasting heavy metal as he slipped dessert into the oven and then got ready to plate their mains.

"If the fruit pie you've got baking is anywhere near this good, you really should open a restaurant," she told him. "It's only right to share your gift with the world."

Sitting back with the glass of wine she'd poured for him, he let her babble. It was just that he was so easy to talk to. He shouldn't have been—the billionaire who was, no pun intended, in the highest-flying circles should have been the last person she could sit comfortably with at her old kitchen table. Although maybe *comfortable* wasn't the right word for it, considering that part of the reason she was babbling was because it was a better use of her mouth than drooling.

Honestly, she should be used to the way he looked by now. His chiseled jaw, his broad shoulders, his big, strong hands—she'd always hated it when men objectified women, so she shouldn't be doing it to him. It was just so darned hard not to wonder what it would be like to be dragged into his arms and kissed, Hollywood style.

Just one kiss, so she'd know if it was as good as he made it look like it would be.

"I'm glad you enjoyed dinner." He was surprisingly modest for someone who could easily win *Iron Chef.* "Should we get our business out of the way before dessert?"

She popped the last snap pea on her plate into her mouth, then nodded. Of course she wanted to resolve the inheritance situation, but at the same time, she couldn't help feeling a little sad that her time with Alec would be over after tonight. Maybe, she found herself hoping, he'd drop in to buy a houseplant sometime. Probably not, though. Once he returned to his glittering world, he'd likely forget she ever existed.

She already knew she wouldn't forget him.

He refilled her glass, then said, "Yesterday, you made it clear that you don't want anything from Gordon, but I couldn't sleep at night if I didn't offer you market value on your fifty percent of S&W Aviation." The sum he named had the wine she'd just sipped go down the wrong pipe, and she almost spat it out all over the table.

"That's twice as much money as I thought you were going to offer." And the number she'd come up with had already been way too much. "How am I going to manage all of that? What if I screw up and give it to scam charities instead of ones that really need it? After paying off my parents' mortgage and buying them a new car and sending them on a great vacation, I have no idea how to pick the best foundations to donate to. All the money Gordon gave me—I know it's a gift. And I want to do right by it, by him. By you too, for all the work you put into building your business. But every time I think about it, I freak out about everything I don't know about investing and charities and foundations."

"There are people who can help you with all of

that. Wealth advisors and donor consultants. With their help, you could start by seeking out groups that need help in things you're passionate about. Like garden programs in schools, and community gardens. I know it seems overwhelming, but it doesn't have to be. Especially if you'll let me connect you with a few people who can help."

"Please, connect away. I can't do this on my own."

"You could, easily. But you don't have to." She wondered if this was the wisdom that came from being a part of a big, close family as he said, "I'll give you the name and number of my investment advisor. You can start there, and if you don't like her, I can find other names for you."

"Do you trust her?"

"I do. And I trust my donation advisor too, who happens to be her husband."

"I like that," Cordelia said, "a husband-and-wife team where she grows your money so that he can give it away."

"So, do we have a deal?"

"Only if you agree to deduct fifty dollars for the hours you put in at my store today and this dinner."

"Surely dinner is worth at least a hundred." She could see he was teasing, but when he smiled at her like that, all of her girl parts started sizzling, melting with lust. "Seriously, though, you don't owe me anything for today or tonight. You didn't ask for any of this to happen, Cordelia. I get that the whole situation is strange and stressful."

She was glad when the timer dinged on the oven and he took out the fruit pie. It would give her a few seconds to try to settle herself down. She brought their wine glasses over to the living room table. "I know I should be grateful to become so rich overnight..."

He moved to sit with her on the couch, the pie cooling on a brightly painted porcelain trivet he'd unearthed from the cupboard. "You were happy with your life the way it was. And now you know that no matter how much you want to keep things from changing, they're going to."

Relieved that he understood, and feeling somewhat mellowed out by a full belly and the merlot, she found herself saying, "All day, all night, you've been so nice to me. So kind."

"Nice. Kind." He said the words as though they were in a foreign language. "Women don't usually say those things about me."

"If you're always like this, cooking and lugging soil and making deals that are way better for the other person than they are for you, how could they not?"

"Because I'm not like this with other women. I'm *never* like this."

The air in the room felt different now. No longer

comfortable. She should have gotten up, should have made an excuse to put some space between them. Instead, she found herself asking, "What are you normally like?"

"Counting the seconds until I can leave. Until I can head back to my own space and do my own thing. But with you—"

He lifted his hand to her cheek, and when he touched her, something inside of her came alive. Something she hadn't even known was there, lying dormant.

Heated sparks.

Desperate desire.

And a soul-deep longing to know what it would be like to be wanted by Alec Sullivan, a brilliant, gorgeous, incredibly sexy man who could have anyone.

"You do something to me, Cordelia," he said in that deep voice that made her shiver and heat up all at the same time, "and I keep trying to find reasons to stay longer."

His eyes lowered to her mouth, and her lips started to tingle from nothing more than his intense gaze. No one had ever looked at her like this, with such hunger. And she'd never felt so greedy for a man's kiss in her life.

But if they kissed, what would happen next? Would he actually want to come back to her little garden cottage next week, and the week after that, to woo her? Because she would never fit into his fancy world of jetsetters and dealmakers and supermodels.

Cold, hard reality was the only reason she was able to draw back. "I'll bet the pie is cool enough to cut into now." She stood on shaky legs to get out the pie cutter and did her best to act like they hadn't been just about to devour each other.

The act of putting slices on plates helped in her effort to slow her galloping heart. "It looks delicious," she said as she handed him pie, silently praising herself for how normal her voice sounded.

She'd thought she would be too nervous to eat now, but one bite of his pie almost made her forget about the tension thrumming between them. "Ohmygoshthisissogood." She'd shoved too much into her mouth as she spoke for the words to come out clearly. She made herself swallow before saying, "I can't believe you made the crust from scratch from nuts and graham crackers. You're amazing!"

But he hadn't taken a bite yet, hadn't shown any interest whatsoever in the pie. "Women don't usually sprint away when I'm about to kiss them."

Her fork clattered to her plate. She'd thought they'd both ignore the almost-kiss and that would be that. But Alec Sullivan truly wasn't like any other man she'd ever met. Which meant that they couldn't just leave the big elephant in the room.

"You and I come from different worlds, Alec. We never even would have met if not for…" She sighed, her stomach churning enough that she put the delicious pie down on the coffee table in front of the couch. "For my surprise inheritance."

"So this is what it's like to be on the other side of the brush-off." He didn't sound at all happy about it. In fact, his tone was downright grumpy as he added, "My sister and female cousins would love to be a bunch of flies on the wall right now."

How was it that the most gorgeous man in the world was the one sitting on her couch feeling like he'd just been kicked in the gut…by *her*? "It's not that I didn't want to kiss you," she explained before she could think better of what she was saying. "It's just that I don't think it's smart to kiss you."

"The other guys you've kissed, did those turn out to be *smart* decisions?"

Okay, so maybe she shouldn't have put it quite like that. "Obviously not, since none of them are here right now," she admitted. "But you and I, we're like chalk and cheese."

"Can you even tell me what that phrase means?"

She bit her lip, realizing she didn't actually know much about the phrase, only that she was pretty sure it was of British origin. "We're like apples and oranges, then."

"Both fruit."

Why was he making this so hard? "Round pegs and square holes!"

His eyebrows went up at that, the corner of his mouth lifting ever so slightly. "I'm trying to decide if I should let the peg/hole thing go or not."

Her face flamed even hotter as visions hit her of the two of them doing something *very* different than talking on her couch. "I don't get it. Why do you want to kiss me—some small-town gardener who isn't in any way connected to your world?" But before she let him answer, she had to ask, "Are you just curious about something you've never had before? Or, maybe, do you hate the thought of not getting something you think you want, even if you don't really want it?"

"I won't deny one and two are a part of it. But there's also three—you're beautiful."

She was completely caught off guard by his compliment. She looked down at her jeans, her T-shirt, ran a hand over the end of her ponytail. She'd showered and changed, but it hadn't made much difference. "I'm a mess."

"You are." He smiled, letting wicked intent shine through. "But you're a beautiful mess. Four, you always say exactly what's on your mind."

"The circumstances have been so strange that I

have to be totally honest with you."

"Five, you like my cooking."

"*Anyone* would like your cooking!"

"And six…I keep wondering if this was Gordon's hope all along. For the two of us to meet."

She didn't have a quick comeback to that. Not when a part of her had been wondering the same thing—if this was some strange master plan her birth father had for the two of them. Matchmaking from the grave.

"No," she finally said, desperate to deny this instinctive attraction to Alec the same way she wanted to deny the money that had landed in her lap. "He couldn't have wanted that. Couldn't have known he'd die at just the right time for you and I to get together and fall in love."

Alec jumped off the couch at the word *love*. "He should have known better than to think I had that in me. I'm the worst possible guy in the world for you." Suddenly Alec cursed, low and frustrated. "He must have thought you could reform me. Make me believe in fairy tales and happily ever afters."

She snorted and actually sounded like a farm animal in front of the veritable Greek god in her living room. Well, that was one good way to make sure he wouldn't want to kiss her again. "He didn't even know me."

"And that was his loss," Alec said, his words warming her in a way few things had in the past forty-eight hours. "But what he must have seen of your life from the outside was probably enough for him to paint a fantasy." Alec looked around her cottage, then out the window to the lush gardens beyond. "A fantasy I never realized until now that he must have wanted for himself." He shook his head. "I never asked too many questions about his past. He never wanted me to. And I didn't want him to ask about mine either."

"You're guys, so that's normal, isn't it? Not to talk."

"Sure, it's normal. Until one of them turns up a secret daughter and tries to present her to you on a silver platter."

"Oh my God, that's totally what he did, isn't it?" She stood now too, and stared at him in horror. "Good thing we figured it out before we fell for it."

But instead of nodding, Alec said, "It doesn't change the fact that you're beautiful." He moved closer, close enough for her heart to beat a little too fast. "Or that you have the softest-looking skin." His fingertips skimmed across her cheek. "Skin that feels even softer than it looks." His words were hushed now. "Or that your mouth was made for kissing." His thumb moved like a breath over her lower lip, and her knees went weak.

If he tried to kiss her again now, she wouldn't be

able to walk away, wouldn't be able to think of some excuse to put distance between them. She'd simply give in to it. Give in to the desire curling in her belly. Give in to the near desperate urge to reach out and touch his hard muscles. Give in to letting herself be held in his strong arms, if only for one short night.

But this time, he was the one taking a step back. "But I'm never going to be reformed, never going to believe in fairy tales or happily ever afters for myself. So if that's what he was after—and the more I think about it, it had to be—you're right, kissing each other wouldn't be smart."

She should have been happy he'd finally agreed with her. And she swore she *was* happy that they'd just sidestepped a potential minefield, somewhere deep beneath the roiling need coursing through her veins.

"I've taken up enough of your time today," he said in the same tone in which he might have concluded a business meeting. "Do you want me to help you clean up the kitchen?"

"No. Thanks. You were nice enough to cook, I can easily take care of cleanup." It suddenly felt like they were strangers—which they were, for all intents and purposes. But it still didn't sit quite right with her. Not when, from the start, they hadn't talked to each other like strangers. As she'd said earlier, the strange circumstances in which they'd been thrown together meant that they hadn't been able to start off in any normal way.

She'd always been comfortable with normal. Perfectly happy with easy and smooth. But on the precipice of watching Alec Sullivan walk out of her life, for the first time ever she wondered if she'd actually been missing out on something her entire life. Something big that she couldn't define, something difficult and yet still worth it. Like the weeds that just kept growing no matter how you tried to block their path, but then turned out to have the prettiest flowers in the entire garden—more hardy and colorful and unexpectedly beautiful than any of the fancy plants that she was supposed to like more.

"Thanks for making this easy for me," she said, "and for buying me out so generously."

"Anyone would have."

But she knew that other powerful businessmen would have enjoyed toying with the little gardening bumpkin. Either that, or used their lawyers to rip her and her sudden ownership of their company to shreds.

"So," she said as she walked him to the door, "I guess this is it. The part where we tell each other to have a nice life and go our separate ways." She made herself smile even though she felt inexplicably sad. "I hope you have a nice life, Alec." On impulse, she grabbed a potted orchid from a side table. "For your office. It will do great with all that light coming in through the big windows."

He looked down at the plant she'd shoved into his hands. "It's going to die if I take it."

"It won't." Her smile shifted into a real one. "You were a natural in the garden today. And not just because my customers couldn't stop drooling over you. Something tells me you've got a greener thumb than you think."

He looked up from the orchid and pinned her again with his intense gaze. "And something tells *me* that you're tougher than you give yourself credit for." He paused, before hitting her with, "Gordon's funeral is this Saturday, seven p.m., at the Westchester Country Club. You wouldn't have to tell anyone who you are, if you didn't want to. We could just say you came with me."

He didn't wait for her to reply. Didn't give her a chance to protest that going to her birth father's funeral was the very last thing she wanted to do. He simply leaned in and kissed her on the cheek, lingering for a moment too long. A moment she couldn't help but cherish, even if the smart part of her knew better.

CHAPTER SIX

The following Saturday, ten minutes before Gordon's service was to begin, the sun was just setting, the breeze was light, and the crowd clearly couldn't wait to be done with the eulogy and speeches so that they could hit the open bar.

Gordon had been the master of making the rich and famous feel like kings, even when it was the last thing some of them deserved. He'd often joked that Alec couldn't be trusted not to tell them precisely what he thought of them. Alec had been more than happy to leave the spoiled rich clients to Gordon and spend the bulk of his workday growing the financial side of their business.

Now, Alec was the only partner left at S&W Aviation to schmooze their clients. He was impressed by how many of them had come today. Then again, Gordon had spent many a night getting drunk with an actor who had just lost a key role, or playing to the vanity of a supermodel, or letting a royal beat him at poker.

Alec wasn't looking forward to having to take over that side of the business. But he liked the idea of bringing in a new partner less, even one as pretty and intelligent as Cordelia. No question about it, she would hate every second. And who could blame her, when the garden center she'd built around herself was a perfect fit?

Alec had managed to keep the orchid alive so far, out of sheer will. Killing it would be like severing his last tie to her.

She wasn't going to come today. And he understood why. Cordelia might be more curious about Gordon than she wanted to admit, but ultimately he hadn't been anything more to her than a stranger. Just as Alec knew that he hadn't come to be anything more to her than a temporary business partner.

Chalk and cheese, she'd called them. He'd looked it up online the night he'd left her cottage, when he hadn't been sleeping. The origins of the phrase were Middle English, 1390, from a text by John Gower. Alec had a crazy thought about driving back to her cottage and knocking on her door so that he could tell her.

He'd gone to the gym instead, certain that a bruising workout would sweat this strangely emotional nonsense out of him. When she'd lingered in his head, he'd upped his weights, his speed on the treadmill, his laps in the pool. But still he thought of her.

Even when he knew he shouldn't.

Alec's father moved to his side. "How are you holding up? Do you need anything?"

Drake and Suzanne had both made big strides with their father in the past year. It seemed that meeting the love of their lives had pushed them to finally break through their issues with him. For Alec, however, nothing had changed. He could see that his father was making an effort, but to what end? They couldn't go back and fix what had happened. William Sullivan would never be the father Alec and his siblings had needed when they were kids. Thankfully Alec, at least, was past the point of needing him.

"Gordon would have appreciated the turnout," Alec said. It didn't answer either of his father's questions, but was true nonetheless.

"He was a good man." Alec could feel his father's gaze on him. "I owe him a great deal for being there for you when I wasn't."

His father didn't really think they were going to do this right now, did he? Have some sort of father-son bonding moment where tears were shed and all was forgiven?

No. Not now.

Not ever.

"Alec—" his father began, but before he could say anything more, Alec was saved by the most unexpected thing in the world.

Cordelia was walking in.

"Excuse me." He made a bee-line for her.

She didn't gape at people she'd probably only seen on TV and in magazines. She simply moved toward the open casket.

"Cordelia." Alec stopped her a dozen feet from it. "I'm glad you're here."

It wasn't until he got up close that he realized she was trembling, the faintest shaking of her entire body, head to toe. He didn't think, didn't second-guess his actions, simply put one arm around her, took her closest hand in his, and lowered his mouth to her ear. "Tell me what I can do to help."

He heard her breath hitch in her chest. "Don't let go."

Good thing that was her request, because there was literally nothing that could have made him let go of her. Not when she obviously needed someone to help get her through the moment when she was face to face with her father for the first—and the last—time.

"I'm not going anywhere." He'd never said that to a woman he wasn't related to. It should have filled him with panic, should have made him want to bolt. But Cordelia didn't want anything from him beyond some support in a difficult moment. The kind of support he hadn't known how to ask for when he was a kid—

support he had been too proud to accept.

"I wasn't going to come today," she said softly. "But I couldn't stop thinking I'd regret it if I didn't."

"If you take one look and then need to bolt, I'll help you do it. If you need me to kick everyone out of here so that you can be alone with him, I'll do that too. Just let me know when you're ready, and we'll go. Together."

She lifted her beautiful eyes to his, as vibrant a green as anything growing in her garden. "I'm ready."

He wasn't sure he believed her, but who could be ready for something like this? Sticking with her like glue, her skirt swishing around his legs as they walked together, he tuned out everyone else as they made their way to Gordon's casket. His family and their partners, his friends, Gordon's friends, more than a hundred clients—none of them mattered right now.

Only Cordelia.

★ ★ ★

Cordelia's heart had never pounded so wildly, and she was only barely preventing herself from running as fast and far from this place—and from the man lying in the open casket—as she possibly could. Without Alec's arm around her, without his hand over hers to calm her, she wouldn't have made it this far. Would have turned and fled long before now.

She hadn't told her parents anything about today. Hadn't even shared the news of her inheritance with them yet. She'd told herself she hadn't wanted to taint what they were to her, all they'd done for her, hadn't wanted them to feel inferior to all of Gordon's money showering down upon her.

But that wasn't the real reason she hadn't told them yet. The truth was, she didn't know what to say. Didn't know if she should be sad, happy, or angry.

She'd come here today in search of that answer, hoping that the moment she set eyes on Gordon, she'd settle down into choice A, B, or C. Or some combination of the three.

But when she was finally there, was finally able to look down at the man with the strong chin and thick dark brows, the man from whom she'd obviously inherited her cheekbones and the shape of her ears, someone who looked so hearty that nothing could fell him, especially not a heart attack—she didn't feel anything at all.

Every part of her, head to toe, was numb. Her ears were no longer working either, since all she could hear of the people around them was a steady hum, like a motor running.

"Cordelia?"

She had no idea if Alec had said her name once or a dozen times. The only reason she'd noticed at all was because he'd turned her with his hands on her shoulders so that she was looking into his face.

"Are you okay?"

She heard the words coming out of his mouth, understood what he was asking, but didn't have it in her to reply. Not yet. Instead, she turned to look one more time at the father she'd never had the chance to know, captured him in memory, then turned away.

Alec guided her over to an empty seat and sat beside her, never letting go of her hand, just as she'd begged him not to. And in that moment, he was her only lifeline. He didn't ask her any more questions, simply stayed quietly with her, holding both hands now. She thought he might have said something to one of the men sitting nearby, but her numb haze was so thick she couldn't make out what was said.

And then, a voice suddenly spoke through the microphone.

"Thank you all for coming. Please take your seats." A man in a dark suit was standing at the podium, the same man Alec had spoken to just moments earlier. "My cousin Alec has asked me to say a few words for him." Suddenly it hit her—Smith Sullivan, the movie star, had stepped in for Alec. Somewhere in the back of her brain it occurred to her that they must be related, that Smith must be one of the many cousins Alec had mentioned.

She wanted to tell Alec that he could go do what he needed to do, but when the words wouldn't come out, she nodded her head toward the front instead.

"I promised I wouldn't let you go," was all he would say, and then he tucked her hands tighter into his.

"I'd like to begin," Smith said, "by reading something Alec wrote for Gordon." He looked down at the paper in his hands and paused for a solemn moment before he began to speak. "Gordon used to joke about this day. About how it would probably rain and no one would come. But we both knew the sun wouldn't dare not to shine for him and that his friends would drop everything to be here to celebrate his life. He was a brilliant business partner, one I was lucky to connect with when I was still wet behind the ears. He was an even better friend. And that's who I'll miss most. You weren't perfect, Gordon, and I won't ever understand some of the choices you made, but I'll still miss you forever."

A little part of Cordelia came back to life during the speech, enough that she squeezed Alec's hand. "I'm sorry," she whispered, but he just shook his head. And strangely, in that moment, she almost felt as if he needed her there as much as she needed him. So that *he* would have someone to hold on to.

Especially as the speeches from Gordon's friends

came. One long gush of emotion—whether laughter or tears—that spilled out for long minutes over everyone in the audience.

Gordon was brilliant.

Gordon wouldn't take any crap.

Gordon was the hardest-working man I ever met.

Gordon had a magnificent, booming laugh.

Gordon liked—and was liked by—everyone.

The words, the sentiments, crashed together in Cordelia's head. Inside her chest. Just when she thought she couldn't take any more, the speeches were done, and people were rising from their seats, all of them heading toward Alec. She needed him with her— but she needed to be away from everyone else more.

"Go." The one word from her lips was frantic. "You need to accept everyone's condolences."

When it became obvious that he was going to refuse to leave her, just as he had when the service began, a woman sitting to Cordelia's left said, "I'll stay with her, Alec."

But Alec didn't let go as he said, "Cordelia—"

She yanked her hands from his, all but shoving him out of his seat and toward the throngs that were getting closer. Too close. "They need you." She'd already taken too much from him. He had already been far too kind.

Finally, reluctantly, he got up and walked away.

And she had to bite her lip to keep from calling him back.

"I'm Suzanne, Alec's sister," the woman on her left said. "And these are our brothers, Harry and Drake. There are lots of other Sullivans here too, including our father, who is just over there." Alec's father was standing a few feet away from his son, close enough to step in if he needed him, but not close enough to crowd him.

Cordelia finally looked into the faces of the people who had surrounded her and Alec like a protective bubble during the service. Harry and Drake looked a lot like Alec—handsome, strong, with kind eyes—and Suzanne was gorgeous. This was the family he'd spoken about. His beautiful, perfect, connected family. Alec hadn't had only them—he'd had Gordon too.

"I need some air."

Cordelia wasn't usually rude, but she was desperate to escape the emotions that had come roaring back out of that numb place it had been so nice to hide in for a little while. Anger. Hurt. Betrayal. Sadness.

She knew she was a swirling mess—inside and out—as she ran from Alec's family. She'd taken a taxi here, hadn't trusted herself to drive safely to the service, and now she called another to come pick her up. She was told it would be there in ten minutes, which meant she now had a sixth of an hour to try to get back to that numb place. A little bit of the way there, at least. Thankfully, one of the many stand-up bars was directly in front of her.

Cordelia had never been much of a drinker. Then again, she'd never been to the funeral of the birth father she'd never met either.

She ordered the first drink that came to mind. "Gin and tonic. Light on the tonic." When it came, she tipped her head back and downed it in one long gulp, then handed back the empty glass. "Another, please."

She was halfway through throwing back the second when Suzanne materialized at her side. "I know you probably don't want company right now, but I promise I'll just stand here in silent support if that's what you want."

"It's fine," Cordelia said with a wave of her hand before she slid the glass back to the bartender and asked for a third. "Were you and Gordon close?"

"Pretty close," Suzanne said with a nod and a smile. "He was in our lives for the past fifteen years that he and Alec were in business together. What about you?"

"Never met the guy before." Cordelia grabbed her third drink, took a great big glug of it.

Suzanne's eyebrows went up. "Wait. You've never met Gordon?"

"Nope. So I'll bet you're wondering why I'm here, aren't you? And why I'm falling apart right in front of you."

Suzanne paused a beat before saying, "You don't have to tell me if you don't want to."

Cordelia shrugged. "Why not?" She wasn't feeling much pain anymore. Thankfully, with the help of the gin, she'd almost achieved that numb feeling again. "Gordon was my father." She thought Suzanne might have gasped, and it actually pleased Cordelia to have shocked her. The last of her third drink went down smooth. Real smooth. "Sperm donor, anyway. My mother died having me and he gave me away. Hello and good riddance in one fell swoop." She put the empty cocktail glass on the tray of a passing waiter and grabbed a glass of bubbly for a change. "And now it turns out he willed me his half of the company. Just out of the blue, *here's a billion dollars.*"

"My God." Suzanne just stared at her. "No wonder Alec is acting so—"

"Cordelia." Alec's arm slipped around her waist, and he looked down into her eyes. "How many have you had?"

She shrugged again, wobbling when the small movement made her head spin. "Not enough."

He turned to his sister, scowling. "Suz, I trusted you not to let things go south."

"I know, and I'm sorry I didn't do a better job." Cordelia watched as his sister pinned him with a serious gaze. "But if it were me, I'd be drinking too."

Both of Alec's eyebrows went up. Cordelia guessed that they were talking about her, but she was having a hard time following their conversation.

He reached out to take the champagne from her hand. "Time to go."

"No." She gripped her glass. "I'm having a good time." She took a defiant drink to show him just how much fun she was having. "Best time ever. How could I not, after hearing everyone wax on and on about how generous, how loving, how *fatherly* Gordon was to them?"

"Anything I can help with?" A good-looking—and very large—man put his arm around Suzanne and gave her a kiss. "I'm Roman," he said to Cordelia.

"Nice to meet you." The words didn't come out quite right. Nonetheless, Cordelia held out her empty glass to a waiter. "How about a refill?"

Alec snatched it from her. "You've hit your limit."

She went face to face, chest to chest, toe to toe with him. "I haven't even come *close* to hitting my limit yet."

"Suz, Roman," Alec said over her shoulder, "let everyone know I appreciate their coming today, would you?"

The next thing she knew, one of his hands was wrapped around her wrist and he was dragging her away from his perfect sister and his sister's gorgeous lover, away from the bar, away from the crowds. Away from the casket.

And though Cordelia was glad for that part, if nothing else, she had to ask, "What do you think you're doing?"

"Saving you from the worst hangover of your life. Although I'm worried I might already be too late."

A sleek black sports car materialized from out of nowhere, and she was soon inside beside Alec, buckled up in the passenger seat, speeding away from the funeral.

"I'm not drunk," she tried to say. But this time the words definitely didn't come out right.

"Don't worry," he said as he turned his gaze briefly from the road to look at her. "Once we get some coffee into you, you'll feel more like yourself."

But she didn't want to feel like herself. Didn't want to let all those *SadAngryHurt* feelings back in. No, she'd much rather just keep floating between reality and fantasy.

Before she could say any of this, however, he was stopping the car and undoing the buckle to help her out and into his home. And she supposed it was fortunate he was there, because her legs didn't work right either.

"Jesus." He lifted her into his arms, and her breath whooshed from her lungs as she reached out to grip his shoulders. His very muscular shoulders. "How many glasses of champagne did you have?"

"One."

He looked down at her in disbelief, not missing a step as he took her into his fancy apartment. Then he leaned in closer, so close that she wondered if he was going to kiss her. He looked like he'd be an *awesome* kisser.

Only instead of putting his lips against hers, he seemed to be sniffing her face.

"Gin." He scowled. "You were drinking gin."

"My parents drink it sometimes. On sunny afternoons."

He laid her on the couch and knelt so that they were face to face. "Can I trust you to stay here while I make coffee? Or are you going to go rolling off the couch so you can root around for more gin?"

He really was a beautiful man. And even though he'd carted her away from the funeral like a sack of potatoes, he had been surprisingly nice before that. "I don't want coffee."

She didn't want gin anymore either. It wouldn't help her forget, she knew that now. But something else might help her forget for a little while. *Someone* else might.

"I want you to show me how you are with other women," she said. "I want you to show me how *not nice* you can be."

CHAPTER SEVEN

A string of curses shot through Alec's mind.

That urge he'd had to kiss her in her cottage earlier that week hadn't gone away. On the contrary, it was stronger than ever now. So strong that he only barely managed to shift away from her.

But despite the gin she'd guzzled like a fish, she moved quickly. The next thing he knew, her arms were around his neck.

And, less than a heartbeat later, her mouth was on his.

His first thought was amazement that she tasted like flowers. As though the essence of her garden surrounded her always.

His second thought? That no lips had ever been so soft...or made him so greedy for more.

There was no finesse in her kiss, just a smash of her lips against his. But somehow, that made it all the better. Made him feel like he was a teenager making out with the one girl he'd thought he could never have, the one he'd watched from afar and had secret, late-night fantasies about.

Lord knew he'd had enough fantasies about Cordelia this week. But they had nothing on the sweet reality of her lithe body in his arms, or her soft mouth against his, or the little sounds of pleasure she made as she swept her tongue against his.

When Alec wanted a woman, he immediately got her. There was never time for anticipation. But all week, from the first moment he'd set eyes on Cordelia, he'd wanted her and hadn't been able to have her.

At long last, she was offering herself to him. And he was so starved for her that unquenched desire temporarily overcame everything else, including the sure knowledge that she'd had far too much to drink to be making good decisions right now. It was up to him to make those good decisions for both of them, but first, just one taste. That's all he wanted. And then he swore he would stop.

Taking her face in his hands, he moved her right where he wanted her. Soon, his hands were in her hair, tangled up in the silky strands, and they were lying on the couch, his body levered over hers.

Her legs went around his waist and her hands clutched at his shoulders in the same moment that he began to run kisses from her mouth, over her cheeks, her eyelids, her chin. Despite his vow to take only one tiny little taste, he wanted to cover every inch of her with his mouth, wanted to taste, to adore, every part of her.

She arched her neck so that he could rain kisses over her throat and shoulders. When the fabric of her dress got in his way, he was so overwhelmed by the need to make her his that before he could think like a rational human being and stop himself, he took a fistful of cotton in his hand and tore.

She gasped as his tongue laved a wet path over her fabric-covered breasts. And when his mouth latched on to the taut tip, she gave an even louder gasp. One that compelled him to draw down the fabric and to repeat the motion over bare skin this time. Perfect, sweet, soft, naked skin.

"Alec."

God, he liked the way his name sounded on her lips, especially when it came out this aroused. This lush and heavy with pleasure.

Suddenly, his cell phone rang, the sound not far from that of alarm bells. Alarms that had been playing from the second he'd found Cordelia guzzling booze and blurting out everything to his sister at the funeral.

Sensual desperation was one thing, and he was all for that. Hell, he almost felt as though he and Cordelia had *invented* desperate desire. But while he could tell that she wanted him, when he could think rationally for a split second, he also understood that her desperation didn't really have anything to do with him.

The funeral—along with finding out about Gordon and the inheritance—had done a number on her. He completely understood why she'd want to use sex to try to blot out the day she'd just had. The whole damn week, in fact.

Another time, with another woman, he might have been willing to let her use him for help-me-forget-everything-bad-in-my-life sex. But with Cordelia, he couldn't ignore the feeling that escape-sex would be wrong. Really, really wrong. Not just for her, but for him too. Especially after she'd had so much to drink.

Somehow, he managed to pull his mouth from hers, even though it was the last thing he wanted. "Cordelia." She tried to kiss him again, but he drew back far enough that she couldn't. "We can't do this."

Her eyes were still fuzzy from the drinks she'd had, but less so as his words registered. "You don't want me?"

"I do. Of course I do." They were still tangled up enough for her to feel the proof of his words. "But it's been a hell of a day." He sat up, tried to move her into a sitting position as well. "I get why people have grief sex, but I don't think—"

The words *grief sex* made her soft mouth settle into a hard line. "This doesn't have anything to do with grief. You wanted to kiss me before and now I want to kiss you too."

Alec was wealthy enough and powerful enough that he rarely had to watch what he said. But he knew he was treading on uneven ground here. "This has been a rough day for you, seeing your father for the first time at his fu—"

"It *wasn't* a rough day! Seeing him in his casket didn't even matter!"

She jumped off the couch as she tried to convince Alec to believe things he knew weren't anywhere close to true. When her legs didn't cooperate as she must have thought they would, and she stumbled, he stood and steadied her. The top of her dress was ripped so that it pooled at her waist, leaving her clad in only her cotton bra. A way-too-sexy-for-his-peace-of-mind cotton bra.

Not, however, that she seemed to be aware of her clothing being in disarray at all. Nope, she was far too pissed off at him to do anything but glare and fume. "Why are you making such a big deal about everything?"

Normally, he wouldn't have. But Cordelia wasn't just some woman he'd picked up at a bar or charity event. She was Gordon's daughter. He couldn't give her forever, but he could sure as hell do better than this.

"You deserve better than a drunken screw on my

couch."

"I should have known you wouldn't understand." She was trying to push out of his arms now, succeeding as she finally broke free. "With your big, perfect family always there to support you!"

"Wrong." His voice abruptly turned hard as his answer whiplashed back at her. "My mother killed herself when I was five. My father went completely off the rails. Which left it up to me to make sure Harry, Suz, and Drake didn't fall apart too. That song I couldn't stand to listen to in your kitchen? It's what my father used to sing to my mother. 'Something in the Way She Moves.' And then after she died, all we ever heard was 'Fire and Rain' on repeat. If I never hear a James Taylor song again, it will be too soon."

Cordelia was halfway to the door, ripped dress, tangled hair and all, when she abruptly steadied herself on the kitchen island and turned around. "Wait. What did you just say?"

But he already regretted it. Was silently cursing himself for giving away more of himself to a woman than he ever had before. Sure, any stranger could get some of what he'd told her on Wikipedia due to his father's fame, but Alec had never admitted the rest to anyone. Never even talked about it with his siblings in those heartsplat-words—*trying to keep the people he loved from falling apart.* Never admitted that just hearing certain songs on the radio could shred his insides to pieces.

"Nothing." He moved into the kitchen. "I'll get coffee going and will take you home once I know you're not going to fall over if you're left alone."

With her hands on the kitchen island to stop herself from wobbling while she walked, she moved closer to him. "Your mom." She looked sad. For him. "I'm so sorry she—"

"Forget I said anything." What had he been thinking, shooting off his mouth like that? It was bad enough that he hadn't been able to keep from kissing Cordelia, from climbing on top of her and ripping off her clothes. Blurting out his secrets made it infinitely worse.

Turning around and seeing Cordelia standing there in her bra and torn dress wasn't going to help matters any. He unbuttoned his shirt and yanked it off. By the time he turned around, she had moved to stand right behind him. The urge to kiss her again was strong. So strong that he nearly lost sight of why he shouldn't.

But the fabric in his hands reminded him—he needed to cover her up so that he wouldn't be tempted to touch her again.

"Here." He wrapped the shirt around her, tucking her hands and arms through it when she just stood there and blinked up at him with her too-big, too-pretty, too-honest eyes. Eyes that, even when she was plastered, seemed to see too much. "I'm sorry I ruined your dress. I'll buy you a new one."

That was when she finally seemed to notice that he was buttoning up his shirt over her. "I never liked it anyway." And then she was putting her hands over his to still them over her chest, right where he could feel her heart beating. As fast as his was beating. "Your brothers, your sister—they would do anything for you. I was barely there at the funeral, barely able to see anything at all, but I could still see that."

The coffee machine dinged, and he was beyond glad to be able to step away, to pour her a cup, and one for himself too. He hadn't had a lick of alcohol today, but what he'd tasted of her had made his head spin. Around and around and around until he could barely remember why he shouldn't just keep tasting her until he'd had his fill.

"Drink this." He wrapped both of her hands around the mug so that she wouldn't drop it.

Thankfully, she followed his direction, carefully sipping at the strong brew. However, she wasn't yet inclined to drop her line of inquiry about his family. "Your sister said your father was there today. But he wasn't sitting with you like your sister and brothers, was he?"

Instead of replying, he said, "Give me your cup. You need a top-up."

"Gordon was there for you when your own father wasn't." This time, her words weren't a question. She was simply stating a fact, one so obvious that she'd been able to figure it out even with gin still sloshing around inside her.

One more word out of her, and Alec was going to say something he would regret even more than what he'd already told her—if only to get her to stop talking about his father. About Gordon being gone now too. About what a mess it all was, top to bottom.

Yes, he wanted her more than he'd ever wanted anyone else.

No, he didn't want to talk about his feelings. Especially the ones that were mixed up with his father.

Which meant he needed to get her home and then forget about Cordelia Langley and her colorful garden and her sinfully sweet kisses and the feel of her arms and legs wrapped around him as she made those breathlessly sexy sounds.

But before he could do or say anything to speed the end along, she laid her head on the island with a groan. "I don't feel so good."

Alec swept her up into his arms before she could fall. Her lashes were long against her cheeks, and she was half asleep as he took her out of the kitchen and down the hall to his bedroom. He was going to have to watch her while she slept off the drink, make absolutely certain that she wasn't going to be sick.

"Don't let go," she whispered, the same thing she'd said when they'd been mere feet from her father's casket.

"Don't worry," he murmured. "I'm not going anywhere."

At least for today.

* * *

It was several hours later before Alec felt comfortable leaving Cordelia's side. Her rest had been fitful at first, but finally she settled down.

He was more than ready to collapse on the couch himself, but first he needed to deal with the phone calls from his father that had kept coming all night long.

William picked up on the first ring. "Alec, how are you doing?"

"Fine." Strangely, though he'd missed the bulk of Gordon's service, getting to share the experience with Cordelia had made it more bearable. It might have been one of his worst days ever, had it not been for her.

"I'm not just talking about Gordon's funeral. Suzanne told me about the bomb he dropped in his will. On you and his daughter."

Alec couldn't dispute that. But he still had to defend Gordon. "He must have had his reasons."

"I'm sure he did. Families…they're complicated. We know that better than most, don't we?"

What the hell did his father expect him to say to that?

When Alec didn't respond, William asked, "What can I do to help?"

"Nothing." Surely his father had to realize he was the last person Alec would turn to if he needed help. "Everything is taken care of."

"I wanted you to know that I'm not planning on heading back to the lake yet, so I'm here if you want to grab a beer or—"

"Go home, Dad." Alec was too tired for subtlety. "Thanks for calling, but I've got to get some sleep."

"Okay." He tried not to hear the hurt in his father's voice. "I just wanted to make sure you know I'm here for you. If you ever need me."

"Great. I've got to go now." Alec dropped the cell phone onto the kitchen island, grabbed the blanket draped over the back of the sofa, and lay down, deliberately blocking out thoughts of his father as he let the darkness claim him.

CHAPTER EIGHT

Loud knocking at his front door woke Alec, sleeping on the couch. The bed in his guest room would have been more comfortable, but the living room was closer to Cordelia. If she called out for him, he needed to be able to hear her.

It had been a heck of a long time since he'd tossed and turned on a couch all night. And no wonder, he thought as he stood and stretched out his back. It was damned uncomfortable.

Wearing the T-shirt and jeans he'd changed into last night after putting Cordelia in his bed, he walked barefoot over to the door. He usually had no problem with early mornings, but yesterday had been particularly trying.

Especially the part where he'd had to strong-arm his libido so that he didn't take complete advantage of Cordelia while she was drunk. He grimaced as he remembered the way he'd ripped her dress so that he could get at her. He'd stopped them from having sex, but he hadn't stopped nearly soon enough. It didn't matter that she'd been the one begging him to kiss her, begging him to take her. He still owed her an apology.

He didn't bother looking through the spyhole, just yanked the door open. His sister was holding two to-go cups of coffee. "I came over because I was worried about you. But you look even worse than I thought you might."

He took one of the cups from her and downed half in a long gulp. He didn't invite her in, but she followed him anyway, closing the door behind her.

"I'd ask if you're doing okay," she said, "but I think I already have my answer."

He put down the coffee on the kitchen island, then opened the fridge. Cooking always settled him. "It's complicated."

"Obviously," Suzanne said as she took a seat on one of the stools. "I couldn't believe it when your friend Cordelia said she was Gordon's daughter. How long have you known?"

The word *friend* pinged around inside his brain. He and Cordelia hadn't known each other long, but the time they'd spent together had been intense. He knew for sure that he wanted her—and couldn't have her. He also knew that she was meant to have a family in her flowery cottage—a perfectly nice, uncomplicated husband and cute, happy kids—while he would always be the confirmed bachelor.

"Same as she has," he finally replied. "About a week." He had everything he needed to make a full English breakfast, something he always enjoyed when he was in England visiting family or clients. "I take it you're hungry?" His sister's brain worked so fast that he swore it actually burned calories.

She grinned. "Starved." But then her smile fell away. "It must have been a shock, not only to find out about Cordelia, but that Gordon left his half of the company to her." His sister wasn't at all subtle as she asked, "So are you two going to be partners now?"

"No. She has a great garden store in Yorktown. She doesn't want any part of S&W."

"And you don't want her to have it." He paused long enough before answering that Suzanne's eyebrows went up. "Wait, *do* you want her to have it?"

"Cordelia is smart. Friendly. Even-tempered. Just like her father. Birth father," he corrected himself. "I have no doubt she would be an asset to the business, that she would quickly learn the ropes. But making her sit in an office, forcing her to schmooze with celebrities, would be like tying a weight around her ankles. Hell, around every part of her. She belongs in her garden, in her cottage."

Suzanne was looking at him in a very considering way. "Sounds like you and Cordelia have gotten to know each other pretty well this week."

He looked up from the stove where he had potatoes, bacon, and eggs going. The tomatoes and beans waited their turn. "You're literally the least subtle person on the planet."

His sister grinned again. "Subtlety is a waste of time."

Since he agreed with her, he didn't bother arguing. "Cordelia's here."

"Here?" Suzanne spun on the stool to look around his apartment. "Where?"

"In my bedroom."

"Alec!" His sister was fierce as she said, "How could you? She was *drunk* when you left the service last night."

He shot Suzanne just as fierce a look. "Why the hell do you think I got her out of there? If she'd blurted out the news of her paternity to anyone else, it would have gone straight onto Page Six this morning. A bunch of money- and gossip-hungry vultures are the last thing she needs right now." He continued to scowl as he said, "I slept on the couch."

"No wonder you look so crummy."

He didn't care what he looked like. All he cared about this morning was the woman sleeping in his bed. She probably wasn't going to wake up feeling much better than she had when he tucked her in last night. Not because of the hangover she was sure to have. Not even because he'd taken things way too far with her last night on the couch.

But because she still had to be reeling from finally seeing her father…in his casket.

"She was brave to come to his service," he said in a low voice.

"She was," Suzanne agreed, before adding, "You like her, don't you? *Like* her, like her, I mean."

"You're talking like we're six years old on the playground."

"That wasn't a no," she pointed out.

He reached for the coffee, drank the rest of it. "Drake and Rosa got the big romance. So did you and Roman."

"You actually managed to say Roman's name without curling your lip for once," she teased. "Good job."

Ignoring her remark about the boyfriend he was still getting used to her having, he continued, "Cordelia and I met under strange circumstances and have connected because of it. But we don't live in the same world. Don't want to live in the same world."

Clearly not believing a word of his denial, Suzanne said, "Should I mention the fact that you couldn't take your eyes off her yesterday? Or should I just drop it?"

He shot her a warning glance. "It's long past time for you to drop it."

"For now, big brother," she agreed. "How are you doing without Gordon? Personally, I'm still having a hard time believing he's gone."

"It sucks." He wasn't going to sugarcoat it—didn't need to with Suz.

"Anything you need, you know I'm here for you. We all are." She paused before adding, "Including Dad." When Alec simply grunted, she went on, "He's really worried about you. He wanted to come here himself this morning. But he wasn't sure how that would go—none of us were, actually—so I came instead."

While neither of them believed in beating around the bush, their reticence to talk about their father was something else entirely. There was so much history, so much darkness. Too much for easy words and simple answers.

"I'm glad you're here, Suz." Alec finally smiled at her. "Did the rest of Gordon's reception go okay?"

Though he hadn't answered her unspoken questions about whether it would have been okay for his father to come comfort him, she let it go. And as he began to plate their food—putting a third plate in the warming drawer for Cordelia, just in case she had the stomach for it when she woke up—his sister regaled him with stories of celebrities behaving badly.

* * *

Cordelia woke with her head pounding and her mouth feeling like she'd been sucking on cardboard. She made the mistake of opening her eyes and sitting up too fast, before slowly sliding back down into the pillows and sheets.

Alec's pillows and sheets.

Even feeling as rotten as she did—she swore she'd never, ever drink again, not even one drop of gin or champagne—every part of her started to tingle just from knowing she was in his bed. She lifted the sheets and saw that she was fully covered, with the extra layer of his shirt no less.

Why would he have put her in his shirt? Oh God…had she been sick all over her dress last night?

Humiliation washed over her at the thought of barfing in front of him. Seriously, there was no other man in front of whom she'd ever managed to look this consistently awful. She needed to get into a shower, gargle with some toothpaste, and then get out of here before she embarrassed herself any further.

As long as she made sure to move slowly, her legs remained fairly steady. Aspirin for her headache, a hot shower, and a big cup of black coffee would hopefully set her to rights. Hoping Alec wouldn't mind that she was using his shower without asking, she turned on the water, then began unbuttoning the shirt he'd lent her.

The state of her dress beneath the shirt—ripped open to her waist—momentarily shocked her, until the memory of how it had gotten that way suddenly tore through her brain.

How could she have forgotten?

She scrunched her eyes shut. "No. No. No. No. No." But all the wishing in the world couldn't rewind time to the hours before she'd showed up at the funeral. She couldn't not see Gordon in the casket. Couldn't refuse the gin.

And she definitely couldn't forget throwing herself at Alec and begging him to have sex with her.

She dreaded making the walk of shame into his kitchen this morning. How was she going to face him?

Alec had been nothing but nice to her from the start. He'd understood that she was a mess over the revelations from her birth father, and he'd tried to make it easy on her in any way he could—from his buyout offer to his help at the funeral to letting her kiss him when she was drunk.

She was just toweling off when the rest of it came back to her—the shocking things he'd said about his father, his mother, and about how he'd been in charge of caring for his siblings from such a young age. Cordelia might not have known her birth father or mother, but she'd had parents who loved her, cared for her, watched out for her every single second. Whereas Alec had lost his mother in the worst possible way—and then hadn't even been able to wallow in grief. Because he'd been a child carrying the burden of keeping the family together when his father had fallen apart.

Cordelia's heart ached for him. He obviously hadn't meant to let the information about his past spill out, but he'd been pushed too far by a day that must have been just as hard for him as it was for her.

As mixed up as her feelings were about her birth father, Cordelia understood that Gordon Whitley had been as good as a father to Alec. And it wasn't fair of her to try to take that away from him out of misguided jealousy that she hadn't been given the same love, the same attention from Gordon.

She'd been in Alec's way all week—not only keeping him from running his business and from his family, but also from processing his own grief over losing Gordon. It was long past time for her to make her apologies for everything she'd put Alec through, say her thank-yous for all of his help, and then get out of his life. Completely.

Her chest squeezed at the thought of never seeing his handsome face again, of never feeling the warmth of his arms around her, of never sharing another breathtakingly sensual kiss.

Her heart heavier than ever, Cordelia carefully hung up the wet towel and picked up her clothes and his shirt from the floor. She'd have it cleaned and pressed and sent back to him, along with the clothes that she would have to borrow this morning.

She didn't want to snoop through his things—she already felt bad enough about using his bed and shower, not to mention the horrifyingly embarrassing *please-have-sex-with-me* part of her stay in his home—but she needed to find something to wear. A sweatshirt and sweatpants, maybe? In the third drawer she tried, she found a stack of T-shirts. Putting her bra and panties back on, she slipped the navy blue shirt over her head and found that it came to her knees. With the belt from her dress, she cinched the T-shirt around her waist. Honestly, she liked the look of it better than the dress she'd had on for the funeral. T-shirts and jeans were her comfort zone, whereas she always felt as though she was playing dress-up in skirts and heels.

Her heart was pounding like crazy as she gathered up her dress and his shirt, then opened the bedroom door, her cheeks flushing all over again at the memory of what they'd done on his couch. At what she'd *begged* him to do. It was thanks only to his honor that he'd stopped them from going even further. She already felt bad enough about how she'd behaved—she would never have forgiven herself for using him to blot out her grief had they continued.

But when she stepped into the hallway, she realized he wasn't alone. A woman was with him, laughing.

Jealousy seized Cordelia before she could stop it. Even though she knew she had no hold on him. Even though she'd already decided to leave him alone from here on out, rather than continuing to be some sort of weird piece of Gordon's legacy that just kept hanging on to him.

She recognized the woman's long dark hair first, and then her slightly husky voice. Suzanne, his sister. She must have stopped by this morning to check on her brother. Because she knew he was hurting from the loss of his friend.

Shame swamped Cordelia all over again at the fact that she'd been so busy thinking about herself, about her confusion, about her pain, she hadn't tried to help soothe Alec's grief. Why couldn't she have dealt better with everything that had happened, instead of dissolving into a mess every other second?

A mess that Alec kept having to clean up.

Well, she wouldn't lose it again this morning. She'd apologize for ruining Gordon's service, make it clear to Alec that he was safe from her throwing herself at him again, and then she'd get out of his hair.

Last night, she'd been too tipsy to really notice her surroundings. But in the light of morning, she took in the sleek contemporary lines and the furniture and sparse decorations that made his apartment look like something straight out of a magazine. And yet, this place made of glass and steel and concrete, while fancy and impressive, didn't feel quite right for him, not when he'd fit so well in her flowery cottage.

It struck her that Alec, more than anyone, needed a warm, loved-up home. Maybe that was why he loved cooking so much—because it was the only way for him to get those home-cooked meals he must have longed for after his mother's death and the splintering of his family.

"Cordelia." He pushed out of his chair at the kitchen table where he and Suzanne were sitting. "How are you feeling this morning?"

"Okay." The word croaked out of her throat. She was desperate for a cup of coffee. "I hope it's all right," she said as she gestured to what she was wearing. "I borrowed one of your shirts."

"Borrow anything you need." He handed her a steaming cup and she put down the bundle of clothes to take it gratefully. "I've got breakfast ready, if you think you can handle it."

She hadn't thought she would, but he was such a brilliant cook that the smell in the kitchen had her mouth watering. "I could maybe eat a little."

He smiled at her then, that beautiful smile that

made her heart dance inside her chest. "Sit—I'll bring it out."

Suzanne was standing now too, arms open. "I'm so happy to see you again."

Cordelia couldn't resist falling into the hug from Alec's sister, even though she felt like a fool, remembering everything she'd said to her at the service. "I don't mean to interrupt your breakfast together."

"You're not interrupting anything." Alec put a loaded plate of food in front of her, along with what looked like freshly squeezed orange juice. "Suz stopped by to let me know which clients behaved badly at the service after we left last night."

"And to see if I could convince Alec to make breakfast for me." Suzanne stole some potatoes and sausage from Alec's plate. "He's the best cook in the world."

Cordelia's mouth was already so full that all she could do was nod. When she'd finally washed down her way-too-big bite, she said, "This is amazing, Alec. As good as the dinner you whipped up from my garden."

Suzanne's eyebrows went up as she looked between the two of them. "You cooked Cordelia dinner?" she asked Alec. And then to Cordelia, "From vegetables in your garden?"

Thinking it would help if she explained, Cordelia said, "One of my part-time staff at the garden center had to leave early, and when a rush came in, Alec saved me by pitching in. My customers keep asking about *that lovely young man who was in last week.*" She smiled as she forked up more eggs. "I don't have the heart to break it to them that you don't actually work for me."

"Lovely young man? Someone actually called you a *lovely young man?*" Suzanne gaped at Alec. "Who are you? And what have you done with my brother?"

"Roman's probably wondering where you are," he said in lieu of a reply as he reached over to take his sister's plate.

"He's busy at the gym this morning, teaching a group of kids how to box." She batted Alec's hand away from her plate. "And I'm not done eating yet. Besides, I can't leave until we discuss Dad's seventy-fifth. It's long past time to figure out where we're throwing his party. I was thinking it would be fun to surprise him this year. If we have the party at Summer Lake, someone in town is bound to tell him." She looked expectantly at Alec. "Got any ideas for alternate locations?"

He shoved away from the table, taking his plate over to the sink. "I don't know yet if I'll be there."

"What are you talking about?" Suzanne frowned. "Of course you have to be there."

"With Gordon gone, I've got twice the load at work. And you know he was always the one who did the bulk of the interfacing with our clients. Now that's on my shoulders."

Clearly, Alec wasn't thrilled about the new work he was having to pick up in Gordon's absence. Nor did he seem at all happy about attending his father's party.

"You can't miss Dad's birthday," Suzanne snapped. "It will break his heart if you do."

Alec stood with his back to them at the sink, and without thinking, Cordelia got up and went over to him. She took the plate out of his hands. "You know our deal—you cook, I clean."

"Thanks." In a low voice, he added, "I'm glad you seem to be feeling better this morning."

She smiled at him, wishing he would do the same. Wishing everything wasn't so confusing. So difficult. "I do, actually." Now that she was fed and caffeinated, she was surprised to realize that she felt quite a bit better. Even hearing Suzanne and Alec talk about Gordon didn't hurt quite so badly anymore. And she knew the reason why.

Because Alec had been there for her. He'd helped her deal with her emotions over Gordon's passing and her surprise inheritance in a way that no one else could have—not her girlfriends, not her parents.

Suddenly, it hit Cordelia that leaving Alec alone wasn't the answer. Just the opposite, in fact. She needed to stay by Alec's side so that she could help him with *his* father. She needed to be there for him in exactly the way he'd been there for her—by showing up, holding on, and not letting him deal with everything on his own, even if he swore that was what he wanted to do.

"I'll see what I can do to fit his birthday party into my schedule," Alec said grudgingly to Suzanne.

"Good," Suzanne said with obvious relief. "And don't forget to let me know if you think of anywhere that would work. It's got to be able to fit at least a hundred people." Suzanne got up from the table and brought her empty plate over to the sink. To Cordelia, she said with a smile, "I don't know if Alec told you, but our family is enormous, and growing by leaps and bounds every year as our cousins get married and have kids."

Cordelia wasn't normally impulsive. She didn't usually choose to walk head first into conflict. And she'd never in her life known a force of nature like Alec Sullivan—or his sister, for that matter. But she knew exactly what she had to do... even though Alec wasn't going to like the idea she was about to toss their way. In fact, he was sure to fight her with every step.

But Cordelia needed to help him, darn it. The same way he'd helped her. Whether he liked it or not.

"I know a place that could work." Drying her hands on the towel by the sink, Cordelia gave Alec and

Suzanne what she hoped was a calm and reassuring smile. "I have a barn on my property. Alec, you must have seen it when you were helping out the other day. I've hosted a few events in it this past year—a baby shower, an engagement party. I was actually thinking of trying to put on one of those farm-to-table dinners that are so popular now, but I don't know any chefs who could pull it off."

"Alec could," Suzanne put in, while he remained dangerously silent.

Cordelia's heart was thumping fast—too fast, given the lingering hangover—but she vowed to see this through. Best case, this birthday party would help Alec to be not only a part of his father's birthday celebration, but also one of the most important parts of it as the chef. She blocked out all thought of a worst case.

"My barn could fit up to a hundred and fifty people," she continued, "so depending on how you wanted to set it up, we could have a stage at one end for music and dancing and have tables at the other for a meal."

"A farm-to-table dinner for Dad?" Suzanne said. "He would *love* that! And Alec, if you were the chef, it would be even more amazing!" Alec still hadn't said a word as Suz went on, "I've got to get going now. We're working on a new software release, and it's spilled over into the weekend. I can't wait to spend more time with you, Cordelia. And thanks for breakfast, Alec." Despite the fact that he looked like he was about to erupt, Suzanne gave her brother a peck on the cheek. "Bye!"

CHAPTER NINE

The door had only just closed behind Suzanne, and Alec's head was still spinning even though he wasn't the hungover one, when Cordelia said, "Before we talk more about having your father's birthday party in my barn, I need to tell you how sorry I am for the way I behaved yesterday. I was tempted to crawl out your bedroom window this morning, actually, so I wouldn't have to face you."

"You don't need to apologize for anything you said or did yesterday." Despite the fact that Alec wasn't at all happy with her offering her barn for his dad's party, he refused to take it out on her by making her feel bad about her reaction to Gordon's funeral. "I'm the one who should be apologizing."

"I can't believe you think you need to say sorry to me for anything," she said with obvious surprise. "*I'm* the one who's horribly embarrassed by how I behaved, both at the service, and then after, when you brought me back here to sober up." Her cheeks were a deep pink as she added, "You should never have had to leave

Gordon's service early to take care of me. And you *really* shouldn't have had to fend off my—" She winced. "My amorous attack."

"First of all, I was all for your amorous attack. Which I'm sure you remember, given that your dress is unwearable today. *You* didn't rip it to shreds—*I* did. I never say things I don't mean, so when I told you that I want you, I wasn't lying, even though I am sorry for being so rough." He moved closer, put his hand on her cheek. They'd been completely honest with one another from the start, so it didn't feel right to be anything but honest now. "But I'm not a forever kind of guy, so if that's what you're looking for, we need to call me-and-you done right now."

Her eyes seemed bigger than ever, her face even more beautiful, as she looked up at him from beside his kitchen sink. "I grew up with parents who loved each other," she said softly. "I've always believed in forever, always wanted happily-ever-after for myself, just like they found." But she didn't move away from him, didn't shake off his touch as she spoke. And though he should have stopped touching her, he couldn't. "Your parents are the reason you don't believe in those things, aren't they?"

Bringing up his parents was the one surefire way to get him to drop his hand. And to remind him that it was long past time to shut down her idea about throwing his father's party in her garden. "I know Suz was excited about having the party in your barn, but it's not a good idea." Just as it wasn't a good idea for the two of them to be alone for much longer, when he could barely control himself around her.

Cordelia obviously wanted a fairy-tale relationship to go along with her fairy-tale cottage. But when she was this close, when she was wearing one of his T-shirts and her bare, tanned legs were tempting him like crazy, he could barely think for wanting her.

"I disagree," she said, then licked her lips, making them so shiny and kissable that he had to shove his hands deep into his pockets to keep from yanking her against him. "You've gone above and beyond to help me deal with things. It's my turn to help you now."

"Help me with what?" If he could only get his mind away from all the things he wanted to do with her, things that went *way* beyond ripping off her dress, he might be able to follow what she was saying.

"With your father."

Those three words succeeded in throwing ice water over him. "No."

"I get why your relationship with him is tough," she persisted, "but—"

"It's not tough. It's fine. We're fine."

"You're not!" The words burst from her. "I never even had a chance to know Gordon. The closest he ever came to being a father to me was leaving my parents a note that said, *Please give my daughter every-thing I can't. I'm trusting you both with her life, with her happiness.*" Alec was reeling from that information when she continued, "But your dad is still right here. Don't you want to at least try to make things better while you still can?"

Alec's phone buzzed on the counter. He grabbed it as though he were reaching for a lifeline and was relieved to see a message from his assistant about an emergency, even though it was with his least favorite client. Mona was a self-absorbed supermodel who had been angling to make him another notch on her belt for the past several months. The less interested he was, the more focused she'd become on her goal of claiming him as one of her boy toys.

"I've got to go. There's a problem at work."

"I'll go with you." Cordelia's expression was de-termined. "We can talk more about your father's party on the way—and what you want to make from my garden for his big birthday dinner."

"There's nothing more to talk about." He was just as determined. She needed to understand that about him. "We're not going to have his party in your barn. And I'm not cooking." He grabbed his keys. "I'll drop you off at your cottage on the way in to the office."

She didn't argue again as she went to pick up her

bag and the bundle of clothes she'd set down earlier, then got into his car. With anyone else, he would have thought he'd won, would have believed the birthday party subject would remain closed. But he'd spent enough time with Cordelia to know better. One mile turned into five, five into ten. And still, she remained silent. But he could hear her wheels turning the whole time, damn it.

When he couldn't take it anymore, he said, "Go ahead. Get it out. Every last bit of it this time, so we can be done with it once and for all."

She shifted to face him from the passenger seat. "What are you afraid of?"

He slammed on the brakes at a stop sign. "Nothing." His phone dinged again, this time with the SOS ring tone from his executive assistant. He verbally instructed his phone to text back with the message that he'd be in ASAP to deal with the customer. "We've got to head to my office first, otherwise my staff will quit on me. I'll have to take you home after my meeting." Gordon had stepped in to deal with the supermodel several times these past few months. If only he were still here. But then, that would mean his daughter wouldn't be…

"Good," Cordelia said, "that will give us more time to hash things out about the party."

"How many times do I need to tell you," he said in

as calm a voice as he could manage, "there is nothing to hash out?"

"Okay, then if everything is butterflies and rainbows between you and your father, why not commit to cooking a farm-to-table birthday dinner for him with fruits and vegetables from my garden?"

"Fine." The word shot from his lips like a bullet. "I'll make the goddamned dinner for him from your goddamned garden." Anything to stop talking about it, about his father and their non-relationship. "Right now, I've got to focus on dealing with Flyzilla."

Obviously pleased that she'd gotten him to bend his no to a yes—something very few people had ever managed, especially in record time like this—she sat back in her seat. *"Flyzilla?* Do you have nicknames for all your clients?"

"No. S&W Aviation is always professional, always happy to go the extra mile for a client." He ground his teeth together. "She's an exception."

"I can't wait to see if she's as horrible as you're making her sound."

"Not going to happen." Mona would chew Cordelia up and spit her out. "You can wait in my office while I deal with her alone."

"I know I said I didn't want anything to do with Gordon's airplanes, but after seeing him yesterday at the service…" She paused. "Even though I had to get ragingly drunk last night to deal with my feelings, I actually do feel better about things today. At least to the point where I'm willing to give in to a little curiosity about the business you and he built together. All my life, I've lived with so many unanswered questions. I guess I'm just starting to realize that some of the answers might still be out there. Because of you."

"I haven't done anything." Except rip her dress off her like the lowest kind of life-form and then jump down her throat over something as harmless as a birthday party.

"You have," she insisted. "This past week, you've told me things about him, things I didn't think I wanted to hear, but did. How he would get airsick like me. And how he had a vegetable garden. And how he never really seemed comfortable in his fancy homes. It's like finally finding some of the puzzle pieces that I'd thought would be lost forever—and now the picture, *my* picture, is starting to come together in a way it never has before." She let out a breath. "So that's why I want to see his planes. If I happen to run into Flyzilla, I promise I'll be on my best behavior."

"You might work in a garden all day rather than in a corporate office—but you are *definitely* Gordon's daughter," Alec muttered. "He never took no for an answer either."

From the corner of his eye, he saw her smile. "You

wouldn't respect anyone who did."

She was right about that. Alec had always found it way too easy to steamroll people. But that didn't mean she was right about his father. Alec would cook the meal for the birthday party, but it wouldn't change anything about their past…or their future.

★ ★ ★

Cordelia had never been an in-your-face kind of person. She'd always been happy just to hang out in her garden and listen to the birds chirp and the bees buzz. But Alec brought out the stubbornness in her. On a level that she hadn't known she possessed.

She'd never met anyone so hardheaded. Never thought she could want to shake a man and kiss him at the same time.

They hadn't formally agreed to be done with all the kissing. But he was right that she wanted a forever with someone someday—and since he didn't, it was definitely wiser not to go farther down a road that would ultimately go nowhere.

And yet…

It didn't make the urge to kiss him any less strong. In fact, sitting with him in his car, sparring over plans to use her barn, she found she wanted him more than ever.

No. She needed to focus on the things that made

sense. Like learning more about her birth father, while helping Alec with his. That way, in the end, the two of them would come out of this as friends. No harm, no foul. Just two people who had been there for each other during a difficult time.

As they pulled into the parking lot in Scarsdale, he said, "I don't know why I'm wasting my breath, but I'm going to suggest again that you wait for me in my office until I'm done with my client and can give you a tour of the planes."

"Actually," she said as she unclipped her seat belt and got out, "I'm thinking maybe I can help you with Flyzilla. A woman's touch, and all that."

"Your *help* is going to be the death of me."

"You mutter really loudly, you know."

"That's because I want you to hear every word," he shot back.

Despite their banter—or maybe because of it—he didn't seem nearly as grumpy anymore. Or as scowly. Which meant she was already helping, right?

The first time she had been to S&W Aviation, she had been too shell-shocked to appreciate any of it. This time, she made it a point to take everything in. The brilliant contemporary artwork on the walls, the luxurious furnishings that made the interior feel more like a five-star hotel than an office. And of course, the man who was the undisputed king of his world, a man more striking in a T-shirt and jeans than any other man would have been in a bespoke three-piece suit. The only surprising touch was the abundance of greenery in the building.

"Who takes care of the plants?"

"Gordon did. Now I am, until I can get a good service to take over. Everyone we've interviewed so far is a joke."

One week was long enough for many of the indoor plants to start to fade. But they all looked to be in very good health. "Just like I thought—you've got a secret green thumb."

"Don't say that too loud. If anyone hears, it will ruin my reputation."

She didn't know if he was joking—couldn't tell from his tone or expression. "What's your reputation?"

"Charming when I want to be. Hard when I have to be."

Funny, she hadn't really seen either yet, not when their circumstances had been so strange thus far. She could easily imagine the charm—how powerful it would be when Alec decided to turn it on. But hard? No. That didn't ring true to her, just the way his home hadn't fit him either.

It would be easy to be blinded by Alec's looks. And if money or power were what you were after, those could warp your opinion of him as well. But underneath it all, as far as she could tell, he was just like her, just like everyone else: searching for happiness the best way he knew how.

Cordelia knew how lucky she was that she'd found her passion for plants so young, and that her parents had encouraged her love of gardening. She wanted to believe that planes and celebrity customers made Alec happy too. But the way he was frowning as they headed through the building and out to the tarmac to deal with one of those customers made her wonder if he really was. And she couldn't forget his childhood dream to open a restaurant—or how content he seemed when he was in the kitchen.

"I wanted to give you a proper tour your first time out here," he told her. "Wanted you to really be able to appreciate just what Gordon built."

But she didn't need a "proper" tour to be hugely impressed. "Don't worry, my mind is being blown as we speak."

It was one thing to conceptualize dozens of multi-million-dollar private planes, or even to look at them from a distance through Alec's office window. But to be walking out among them, surrounded by the magnificent aircraft...

It was dizzying, to say the least. Even to someone like her, who had never longed to get into one and fly away.

They bypassed the smaller jets—she almost laughed at herself for thinking that any of them were *small*—and headed for what looked to be the biggest.

"Your customer spares no expense, does she?"

"She's got plenty of her own money," he said in a low voice, "but her father insists on paying for her membership with us. Gordon always figured it was a control thing with the two of them."

"So she has daddy issues too?" Maybe she shouldn't have gone there, but when Alec's only response was to roll his eyes, she kept going. "See? I knew I could bond with her over something."

His mouth twitched ever so slightly at one corner, and she felt a burst of happiness inside. Despite the surprise her birth father had thrown at her in his will, despite the pain of the funeral, despite the headache still lingering behind her eyes—when she was with Alec, everything felt better. And though he was doing his best to be a serious businessman right now, it seemed as though he might feel the same way.

Her birth father might have had plans for wedding rings and babies for the two of them, but something told her he would be happy with their being friends. With knowing that the man he'd cared for like a son and the daughter he'd watched from a distance—two people who were truly as different as chalk and cheese—had somehow managed to find kindred spirits in each other.

"After you." Alec put his hand on the small of her back as she began to climb the stairs at the front of the jet. "The steps can be slippery," he said, as though he felt he needed to explain why he was touching her. "I don't want you to slip in your heels."

They were the shoes she'd worn to the funeral. The only heels she owned, actually. Made of soft, light blue leather with a three-inch heel, they were fairly comfortable—she wouldn't have bought them if they weren't—but they were still far more wobbly than the tennis shoes or boots she usually wore.

Ducking her head slightly through the jet's door, Cordelia barely had time to take in the luxurious surroundings, due to the fact that there was a handful of people waiting inside, all madly clicking away on their cell phones. Cordelia quickly guessed that the stunningly beautiful blonde must be Flyzilla.

The woman frowned at Cordelia, but when Alec stepped through the door behind her, she lifted her painted lips into a sensual smile.

"Alec, aren't you a sight for sore eyes?"

His face was completely devoid of expression as he said, "You're looking lovely, Mona."

"You're so sweet to notice." She ran a hand over the red dress that fit her like a second skin. "I just grabbed whatever was closest in my closet today."

Cordelia nearly snorted out loud at that obvious lie. No one, not even a supermodel, looked this good without putting some effort into it.

"What can I help you with, Mona?"

Instead of answering his question, she pointed at Cordelia. "Who is *she*?"

"A friend." Cordelia appreciated how quickly he said it, and that he seemed to mean it.

"Well, tell her to go away," Mona demanded. "I need to talk to you." She got way too close to Alec and put both hands on his chest to run blood-red fingernails down it. "Alone."

"Cordelia," he said, the apology clear in his tone, "I won't be long."

He was doing his best to hide his revulsion at the way Mona was pawing him, but Cordelia saw it. And it infuriated her that one of his customers thought she could treat him like this. Like a prize she should have because she was rich enough to use one of his planes.

"Don't worry about me," Cordelia said, not planning on leaving Alec alone with the horrible woman for so much as a second. "I'm happy to hang out here while you two talk."

"Cordelia." Mona's lip curled. "What a quaint name." She scanned Cordelia from head to toe. "You've got to tell me the name of your designer. Simple and earthy is so in right now."

"I just grabbed the first thing in *Alec's* closet when I woke up this morning," Cordelia replied in a honey-sweet tone. She'd never played this kind of game before, but her urge to protect Alec trumped however off-base she might have felt going toe to toe with a woman like Mona.

Mona looked as though Cordelia had hit her with a baseball bat across the solar plexus as she turned to Alec in fury. "You're with *her?*"

Before Alec could reply, Cordelia instinctively said, "You bet he is," then grabbed him and kissed him, a smack on the lips that was so fast it shouldn't have made her go hot all over.

But it did.

Stunned by what she'd just done, she quickly pulled away, but he didn't let her go. Instead, he kissed her back. And even though she knew they were just playing a game to keep Mona from getting her claws into him, Cordelia nearly melted into a puddle of lust and longing in the middle of the fancy private plane.

Earlier, she'd wanted to punch and kiss him. Now she just wanted to keep kissing him. Again and again and again.

"Now," he said to Mona when he finally let Cordelia's lips go, then tucked her in beneath his arm, "what can I help you with before your flight?"

"Your standards have fallen," Mona said in a hard

voice, one that made it clear she was talking about his taste in women rather than the planes his company rented out.

"On the contrary," he replied, with one of those shark smiles Cordelia hadn't seen since their first meeting in his office, "I'd say my standards have never been higher."

Mona snarled. Actually sounded like a rabid dog. "Get off the plane, people!" Her entourage hurried to collect the bags and phones and tablets that they'd strewn around the cabin. "I wouldn't fly on one of your jets if they were the last planes on earth," she spat. "Gordon was always happy to do whatever he needed to make me happy. He would be rolling in his grave if he knew this was how you were treating your customers."

"You can say anything you like to me," Alec said in a deadly tone, "but leave Gordon out of it."

"I'll say whatever I want to!" Mona spat, doubling down in the worst possible way.

Cordelia stepped between them, coming face to chest with the horrible woman. "Either apologize to Alec for your behavior, or take your bad manners elsewhere. *Now.*" This wasn't just about Alec anymore. Not now that Mona had made the mistake of bringing Gordon into it.

"You can't tell me what to do, you little nobody!"

Mona's nostrils were flaring so wide Cordelia had a clear shot to her brain. It was not her best look. "I'm going to make sure *all* my friends pull their business," she said to Alec. And then to Cordelia, "You're going to pay too. And not just because it will be fun to tear you apart like the little rag doll you are." Her voice dripped with pure malice. "But because you're way out of your league with a man like Alec."

"*Mona.*" Her name was a serious warning from Alec, one anyone else would have heeded.

But the supermodel clearly didn't know when to back off. "You think you're so smug right now, wearing his shirt with your ratty hair and cheap shoes, but once he's through with the novelty of slumming it, you're going to be out on your ass with a little trinket from Tiffany." She raised a haughty eyebrow at Alec. "Likely the same bracelet he sent to my friend when he broke their date last week. If you're that lucky."

"Get the hell off my plane." Alec all but snarled the words.

Cordelia suddenly knew what *hard when he had to be* looked like. Gone was the charm. Even the shark smiles were in the rearview now.

Mona didn't bother to mask her fury. "There are a hundred guys willing to take what you could have had." She was anything but beautiful as she said, "Your loss," and stalked out of the plane.

"You were right," Cordelia said in a regretful tone once they were alone. "I should have stayed in your office. You've just lost a bunch of business because I couldn't keep my mouth shut."

"Are you kidding? You were magnificent." Alec surprised Cordelia by reaching for her hands and pulling her closer. "Gordon would have been so proud of the way you defended him. And me too."

"She was just so *awful*." She looked down at their linked hands, surprised by how well they fit together. "I couldn't sit back and watch her act that way. Not only because of the things she said about Gordon, but also because I hated her acting like your feelings didn't matter at all. Like she was sure you'd take one look at her and be unable to think with anything but your—" She flushed as she cut herself off. "I didn't know Gordon, but I'm positive that anyone you would have trusted enough to share a business with would have done the same thing."

"You're right. He wanted to send her packing a long time ago." Alec didn't give her time to fully process this information before he asked, "Do you want to see his favorite aircraft?"

"It's not this one?"

"God, no. This jet is for the Monas of the world. All flash and no substance. Gordon preferred a big engine over an overblown interior."

They were heading out of the plane, his hand at her lower back again, when she had to ask, "What about you? Which plane do you prefer?"

"It's out for the day, but I hope you'll let me do more than just show it to you. I'd like to take you up in it, Cordelia."

She almost slipped on the stairs, but he caught her around the waist before she could. "That's a seriously bad idea. I'd never forgive myself if I barfed all over your favorite plane."

He didn't look worried. "You won't."

"How can you be so sure?"

"Because it was the only aircraft Gordon always felt fine flying in."

But she knew it wasn't the plane Gordon had felt so safe with.

It was Alec.

CHAPTER TEN

Alec had learned how to defend himself at a young age, when his family's problems had become fodder for the world's press. The journalists who hadn't been able to get anything out of his grief-stricken father had turned to the kids. But Alec had fiercely protected his siblings, making sure that no one could ever corner them and find out just how terrible things were in the New York Sullivan household. He'd made sure not to let on with his Aunt Mary or Uncle Ethan either, so that no one would separate Alec and his siblings "for their own good."

From what he'd just seen on the plane today, Cordelia would have been just as fierce a protector. Alec could easily have taken care of the situation with Mona. But he'd enjoyed watching Cordelia get in Mona's face and tell her to back off.

Fact was, he enjoyed watching Cordelia do *anything*.

The only part he regretted, honestly, was that Mona had threatened Cordelia. Because if anyone so much as harmed a hair on her head…

"What do you send the women you break up with?" They were standing outside Gordon's personal jet now, a Gulfstream G650, as Cordelia clarified her question. "If canceling a date warrants a Tiffany bracelet, what do they get when you dump them?"

"Whatever they want."

She frowned. "How do you know what that is?"

"Because by then they've already picked it out." He knew it sounded cold-blooded, but it was all part of the arrangement, one both parties agreed upon at the start. "The women who go out with me aren't after anything more than a good time and something new for their jewelry box."

"That can't be true. I'll bet you've left a string of broken hearts from here to the end of the runway."

"I haven't."

"Have you looked in the mirror lately?"

His mouth quirked up into a cocky smile. "Are you saying you like how I look?"

She didn't further feed his ego. "All I'm saying is, in addition to your good genes, you're actually a really nice guy." She held up a hand to forestall his correcting her on that point. "I'm entitled to my own opinion after spending time with you this past week. Which is why I'm not convinced things with the women you go out with are transactions as heartless as you think." She pinned him with a serious look. "At least, not for them."

"Some women might make the mistake of thinking I can give them more than just a good time, but I never forget that I can't."

"Tell me again." Her words were soft but unwavering. "Why can't you?"

His response came before he could keep it locked inside, just the way it always did with her. "My mother always seemed on the verge of floating away, just disappearing into the ether—and my father was so desperate to keep her grounded—to keep her at all—that he painted her obsessively. In the end, they destroyed each other." He hated talking about his parents, but somehow Cordelia kept getting these flashes of information out of him. Almost as if he'd been waiting all this time for someone he could trust so that he could finally get it off his chest. "Living with them, keeping our lives running around them, *surviving* them, made me who I am."

She cocked her head, looking pensive. "I get how powerful parents can be in shaping their kids, but I'm pretty sure no one could make Alec Sullivan do something he didn't want to do."

How had she done that? Brought the conversation to a place where he couldn't argue with her, even though he didn't want her to be right? One thing was for sure—they were done talking about his parents.

Gesturing to the plane, he said, "This was Gordon's first purchase for the company. In long-range cruise mode, it can cover seven thousand nautical miles. At full tilt, it will cruise at Mach 0.925. He knew the size and speed of the engine, along with the luxurious interior, would make CEOs drool. He was right. Once we grew big enough, he made this plane his own."

He waited for her to push him some more on his past, to probe into his father's fame the way everyone else always did—and steeled himself to bat her questions away unanswered. But she simply said, "How did Gordon know so much about planes?"

"Come inside and I'll tell you."

A week ago, she wouldn't have put her hand in his so readily to walk up the stairs with him. A week ago, she wouldn't have trusted him, wouldn't have put up her dukes to defend him. A week ago, Gordon had been here, and Alec would forever mourn the loss of his friend.

And yet, a week ago, Alec's life hadn't been nearly so colorful...or as full of the simple joy of being with someone he liked. Liked a great deal, in fact.

"Everything about this plane feels powerful, strong." She took a seat in one of the large leather seats. "And yet, comfortable too. All I need is a great book and a blanket to curl up with and I'm set."

She was one of the few women who he believed really *would* be happy with just that. She didn't need gifts from Tiffany. Didn't need to drive the fanciest car or eat in the newest restaurant. Even the cynic inside of Alec couldn't deny the truth of who Cordelia was.

"There's more." He drew her back toward the luxurious bathroom.

"There's a shower on the plane?" She was clearly stunned. "This is like being in one of those spas I've seen on TV."

"Wait until you see the bedroom." He deliberately ignored the voice in the back of his head saying that taking her there might not be his smartest move. "If you thought the seats up front were comfortable, you're never going to want to get up off the bed."

She marveled at the room, which had an inset TV on the wall across from the bed and original artwork on the wall beside it. "How did you manage to make a bedroom on an airplane feel like home?"

"It was all Gordon. He had a knack for it." Just like she did with her cottage. "You've got to lie down on the bed to fully appreciate it."

"I'll bet you say that to all the girls," she teased.

"I like to let the jewelry do the talking," he joked back, then jumped on the bed, lying back with one arm behind his head, patting the empty side. "Don't be shy. There's plenty of room here for two."

"There's enough room there for an entire football team," she said with a laugh, before diving beside him and making a sound of such pleasure that every one of his inner heat gauges shot into the red. "This bed is *heaven.*" She sprawled out as though she were making a snow angel. "Your customers must want to tell the pilot to keep circling so they never have to leave."

He wanted to joke again. But he couldn't. Not when he was barely holding himself back from crawling up over her and showing her another side of heaven. The only way he could keep himself in check was to talk about Gordon.

"He was poor before I met him. Really poor."

She instantly stopped playing on the bed and rolled to her side to meet his gaze. "I know that shouldn't make me feel better. But it helps to know he wasn't a zillionaire already when he gave me away."

"I won't presume to know what he was thinking when you were born, but I'm guessing there was a fair chance he didn't want you to have the same kind of childhood he did."

"How bad was it?" Her words were barely above a whisper.

"He never painted the full picture for me." But Alec wouldn't lie to her about what he did know. "He told me enough to understand that there was abuse. And hunger. Enough of both that he never wanted to feel those things again." Alec wanted to reach for her to make sure she was okay with hearing all of this, but his restraint was already worn too thin from sharing the bed. "He didn't have any other family that I know of. Just parents he wanted nothing to do with."

"He must have loved your big family."

"He did. Although he always seemed wistful around my sister and female cousins." Alec hadn't understood it at the time, but now he knew Gordon had been thinking of the daughter he hadn't dared to claim.

"I know this might sound crazy," Cordelia said after a few moments, "but just being on his plane makes me feel as though I know a little bit about him now. Even more than hearing everyone talk about him at his service did."

She looked into Alec's eyes, not hiding anything she was feeling. He was constantly amazed that she never hid. Never pretended. Never lied about her feelings, even when she was scared. Especially when she was scared.

"I now know that he liked luxury," she continued, "but that he didn't want to be in a golden cage. He liked strength and power, but he didn't need to lord it over anyone. He was an efficient man, who focused on what counted, rather than wasting time on what didn't. I think…" She swallowed hard. "I think I might have liked him, Alec." The next breath she took shook through her, hard enough that the bed vibrated beneath them both. "I wish I could have met him."

Alec put his arms around her then, the dangers of a shared bed be damned. He stroked her hair, then down over her back, wanting desperately to soothe her. He hadn't been lying when he'd told Cordelia he wasn't like this with anyone else. But it was the only way he knew how to be with her.

"If I could turn back time and make it happen," he said, "if I could give you more than just the knowledge that he wanted your parents to give you everything he couldn't—especially happiness—I would."

She lifted her head from his chest, and he saw that her eyes were wet. "You really would, wouldn't you?"

He'd have answered her with words if he could. But all he could give her was a kiss. The kind of kiss he'd never given anyone but her. A kiss full of desire. Of emotion. Longing. And a powerful need to heal her wounds.

Her mouth met his with just as much passion, emotion, longing. Her lips were soft yet fierce as they kissed. She felt so delicate in his arms, yet at the same time she was the most unbreakable woman he'd ever known. He rolled her beneath him, and she arched into his touch, giving herself over to him so readily. So perfectly.

No one had ever fit him the way she did. No other woman had ever tasted as sweet. He lifted his head to tell her, to confess that he was in over his head, but she tangled her hands in his hair and pulled his mouth back to hers before he could.

"Please," she whispered against his lips. "Please don't stop. I need this. I need *you*."

He would have to stop soon. Regardless of how much he wanted her. But not yet. Not until he'd given her what she needed. Pleasure to replace pain, at least for a few minutes. He wouldn't take anything for himself, he vowed.

"I know what you need." He reached for the hem of his T-shirt she was wearing as a dress, stopping to stroke the smooth skin of her bare thighs.

"*Alec.*" His name from her lips was little more than a hitching gasp.

She wasn't the only one losing her breath. Alec was too. From nothing more than what teenagers would have done while making out—touching her thigh while kissing her was barely past first base.

He wanted to tear the shirt off her the same way he'd torn her dress the night before, wanted to rip away anything that came between him and her naked skin, but somewhere in the back of his brain he knew she'd need these clothes to walk out of here in front of his employees and customers.

Only, it was nearly impossible to keep the fabric intact as he slid his hand higher up her thigh and she trembled against him, holding him closer, kissing him harder with every inch. Up, up, up he went. Closer to heaven with every gentle stroke of his hand over her bare skin.

Every ounce of his concentration went to holding on to his control. But when he crossed the final inch of skin, when she arched into him, when his fingers slipped beneath the thin cotton of her panties and he found her hot, and slick, and so damned sweet—his control snapped.

She had become so precious so quickly that he was hell-bent on keeping her safe…even as he couldn't help but lead her at least partway down his dark, desperate path. He'd never forget this moment, never forget the pleasure, the gift, of Cordelia opening herself to him. Giving him something he didn't deserve, but could never in a million years regret taking.

She buried her face in the crook of his neck, her breath hitching out, panting as she rocked into his hand, taking what might have remained simple strokes of pleasure and making them thrusts of pure bliss as everything in Alec's world came down to this.

To *Cordelia*.

To her scent—of a garden even while in an airplane.

To her sounds—unfettered, unabashed pleasure as she climbed higher and higher in his arms.

To the feel of her against him—soft and strong and so damned sexy she made his head spin.

To her incredible beauty—from the flush on her cheeks to the wild heat in her eyes as every muscle went taut, then broke apart in beautiful release.

He had to kiss her again, needed to be there with her in every way he could allow himself. Long moments later, she finally stilled with a sigh of what sounded like relief. The very relief he'd wanted to give her. And yet, as she'd tipped over the edge in his arms, clinging to him to ride out the pleasure, he knew he'd betrayed his vow to only give to Cordelia and not to take anything for himself.

The truth was that her pleasure had been as much for him as it had been for her.

His body throbbed with unquenched need as he gently stroked her hair while she worked to catch her breath. "Better?"

She shifted slightly in his arms so that she could look up at him. He should roll away from her, and he would force himself to do it soon, but he couldn't keep from first stealing a few more seconds of her soft and warm body beneath his.

"So much better," she confirmed. And he could see it in her eyes, that at least for the moment, they'd lost that sheen of hurt. "But why are you stopping?"

"You know why."

She was silent for a moment. "What if...what if I told you it doesn't have to be forever?"

God, he wanted what she was offering. Desire was literally tearing at him. But he wasn't a monster, especially when it came to Cordelia. "I wouldn't believe you."

"I wouldn't believe me either." And yet, her big eyes remained full not only of lingering pleasure, but also of anticipation of all the ecstasy that awaited them, if only they could agree to move to the next level with each other. "But I still want you, Alec." Her honesty continued to stun him. And please him in equal measure. "I want you more than I've ever wanted anyone. Even now, after you just made me feel so good, I can't stop wanting you."

He groaned, pulled her close again, and just held her. "Gordon set us up for a hell of a situation, didn't he?"

"He did." She hugged him tighter. "But I'm glad he did. You're the friend I didn't even know I needed, and now I can't imagine my life without you in it."

Despite the fire raging inside of him, a fire that could never go any further than this, he told her the truth. "It's the same for me." In the most unlikely of situations, he'd found a friend. A beautiful, honest friend he would never forgive himself for hurting. So even though he had no idea how the hell he was going to stay away from her, he made himself say, "Tomorrow will be the start of a new week. Everything will go back to normal on Monday." It had to. He'd make sure of it. He'd buckle down and do the job of two men at S&W Aviation during the day. And at night, he wouldn't let himself fantasize about stripping away every last stitch of Cordelia's clothes and making love to her. Again and again and again.

He felt her take a deep breath, knew she was preparing herself for that fresh start, and forced himself to let her go—even as visions continued to hit him one after the other of all the pleasure yet to be had if he held on to her instead.

She pulled the T-shirt down over her thighs as she sat up. "Thank you for the tour. And for being there for me. Again." Her cheeks were flushed as she said it, but he was glad she didn't look embarrassed or regretful over what they'd just done. "You're right that everything needs to go back to normal tomorrow. And it will." She lifted her chin, pushed back her shoulders, as if steeling herself to make sure the plan didn't deviate off course. "I should probably head home now to check on my shop before they close up for the day."

"Sure." He just barely got his body in check by the time he stood. "I'll drop you off."

CHAPTER ELEVEN

Cordelia woke as the first rays of the sun shone over her bed. Even as a little girl, she'd been up with the sun. She loved listening to the first bird calls, loved getting her hands in the soil when it was still damp with dew, loved breathing in the sweet air, loved knowing she had a brand-new day in which to explore and appreciate the beauty all around her.

Rarely, however, had she needed a fresh morning start more than today. The past week seemed like one big blur to her now. Of emotion. Of pain. Of unexpected pleasure.

And through it all, woven into nearly every moment, was Alec.

Despite the morning chill, she went hot all over at the memory of his kisses, of his hands on her, of how masterfully—how wonderfully—he'd taken her into pleasure. Sharper, sweeter pleasure than she'd ever known. She'd barely come down from the high when she'd wanted to beg him to do it again, to love her with more than just his hands, his mouth.

She threw back the covers, hoping that bare feet on the cold hardwood floor would bring her back to earth. Back to reality.

One where she and Alec were never going to be more than just friends.

Yes, they'd crossed a line past friendship yesterday. And there was no denying that they wanted each other. But she understood that what he'd done had been, first and foremost, to give her a breather, and a release, from her roiling emotions over her birth father.

It was time now to be strong enough to stand on her own again. She would put in a good day's work in her garden center and then she would call the investment/donation team Alec had recommended to ask them to help her make sense of the new—and awesome—responsibility she'd been handed by Gordon and his money.

She also planned to call her parents tonight and finally tell them what had happened. She was sure they would understand why she'd needed to get her head around things first. Now that things might actually go back to normal soon, she wanted them to weigh in on where the money should go, especially regarding which educational foundations could benefit the most from a large influx of funds.

Her regular routine—a shower and a bowl of granola—helped make her feel more settled. She planned to spend a quiet hour in her garden with a steaming cup of coffee in hand, before heading across her property to put up the OPEN sign in the front window of the garden center.

She had just stepped out the front door and into her garden when she abruptly realized she wasn't alone. A dozen photographers were standing just outside the garden gate, and they were all trying to get her attention at once.

"How does it feel to become a billionaire over-night, Cordelia?"

"What are you gonna do with all the money?"

"Did you really not have any idea that Gordon Whitley was your father?"

Shock had the cup of coffee sliding from her fingers to crash and splash on the flagstones at her feet. She stood there unable to do any more than blink in confusion at the flashbulbs going off all around her like a massive disco ball.

How could these strangers have found out about every-thing?

Suddenly, a deep voice broke through. "Get the hell away from the house. You're trespassing on private property." The flashbulbs stopped momentarily as all eyes turned to Alec, resplendent—and fierce—in a dark suit, his eyes blazing. "My lawyers will have all of your asses if you're not gone in sixty seconds."

Cordelia could hardly believe it, but in less than a minute, they were all gone. All the cameras, all the people who had been shouting questions at her as though they knew her. As though they didn't care who they hurt as long as they got their story.

"Cordelia." Alec's eyes were gentle as he turned to face her, but she could see how upset he was. How angry. "Let's head back inside." He put his arm around her and soon had her sitting on her love seat with her cold hands wrapped around a fresh cup of coffee. "That's what the press does—they ambush you. But it won't happen again. I promise you that." His phone was buzzing in his pocket. He pulled it out, sent a text, then slid it back into his pocket and put his hands on either side of her face. "What did they say to you? I could hear them yelling, but not their questions."

Staring into his eyes grounded her better than anything else could have. "They were asking about Gordon. Asking if I knew about him all along. Asking what I was going to do with all my money." She shook her head, trying to make sense of it all. "I haven't told anyone about Gordon, only your sister, and I know she wouldn't have said anything to the press. So how could they possibly know so much?"

Alec's expression was grim. And furious. "Page Six. There was an anonymous tip about you and Gordon. Reporters were waiting outside my apartment this morning too. That's how I knew I needed to get over here ASAP."

"Thank you," she said, hugely grateful that he'd thought to protect her. Again. "Who could have tipped them off?"

It hit her a beat before he said, "Mona." He looked like he wanted to tear the supermodel apart with his bare hands. "My guess is she must have had someone who owed her a favor in one of our attorneys' offices. Or who wanted to get into her bed through any means necessary."

"She really meant it when she said she wanted to destroy me." Cordelia had no idea how Alec worked with people like Mona and kept his sanity.

"She's going to regret it," he said, dark promise in his voice. "I'll make sure she does."

"No. That's exactly what she wants. To pull you into her game. And to believe she shoved me down with this. Neither of us will give her that satisfaction." Now that the initial shock had worn off, Cordelia managed to give him a small smile as she added, "Even after knowing how low she's capable of going, I'd stand up to her again."

"I know you would." He put his hand on her cheek, and for a moment, she thought he was going to kiss her.

She knew it wouldn't erase what had happened

with Mona and the press—and that it would be a further complication their friendship didn't need, especially now—but Cordelia couldn't help but crave his kiss. Could barely keep from begging him to put his mouth and his hands on her again.

When she looked into his eyes, she swore she saw the same heat and longing tangled up inside of him that she felt in herself. But instead of closing the final distance and kissing the breath from her, he shifted back in his seat. "I'd hoped you'd have more time to deal with your inheritance privately, but now that the cat's out of the bag, we're going to have to make a solid game plan. Right away."

He'd barely finished speaking when someone knocked on her front door. "If it's another journalist or photographer…" Alec's expression was menacing as he got up to answer it.

She put a hand on his arm. "I've got it." The past week had been nutso, but she'd always taken charge of her own life. It was long past time to take charge of it again. She steeled herself for a confrontation as she opened the door. But the two people standing on her front step were definitely not strangers.

"Mom? Dad?" She'd never been so happy to see their faces. Or felt so guilty. "I'm so glad you're here. I was going to call you and tell you everything today. I swear it."

Fortunately, they seemed anything but angry as they pulled her close. "Oh, honey," her mother said, "we're just so worried about you and how you're doing."

Tears came then, now that she knew she was safe in her mother's arms. "I should have told you everything before now. I wanted to, but—" Cordelia stopped short as she realized Suzanne Sullivan and her boyfriend were standing behind her parents. "Suzanne. Roman." She wiped her tears away, not at all surprised that Alec's sister had come to help. Though she'd known Alec only a short time, she could see already that this was how the Sullivans operated. As a team. "Please come inside. Alec is here. He got rid of the press who were swarming just outside my picket fence."

"I'm glad he was able to get here so quickly." Suzanne gave her a hug. "We knew that if his place was overrun with press, then yours would be too. Roman is great at dealing with journalists and photographers who won't take *go away* for an answer."

"If it's all right with you," Roman said, "I'd like to stay outside and keep watch in case anyone decides to sneak back onto your property to get a scoop."

"It's more than all right with me," Cordelia said. "You're a godsend, Roman. But at least come in and get a cup of coffee first."

"I'm fine for now," he said, already heading back toward the gate.

She appreciated his determination to scare off trespassing photographers more than she could say. Appreciated Alec and his sister both being here so much, in fact, that her throat was tight with emotion. Especially now that she was finally about to share everything with her parents.

Amy and Walter Langley looked more than a little shell-shocked, not only by the news, but also by all of the Sullivans rallying around Cordelia in support. She was trying to figure out where to start her explanations when another knock came at the door.

"Cordelia," the handsome man with the glasses said, "I'm Harry, Alec's brother. We met briefly at Gordon's service."

Another man standing beside him smiled and said, "And I'm Drake, Alec's youngest brother. We also met at the service."

The beautiful, and very famous, woman beside him smiled warmly at Cordelia. "I'm Rosa, Drake's other half."

"Please, come in." Cordelia's cottage wasn't large to begin with, and now every seat in her living room plus her kitchen chairs would be taken. She'd never been happier to host a crowd, though. Having Alec on her side was a huge relief. His whole family felt like a *miracle.* "I'll brew more coffee."

"We don't want to put you out," Harry said. "We just wanted to see if there's anything we can do to help."

Harry Sullivan was sweet, just like Alec. And yet she could immediately see how different they were. Everything about Alec spoke of business prowess and power. Though Harry was also big and broad and extremely good-looking, he seemed to be a gentle soul who lived more inside his head. Suzanne struck Cordelia as a mixture of both brothers. As for Drake? Cordelia knew only that his girlfriend had been one of the most famous reality-TV stars in the world.

It hit Cordelia that she didn't know much at all about Alec's siblings—not their jobs, or even their birth order, apart from the fact that he was the oldest. She felt more than a little ashamed of herself for not having asked Alec to tell her about them, especially when his family was so important to him. And so close that each of them had dropped everything to come to her aid, simply because they loved their big brother and he was her friend.

She was comforted to know how well supported Alec was by those who loved him. He believed his parents were the only ones who had shaped him. But how could he not see that his siblings had a hand just as big, if not bigger, in making him the man he was today?

Alec handed mugs of coffee to her parents. "I'm Alec Sullivan, Gordon Whitley's friend and business partner."

"We're so sorry about his passing, Alec." Cordelia's mother held out her hand. "I'm Amy, Cordelia's mother."

Her husband shook Alec's hand next. "I'm Walter, her dad."

"Mom, Dad." Cordelia took their hands in hers as her parents sat on the love seat and she took the ottoman facing them. "I found out about Gordon last week from his trust attorney. They told me he was my birth father, that he had passed away the day before, and that he had given me his half of S&W Aviation. I couldn't believe it—couldn't believe any of it was real. Not just the money, but—" She paused to steady her voice. "The fact that he'd been so close. All this time. And he knew who I was. Knew I was here all along."

"Honey," her father said, "if we'd had any idea who your birth father was, we would have told you."

"I know you would. But for whatever reason, he didn't want any of us to know. I wasn't okay with that at first, but I'm getting closer to it every day. Alec has helped. A lot." She scooted over on the ottoman, and their silent code was already good enough that he understood it was an invitation for him to come and sit beside her as she continued. "Alec was nice enough to buy Gordon's half of the company from me, and he's also connecting me with advisors who will help me figure out where to invest and donate the purchase money. I never thought I'd have the responsibility for so much. Or the chance to do so much good with it."

"We'll help too," her mother said, "any way we can."

But there was more Cordelia needed to tell them. "I went to Gordon's funeral. Saturday night."

"Oh, honey." Her mom looked more distraught than ever. "You shouldn't have had to do that alone."

"I wasn't alone." Cordelia looked at Alec again, sitting beside her, ready to do whatever it took to protect her, the same way he'd helped her over and over again during the past week. "Alec was there." She smiled at his siblings. "And his family was there to support me too." She turned guilty eyes to her parents. "I'm sorry I didn't let you know in time so you could be there too."

"No more apologies." Her father was firm. "This has all been a huge shock, and of course you needed time to process it all. We know you're the woman we raised you to be. The strong, resourceful, intelligent woman Gordon wanted his daughter to become. If anyone can deal with a surprise like this, it's you."

"I love you, Dad." She threw her arms around him, and around her mother too.

When they finally let each other go, Alec was no

longer beside her. Instead, he had his jacket off, his sleeves rolled up, and he was cracking eggs in the kitchen. She wasn't hungry, but she didn't tell him that food could wait, or not to bother making breakfast. Not when she understood that cooking was his way of thinking things through. And that it made him happy.

"Looks like Alec is making all of us breakfast." And despite the mess still waiting for her with the press—she seriously doubted they were going to back down until she gave them answers to their probing questions—she smiled as she told her parents, "You're in for a treat. He's the best cook in the world."

★ ★ ★

Before they dove into strategy, Alec knew it would do both Cordelia and her parents some good to relax over a hot breakfast for a few minutes. And, truthfully, he was glad to have something to do with his hands, to fry eggs and sausage with herbs from her windowsill plants. Otherwise, he was going to dash out into the parking lot and start throwing punches at any lurking photographers or journalists.

Cordelia's little kitchen table by the window was too small for everyone to gather around, so Alec's siblings and Cordelia's parents ate from plates on their laps instead. He made sure her plate was full, as well, knowing she'd need the calories to burn through what promised to be a long day ahead.

He also took a loaded plate out to Roman, who informed him that several photographers had indeed come waltzing onto her property in the past half hour. Of course, Suzanne's bodyguard boyfriend had quickly dispensed with them. Alec might still be wrapping his head around the fact that his sister and Roman were a couple—he wasn't sure anyone would ever be good enough for his little sister—but it helped a great deal knowing that Roman was one of the best men he'd ever met.

On the way back inside, Alec checked his phone and saw that among the calls from his employees, clients, and journalists, his father had also called several times. Alec shoved the phone back into his pocket. Everyone, including his father, would have to wait until he'd helped put Cordelia's concerns to rest.

Thankfully, her parents were unconditionally there for her. What's more, the way the couple still held hands after who knew how many years of marriage told Alec a lot about why Cordelia believed in forever. Who wouldn't believe in love with role models like these? If they'd been his parents, he probably would have been looking forward to happily ever after too.

"Cordelia says you're both teachers." He'd never been interested in meeting the families of the women he dated. But Cordelia wasn't anything like those women. She was a friend. One he planned on keeping. "Which grades do you teach?" He ignored the phone buzzing in his pocket—another incoming call from his father.

"I teach eleventh-grade math and physics at the high school," her father said.

"I'm the art teacher for the district, so I roam among the schools during the week," her mother replied, before adding, "You've got to tell me how you made the eggs so light and fluffy. They're the best I've ever tasted."

"Add a little milk and barely whisk it before it hits the pan." He nodded over at Harry. "My brother is a teacher too."

Harry swallowed the bite of sausage he'd speared, then told them, "Medieval history and warfare."

"You must teach at the university level?" Cordelia's mother asked.

Harry nodded, smiling to put them at ease. "Columbia."

"Medieval history at Columbia." Cordelia's father cocked his head. "Wait a minute." He looked at Alec. "Your surname is Sullivan." Then back to Harry. "You're Harrison Sullivan, aren't you?" He looked more than a little awed. "I've read everything you've written—more than once, in fact."

A beat later, her mother's eyes went wide. "*Oh my*

God. Your father is William Sullivan." She pressed her lips together. "I'm so sorry. That was terribly rude."

"Everyone has that reaction," Suzanne said with a warm smile. "You don't need to apologize for it."

"I'm just such a huge fan of his work." Cordelia's mother's eyes went even wider at a second realization. "And you're Drake Sullivan." She almost looked more stunned by this than by learning that Gordon had been Cordelia's father. "Years ago, I saw one of your paintings in a gallery. I was tempted to remortgage our house for it."

Alec made a mental note to find out which painting it was and buy it for Cordelia's mother. If it had already sold, he'd ask Drake to paint something similar. Alec had no doubt that Gordon would have wanted to thank Amy and Walter for doing such a wonderful job as parents to Cordelia. He'd been right to trust them with her life and happiness. They'd given her all that and more.

For the first time, Alec found himself wondering if that could be part of the reason why Gordon hadn't made himself known to Cordelia. Had he been worried that her parents would feel overshadowed by him and his success, even though they'd done all the truly important work of raising and loving Cordelia? Had Gordon thought they might resent him for sweeping in with his big bank account and fancy life?

Both Harry and Drake looked slightly embarrassed by the praise they'd been given, so Alec decided to turn the spotlight on Suzanne. "Suz here, she's a computer genius who puts both of those yahoos—" He gestured to his brothers. "—to shame."

She rolled her eyes. "Says the billionaire aviation mogul."

"What an amazing group you all are," Cordelia's mother said. "Your father must be so proud of all of you."

An awkward silence landed. Hard enough that Cordelia jumped into the fray. "Actually, they're throwing a surprise birthday party for him here soon. In the barn. Alec is going to cook a farm-to-table dinner."

"You are?" Harry raised an eyebrow in Alec's direction.

"We worked it out on Sunday morning," Suzanne confirmed. "I meant to text you and Drake about it, but the emergency coding session I got pulled into after I left Alec's house scrambled my brain."

"*You're* going to cook a big dinner for Dad's birthday?" Drake looked as though he couldn't believe it.

Alec wasn't about to explain that Cordelia had all but cornered him into doing it. His siblings probably thought that because she surrounded herself with flowers and looked so sweet, so gentle, that she couldn't outmaneuver a guy like him. They were wrong.

"It's no big deal," Alec told them, even though they all knew that it was. His phone buzzed again with the ring tone he'd given to his father, as if to reinforce the point.

Cordelia stood and gathered up plates to take to the sink. "Since you're all here now, why don't I give you a tour of the gardens and the barn? That way you can start thinking about how you want to set things up for the party."

Alec stopped her with his hands on the stack of plates she was holding. He knew she was dying to get out to her garden and that it would do her a world of good to lose herself in blooms for a while. But they couldn't ignore the bomb that had dropped onto Page Six this morning, courtesy of Mona.

"I can help out with your customers while you show everyone around," he offered. "But before you leave to do that, we need to figure out a plan. Roman is doing a great job of holding back the press this morning, but you need a strategy mapped out beyond that."

"I'm just going to tell everyone the truth." Cordelia took the plates from his hands and put them in the sink. "That I didn't know Gordon was my birth father until last week and that I intend to donate the money he willed me to a number of charities."

All Alec wanted was to see her smile. Funny how quickly that had become his top goal, before he'd even realized it had happened. But he couldn't sugarcoat things. "It's not that easy, Cordelia."

"Why not?"

"Because you're now rich enough to be a target for every fortune hunter on the planet. *And* for a gossip mill that will make sure to dig up every little thing in your past in the hopes that there's a juicy story there."

"I promise you, there's nothing juicy in my past. Nothing at all."

Obviously, she didn't know about the extra bit of juice Mona had sprinkled over her life while she was sleeping. He hadn't had a chance to tell her before everyone showed up. "They think we're together."

"Together?" She looked confused for a moment before her eyes went wide. "You and me? Why would anyone think—" She broke off with a groan. "Because that's what I told Mona."

He saw her flush at the memory of how she'd kissed him to prove her point. A kiss that had rocked him to his core, just the way taking her over the edge in the bedroom of the plane had only made him want her more. He'd stayed up half the night fighting the urge to go to her.

"Who's Mona?" her father asked.

"One of Alec's customers," Cordelia told him.

"Former customers," Alec clarified.

"I met Mona yesterday on one of Alec's planes," Cordelia explained. "She was behaving horribly toward him, so…" She flushed an even deeper rose, so beautiful that Alec nearly lost his breath from nothing more than looking at her. "I made it seem like he and I were dating."

Alec's siblings eyed each other at her admission. He knew what they were thinking, what they were hoping—that he was falling for Cordelia. But they knew better than anyone that it wouldn't matter if he was. She deserved a hell of a lot more than he could give her.

"Mona is a nasty piece of work," Suzanne said. "I'm sorry you're going through all this today, Cordelia, but I'm glad someone finally put her in her place."

"I didn't think my little white lie would have *these* ramifications," Cordelia said. "We've got to let people know we're not together, Alec."

"I disagree." He ignored the satisfied nods his siblings were giving each other, as if they were all but picturing him at the altar with Cordelia saying *I do*. He shoved away the part of him that took surprising pleasure in a vivid picture of Cordelia in a long white dress, her eyes locked to his as she told him she'd love him forever. "If people think you and I are dating," he explained, "they're far less likely to hassle you for your money and what they think you can do for them."

"But you didn't ask for any of this," Cordelia pro-
tested. "You shouldn't have to cancel dates or explain
things to someone you're actually dating, just to
protect me. Plus, you've already done so much for
me."

"Alec is right." Harry's voice had always been one
of reason, and Alec was glad he was jumping in with
his opinion. "And so are you, Cordelia. Tell the truth
about Gordon in one short press conference—and also
let Alec have your back if the vultures try to swoop. I
believe he's right in saying that they will."

She frowned, clearly torn. "I hate the thought of
making you lie for me, Alec." She looked at his siblings.
"And all of you will have to lie too."

"Don't worry, you won't be stuck with me forever." Everyone knew Alec Sullivan didn't do forever—in
a real relationship or a fake one.

He couldn't quite read her expression as she said, "I
would never ask you for forever, Alec." Nor did he
want to read the ache that spread through his chest at
her words. Along with a sense of loss that made no
sense whatsoever.

"Cordelia." Her mother looked nervous. "I wish
we knew what advice to give you, but we don't know
anything about the press and photographers and
people coming after you for your money."

"We do." Drake lent his voice to the discussion. "We've had to deal with situations like this our whole lives, especially Alec as the oldest."

"I have too," Rosa said, finally chiming in. "I agree that telling the truth is usually the best option. But sometimes…" A hint of pain flashed across her face. "If one little lie will help, Cordelia, then you shouldn't feel bad about telling it. Especially when you have the Sullivans behind you." She beamed at Drake and his siblings. "When they say they have your back, they mean it."

"Fine," Cordelia said, putting her hands up, "you all win."

Though Alec was always ready, always willing, to come to his siblings' aid, he'd never thought to ask them to come to *his*. Without their doing just that today, however, he would never have been able to convince Cordelia to pretend to be his girlfriend.

Cordelia pinned him with a very serious look. "But only if you swear you're okay with playing my boyfriend."

He didn't have to think it over, didn't have to fight with himself over his reply. The only thing he had to fight was his grin. "It will be my pleasure, Cordelia." There was no other woman he would have done this for. But he couldn't imagine not doing it for her.

Nothing had gone back to normal on Monday

morning the way they'd thought it would. But he couldn't deny that a part of him wasn't sorry about it, if only for the excuse it now gave him to stick by Cordelia's side. Not for forever. For long enough, he hoped, to settle her world back to rights, as much as it could.

So he'd pretend to be her boyfriend, while simultaneously not allowing himself to cross any more lines than they already had on the airplane. He'd already made a silent promise to Gordon to respect Cordelia to the highest degree. And now that he'd met her parents, and knew for sure just what good people they were, now that he'd seen for himself that she was the most important person in their world, Alec knew without a shadow of a doubt that Cordelia deserved the happiest ending possible.

She wouldn't find that ending with him. But once he'd helped her clean up the complications Gordon had dropped in her lap, she would be ready to find it with someone else.

The thought of Cordelia in another man's arms was brutal. Beyond brutal.

But it would be far worse to lead her down the path to a broken heart.

CHAPTER TWELVE

Alec wasn't surprised by all the customers clamoring to get into Cordelia's store as soon as the doors opened. Who in town could resist coming by the Langley Garden Center to see if they could get any dirt on the big news that had broken that morning?

After Cordelia had promised her parents that she was okay, she'd insisted that they head off to work. She was currently in the barn with Suzanne, Drake, and Rosa, showing them the space for their father's party, while Alec and Harry worked to keep her retail operation running smoothly.

Harry was brilliant at politely holding off nosy people at the register. If he hadn't decided on academia, he would have been a top-notch mediator with his soft-spoken and sincere manner.

Alec would rather do the dirty work of hauling heavy bags of soil and digging through inventory to find the blooms Cordelia's customers were interested in. His suit shirt and pants were streaked with dirt, and his hand-stitched Italian shoes were done for after all the mud he'd walked through this morning, but he couldn't care less. There hadn't been time to change into jeans, a T-shirt, and work boots before coming over. He'd needed to get to Cordelia as soon as possible.

Forty-five minutes into the rush, both the store and the parking lot suddenly emptied out, leaving Alec and Harry alone for a few minutes.

"Cordelia seems to be handling everything well."

Harry's tone was mild, but Alec wasn't fooled. He knew when his brother was fishing. "She's tougher than she looks."

"She's a beautiful woman."

When Harry paused before saying anything more, Alec knew he was waiting for a reaction. And the truth was, it was taking a heck of a lot of control not to snap at his brother that Cordelia was off-limits.

"She is," was Alec's concise reply.

"Apart from that," Harry continued, "she's not at all like your usual women."

"She's not one of *my women*." At Harry's sound of obvious disbelief, Alec all but growled, "If you have something to say, say it."

"You don't want me poking my nose into your business," Harry reminded him.

"That's never stopped you before."

His brother laughed at the truth of it. "Okay then,

since you're clearly attracted to her—and it's mutual, from what I can see—and you obviously like and respect her, why not give her a chance? Not to become one of *your women*, but to be the one that sticks."

"One week into this mess and against all odds, we've become friends." He needed his brother to understand. And to remind himself while he was at it. "I'm not going to risk screwing that up."

"What makes you so sure you will?"

Alec raised an eyebrow. "You know my track record. You've seen more than one drink thrown in my face. And you know how I feel about love and marriage." He gestured toward the barn, from which Cordelia, Suzanne, Drake, and Rosa had just emerged into the bright sunlight. "Look at her. She's *made* for the perfect happy ending."

Cordelia looked over and caught him staring at her. When she smiled, Alec couldn't help but smile back.

Until he realized Harry was smiling too. At him. As though his brother thought he knew Alec's mind, regardless of what he'd just been told.

Alec's phone buzzed again with the same ring tone he'd been hearing all week. "I've got to take this. Keep manning the register, would you?" He headed off in a direction opposite that of Cordelia and his siblings, to a spot between a bed of roses and a bed of lavender. "What's up, Dad?"

"I've been trying to get ahold of you all morning. I saw the news and figured they must be harassing you and Cordelia."

To head things off at the pass, Alec said, "They were bothering Cordelia, so I came to the garden center to boot them out. That's where I am now."

"I'm glad you're able to be there to support her through this," William said, "but she's not the only one I'm worried about. I know how hard it is to deal with journalists and photographers intruding on your privacy."

"I already know the drill," Alec said. This would be the perfect time for a customer to need his help. Figured that there wasn't a single one to be seen at the moment.

"I'm sorry for everything I put you through when you were a kid," his father said. "And after."

For more than two decades, there had been no apologies. Not until Drake had fallen in love with Rosa and suddenly their father had decided he was ready to earn the name—and for them to be one big, happy family, as well. But Alec didn't buy it. And this was the last thing he needed to deal with right now. "I've got to go."

"The offer still stands," his father said, desperation seeping into his tone. "I can be there if you need me. Wherever you need me. Whenever you need me."

The center of Alec's chest felt tight. Sore. He rubbed his fist over it, telling himself it was from lifting so many bags of soil this morning. He must be getting soft from too much time inside an office.

"Don't worry about me," he said to his father. And then to forestall more phone calls, he added, "You can always assume I've got things under control." The very control he'd had since he was five. When Alec hung up and turned around, he was surprised to see Cordelia standing behind him.

"I was just coming to let you know that we're done touring the property."

"Great." He shoved back thoughts of his father, along with a feeling of guilt over their conversation. "Does everyone agree the barn will work?"

"They think your father is going to love it."

"I'm sure he will."

"Were you just on the phone with him?"

He should have been irritated with her prying. Would have been if it were anyone else. But she wasn't out to hurt him. She simply had a soft heart. "He saw the news and has been calling all morning."

"He must be desperate to help in some way, just the same as my parents."

"I told him he doesn't need to worry about me."

"He's your father," she said. "He can't help but worry about his son."

"He sure as hell didn't worry about me when I was a kid." Damn it, hadn't he promised himself he wouldn't keep talking to her about this? That he'd just do whatever he needed to for the birthday party and keep his mouth shut about his feelings?

She took one of his hands in hers and gave him a heartfelt look. "I'm sorry he didn't, Alec."

Never in his life had he wanted to kiss someone more. Because if he kissed her, nothing else would matter. He could lose himself in her taste, in her soft curves, in the sweet sounds of pleasure she made when his mouth, his hands, were on her.

Only the fierce will to do the right thing—for once—could get him to slip his hand from hers and take a step back. "I don't know if we can trust Harry with the register for too much longer. We should head back."

But instead of moving toward the garden center's main building, she said, "I can't believe how generous your family is, coming to help the way they did this morning. Especially when I know all of them lead such busy lives. Lives I've insisted they all go back to." The floral scent that was uniquely hers made it hard for him to think straight as she said, "You know I love having you here too, and I don't know how I could possibly have dealt with the press and the store this morning without you, but you should also head in to your office now. After changing your clothes and shoes, that is." She looked more than a little stunned by the mess he was. "You've got to let me pay for the dry cleaning."

Ignoring that, he said, "I can't leave you alone."

"Two of Roman's bodyguard colleagues will be here in five minutes. They'll stay until closing and then make sure I get back to the cottage without any problems. Plus, Brian just arrived to put in his regular half day. So you won't have to worry about me."

But he would.

"Come stay with me tonight," he said before he could think better of having her that close. All night long.

"I can't kick you out of your bed again. And honestly, if I leave now, it will feel like I folded." She lifted her chin, beautiful and brave. "I have no intention of folding."

"Then I'll stay with you." Again, he didn't think his offer through before making it. All he knew was that he didn't feel right about leaving her alone tonight. Somehow he'd find a way to keep his mouth, and his hands, off her. "I'll sleep on the couch."

"You don't have to do that, Alec. You've already slept on the couch one too many times on my behalf. Besides, I know you have a life that doesn't revolve around me."

She was right, he did. But nothing else in that life

seemed to matter nearly as much as she did. "We've got to make plans for tomorrow's press conference," he reminded her. "And between the two of us, you've got the better vegetable garden for me to cook from."

"I've got the *only* vegetable garden between the two of us."

He almost gave in to the urge to kiss her then. Came so close that he couldn't keep from leaning in and only barely managed to aim his lips at her forehead instead of her mouth.

"That won't convince anyone," she said.

His brain was scrambled enough from wanting her that he couldn't follow. "Convince anyone of what?"

"That we're together." And then, before he knew it, she was reaching up to thread her fingers through his hair, going up on her tippy-toes, and pressing her mouth to his.

Sweet Lord, she tasted like heaven.

Like sin.

Like everything he could ever desire.

He couldn't keep his hands from moving to her waist, then sliding even lower to her hips so that he could drag her closer as he greedily took what he had no business being offered.

"Now *that* kiss," she whispered when she finally lifted her mouth from his, "the world would believe."

Her eyes were full of sensual promise, her lips were

glistening from where he'd run his tongue over them, and Alec knew if he didn't get out of there in the next thirty seconds, he'd be dragging her behind the hedge, ripping off her clothes, and taking her on the brick path.

"I'll be back before dark," he said as he forced himself to back away. "Call me if you need anything, Cordelia. Anything at all."

★ ★ ★

Cordelia floated on the memory of that kiss all afternoon. Despite the fact that she had a million things to worry about, those worries would hold. She wasn't a virgin, and her parents had taught her to respect and appreciate herself as a woman. But only Alec's kisses had ever made her feel this way.

He'd told her again and again that he didn't want a relationship—even their fake relationship, he'd made sure to point out, wouldn't last forever. And she believed him. She'd be crazy not to.

But at the same time, she was starting to think that pleasure didn't necessarily have to be the sole province of a romantic relationship. Maybe two friends who mutually respected each other, two friends who simply enjoyed being with each other, could have pleasure too. Could have kisses—and so much more—without ruining their friendship.

At five forty-five, she locked up the store, then headed for her cottage, her two guards keeping careful watch the whole way. It had been a bang-up sales day, with customers she hadn't seen in ages coming out of the woodwork.

Perhaps she could have taken offense, but she knew they hadn't meant any harm with their curiosity. Besides, each person had bought something so that it wouldn't look like they were there only to gawk. And she'd been glad when a few customers passed on information about the local organizations they worked for that could use some financial assistance—one for rescue dogs, one for a literacy group, and one for a new playground in town.

She had only just stepped inside her house and kicked off her shoes when Alec appeared at the door. He was wearing jeans and a T-shirt and carrying a suit bag.

Her impulse to kiss him this morning had been a good one, so she let herself give in to tonight's urge to throw her arms around him and hold him tight. "Hi." He was stiff against her when she hugged him, as though he thought he needed to keep some distance between them. But she didn't let go. "I'm glad you're here." Her stomach rumbled and she laughed. "My stomach is too."

He smiled, but she could see the concern behind it.

"Everything go okay after I left?"

"Just like I told you in response to every one of your bazillion text messages this afternoon—yes, everything went fine."

"Good. Now that I'm here, I sent Roman's guards home." He ran his hand across her cheek and then her hair, as though he needed to verify for himself that she was safe and in one piece. "Any requests for dinner?"

"I've got chicken and steak in the fridge, but vegetarian would be great too." She took his suit bag. "I know you're itching to start foraging in the garden beds, so I'll put your things away."

After hanging up his suit in her closet, she stood in the open doorway and indulged herself in watching him. Her first impression of Alec had been all about *power*, though his looks had been hard to ignore. Now, she saw him differently. He was still powerful. Still gorgeous as sin. But with a gentleness—and a hole inside of him from his childhood—that made her chest clench tight.

Moving into the garden before he caught her staring, she helped him pull onions and carrots, radishes and potatoes. As they brought the vegetables inside, she asked, "Did you have any problems at your office? Mona didn't come back to stir things up again, did she?"

"She's not creative enough to come up with another attack," he reassured her. "There were a few nosy customers who wanted the scoop on Gordon and you and the current status of the business—just like there were some curious customers here today. But it was nothing I couldn't deal with. And everything is in place for the press conference tomorrow. I just need you to confirm that nine a.m. at my office will work for you. We'll be setting up in the conference room, which holds fifty."

"That's fine," she said, even as nerves skittered up her spine at telling that many people her story. He pulled out his phone, and when he was done texting his assistant to approve sending the time and location to the press, Cordelia asked, "Tomorrow, when we're at the press conference, are you sure you want to keep up the lie about our being together?"

"Yes." She appreciated that he didn't pause, didn't hesitate at all. "It makes sense."

If everything Alec and his siblings had said this morning was true, it really did make sense. And so, she now believed just as strongly, did this.

Cordelia reached for the hem of her T-shirt and pulled it over her head.

CHAPTER THIRTEEN

All last week, Alec's dreams had run hot, with Cordelia playing the starring role. Kissing her on his couch, making her come on the plane—neither had gone anywhere close to quenching his desire for her. Every tiny taste he'd had just made him want more.

And yet, he knew better than to turn those dreams into reality. Somewhere in the back of his brain—a brain that was barely functioning at the moment—he understood that he needed to stop her from taking off the rest of her clothes. Needed to pick up her shirt from where she'd tossed it and have her put it back on.

But for the first time in his life, Alec wasn't able to think straight. He wasn't able to move away, or to remember all the reasons why they shouldn't do this. Not when Cordelia's strong yet elegant hands were already on the button of her jeans. And then the zipper. All he could do was hold his breath as she let the denim fall in a puddle at her feet.

His mouth was dry, his breath coming faster than it should have, just from looking at her in a bra and panties. The black cotton wasn't skimpy. Shouldn't even have been sexy.

But the way she wore it made every inch of him go hard. Hungry. Desperate to touch. To taste.

To *possess*.

She kicked her jeans away, and he wanted to drink in her gorgeous curves, wanted to memorize every inch of her beautiful body.

He made himself drag his fiery gaze back to her face instead. *"Cordelia."* Her name came out raw. Hoarse.

She put a finger on his lips before he could say anything more. "You helped me on the plane. Helped me release so much stress. I know none of this has been easy for you either." She ran the pad of her thumb over his lower lip, as if she couldn't resist touching him. Showing him what he could have if only he let go of his self-control. "Let me help you tonight."

"You don't have to do this." But God, how he wanted her to. "You don't owe me anything."

"I don't *have* to do it," she agreed. "I *want* to do it."

He was already so far past the point of reason that he could barely get the words out. "I'll hurt you. I can't hurt you."

"You won't hurt me, Alec." She moved even closer and took his hands in hers. "I know what this will mean. And I also know what it won't. You're not going to be my boyfriend. I'm not going to be your girlfriend. We're not going to end up with some magical happily-ever-after. Tonight we'll just be one friend helping another." He could feel the heat radiating off her skin. "And the truth is, it will help me too. Help me get all the way past what happened this morning—and also help me feel stronger to deal with what's coming tomorrow."

There were so many reasons he shouldn't do this, but the final reason she'd just given *to* do it trumped them all: She needed his help. And that was the one thing he could never deny her.

No matter what, he wouldn't let the aftermath be messy, wouldn't let either of them be awkward or weird about it. Fortunately, given how well they'd both dealt with her orgasm on the plane, their track record so far was good.

Alec lifted her into his arms, never so happy in all his life to get to touch someone. To get to be with someone. "I'll stop when you need me to stop." If it was just another orgasm she needed, that's all he would give her. No matter how desperate he was going to be for more.

"Stopping is the last thing I need tonight. What we did on the plane, it was good. So good. But it wasn't enough."

And then she threaded her fingers into his hair and

dragged his mouth down to hers for a kiss so hot he had to stop walking toward her bedroom. Because he couldn't do a damn thing but devour her. Her lips. Her cheekbones. Her eyelids when they fluttered closed. And then back to her sumptuous mouth.

On a groan, he dragged his mouth from hers and stumbled toward what he hoped was her bedroom. He'd never been clumsy, never been out of control. But with Cordelia, nothing had ever been close to normal. Just as he could never have predicted her existence, he couldn't have predicted his reaction to her either. The way she didn't just stretch his control, but snapped it completely. The way one smile from her had his own lips curving up in response.

The way one kiss had him wanting to possess her, body and soul.

Her bedroom wasn't big and neither was her bed. Barely large enough for two, her mattress was covered with a bedspread printed with flowers that looked so real he was almost afraid of crushing them when he laid her on top of it. Her bed frame was antique, a four-poster that immediately sent his brain—and body—reeling with images of using those posts to bind her just tightly enough so that he could torment her with his fingers, his tongue, and bring her to the edge again and again, not letting her pleasure spill over until she was hoarse from begging. But the last thing he wanted was to scare her with the force of his desire, with how all-encompassing his need for her had already grown.

As she grabbed at his T-shirt to yank it up over his head, then scrambled for the zipper of his jeans, he wanted to be skin to skin with her just as badly as she obviously did with him. But first, he needed her naked. Needed to see every inch of her, needed to be able to touch without boundaries of any kind getting in the way.

He put his hands over hers to still them on his zipper, where he was pulsing beneath her palm. "You first." Her eyes went from their hands to his face. "Everything." His mouth was actually watering. "Off."

She smiled, brightly enough to outshine the sun, but there was a flicker of unease there too. Uncertainty he couldn't ignore.

"Tell me," he said. "Friend to friend."

She bit her lip, looking suddenly shy. "I've been with other men, so I'm not a virgin or anything. But I'm still not…"

He tipped his hand beneath her chin so that she couldn't look away. "Not what?"

"Not a beauty queen." She rolled her eyes. "Like you didn't know that already."

"You are beautiful. So damned beautiful, Cordelia."

"And you're sweet. But I'm sure you're used to women who are sleek and polished." Her skin flushed.

"Everywhere."

He almost laughed when he realized what she was worried about—that she was too natural for him. "Silicone belongs in construction adhesives, not women's chests." He curved his hands over her breasts, loving the way her breath went at being touched even through cotton. "And if you ask me," he said as he slid one hand down over her stomach, then past the waistband of her panties, "women shouldn't want to look like hairless dolls either." He found her soft curls damp, her sex slick with arousal. "You're perfect, Cordelia. Just the way you were made." He couldn't keep himself from sliding inside. "Just the way you are."

She arched up into his hand, and from the way her pulse was pounding at her throat, how flushed her skin was, how fast her breath was already coming—he knew he could take her over, just that quickly. But the next time she came for him, he wanted her naked.

"Strip for me," he urged her again as he made himself move his hands from her. "Finish what you started in the kitchen."

She trembled slightly, but from the way her lips were curved up slightly at the corners, he knew it was from arousal now, rather than nerves. She reached behind her for the clasp of her bra, and he held his breath. That night on his couch he hadn't let himself truly appreciate her, because he'd known better than to touch her like that while she was grieving and tipsy.

Tonight, he was going to take his time and appreciate every inch of her.

Her bra dropped away, and he was *this close* to leaping on her like a wild animal, nearly lost to everything but the instinctive urge to capture and possess. "You're gorgeous, Cordelia."

She was lying back on the bed now, her fingers tucked into the sides of her panties. Stilling at his words, she smiled, pure sunshine as she said, "Thank you."

Any other woman would have been preening at his compliment, posing to highlight her best assets and then fishing for more. But Cordelia simply took his words at face value, which was a very rare trait in his dating experience.

Not, of course, that they were dating. This was just sex between friends. A way to blow off steam in a mutually agreeable fashion and take the edge off a damned hard week. Whatever his next thought would have been fell out of his head as she began to shimmy the final scrap of cotton from her hips and down her thighs.

One second he was standing at the base of her bed, the next he was with her on it. He heard her breath whoosh from her chest as he landed, careful not to crush her, but needing to feel her.

All of her.

He crushed her mouth beneath his as he tangled his hands in her hair and kissed her like his life depended on it. And tonight, it felt as though it actually did. As though there was no going forward without Cordelia, her arms holding him tight, her legs wrapped around his waist.

From the first moment he'd met her, she'd held nothing back. She always told him exactly what she thought, always did what she thought was right. And she was just as honest in bed—from her passionate kisses, to the unabashed way she arched her hips up into his, to the wonderfully happy sounds she made as he moved his hands from her hair to her breasts.

He lifted his mouth from hers, needing to see her eyes, needing to know for sure that he was making her feel as good as she made him feel. "I want to watch you. Watch how you respond when I touch you." He cupped one breast, relishing soft flesh, smooth skin. "I want to see every beautiful reaction."

He rolled the taut tip with his thumb and middle finger and she gasped. And when he caressed her other breast and her eyes fluttered closed as pleasure washed over her, he had to kiss her again, had to fill himself with her taste before lifting his head to watch as he moved his hands lower.

The muscles of her abdomen jumped beneath his fingertips as he made a deliberately slow trip south over her body. The more he wanted to rush, the slower he made himself go. And when she begged— "Alec, please, just touch me"—he knew it was the right move.

On the plane, he'd taken her up and over on a quick burst of heat into flame. Tonight, he'd keep her at a slow simmer for as long as he could. Cruise down the runway, then take her up and up and up, so high that she wouldn't ever want to come down.

"Do you have any idea how many times I've replayed your orgasm in my head?" He stopped his hand between her hip bones, just below her belly button.

"It can't be as many as I have." She wriggled beneath him, obviously trying to get his hand where she really wanted it. "Make me come again, Alec. Just like you did last time."

"Don't worry, I'll definitely make you come again." He smiled at her. "But we're going to do things differently tonight."

He saw her eyes go wide right before he lifted his hand from her stomach and replaced it with his mouth. She inhaled sharply as he pressed a kiss to her skin. She smelled like flowers everywhere. Even here, so close to the slick, sweet center of her.

Her hands were restless, tugging at his shoulders,

then the sheets, then his hair, so he grabbed them and threaded his fingers through hers. "Seems like you're as excited about this as I am."

"Yes!" She clenched his hands in hers. "I'm really, really excited about this."

He laughed, kissing her belly even as the surprising sound came from his lips. Sex hadn't always been a serious thing for him, but it had never been like this. Easy. Carefree. Just plain right.

"Hopefully, you'll be even more excited in a few minutes." He followed up his teasing words with kisses that teased even more as he made his way down between her thighs.

"I've never wanted anyone the way I want you," he whispered, and then there were no more words that mattered as he devoured her with long, slow slicks of his tongue, then a deep plunge that had her crying out and her hips bucking against his mouth in a desperate rhythm. Her nails dug into his hands while her body quaked and shook through her climax. He couldn't get enough of her taste, her unbridled response, her boundless passion.

"*Alec.*"

She didn't need to say anything more than his name in that breathless voice for him to know that she was lost to everything but pleasure. And so was he.

It didn't matter what happened tomorrow in the

press conference. All that mattered was that he was holding Cordelia in his arms tonight, and that he'd just made her entire body smile, head to toe.

CHAPTER FOURTEEN

Cordelia's world would never be the same.

Not after what Alec had just shown her—such intense *pleasure* that the word barely scratched the surface.

She'd thought she'd known what was coming tonight. After all, they'd already kissed, and he'd given her that beautiful release on the plane.

But she'd had no idea at all.

She felt like she could float away on a cloud of ecstasy. Were it not for the hard, heavy weight of his body over hers and the kisses he was pressing along her skin as he made his way back up her body with her hands still in his, she was sure that she would have.

"Good?" His question sounded against the underside of her breast, where he was nuzzling her, his evening shadow scratching her skin in just the right way.

"So good." When he didn't respond, she realized she'd only mouthed the words. Working to get enough breath in her lungs to actually speak the words aloud, she tried a second time. "So good."

His face was level with hers by then, and when he smiled at her—a wonderfully wicked smile—she lost her breath all over again.

"I could do that all night." He pressed his mouth to hers for a soft kiss, before asking, "What about you?"

She did want that. What woman wouldn't? But tonight, she was even greedier. "I need you." Without her hands free, she couldn't strip his clothes off. But she could tell him, "All of you."

He stared down at her, his eyes dark and intense. "Are you sure?"

A week ago, she'd thought they were going to have as little to do with each other as possible and had assumed that lawyers would take over after their initial meeting. The last thing in the world she would have thought could happen was this—the two of them in her bed, with her begging him to take off his clothes and make love to her.

"I've never been this sure of anything in my life," she told him. But this wasn't just about her and what she needed, what she wanted. Alec had to be sure too. "What about you?"

He didn't answer right away. And though she was hovering on a breathless edge, she was glad for it. Because if they both thought things through, there would be less chance they'd regret them.

Not that she'd be regretting *anything*. Regretting making love to Alec would be like regretting a lavender bush's fragrant bloom, or a hummingbird drinking nectar from honeysuckle.

"I'm sure that I want you," he finally replied, his deep voice thick with the very desire he spoke of. "I'm sure that everything about you and your garden and even the sheets on your bed makes me smile." But he wasn't smiling as he continued. "And I'm sure that I'll never forgive myself for hurting you."

"You won't. I promise you, I'm not going to fall apart, or cry, or even stalk you online when this is over."

Finally, she got a hint of a smile from him. "Do you even have a computer?"

"I do, but I try not to use it if I can help it. I'd rather be out in nature."

The wicked spark came back into his eyes. "Speaking of nature, I can't get this crazy picture out of my head of you gardening *au naturel.*"

She laughed. "Actually, once when a yellow jacket was after me in the shower, I ran outside to get away from him, and somehow the front door slammed shut and locked behind me."

He let go of one of her hands so that he could run his from breast to hip. "Did anyone see you?"

"God, no! I grabbed a tarp and wrapped myself in it

before climbing in through a window."

"You can get into your cottage through the windows?" He looked around her room in dismay.

Using all her hard-won gardening strength, she flipped them over before he could jump out of bed to start installing deadbolts on every possible point of entry to her cottage. And, oh, it felt good to straddle him like this.

But it would feel *so* much better once he didn't have any clothes on.

She scooted down so that she could work on the zipper of his jeans, then tug them off along with his boxers. Once she did, she had to stop to gaze in awe at him. "Do you know what I thought the first time I saw you?" She didn't wait for him to reply. "Even in the midst of the craziness, all I could think was that it should be illegal for anyone to look as good as you."

She bent down to press a kiss to his chest, but couldn't bear to stop there. She wanted to run her mouth, her hands, over every incredible inch of him. There were no words to describe the sight of Alec Sullivan in her bed, lying beneath her, his big hands inciting sensual explosions everywhere they roamed.

"I wanted you too, Cordelia. Wanted you like this, straddling me, with your breasts in my hands and your taste on my tongue." Arousal flooded her at his deliciously dirty words. "Wanted to feel your heat sliding over me." She rocked her hips against his, moaning at how good it felt to finally be skin to skin, in all the most wonderful places. "Wanted to kiss your sweet mouth…kiss every sweet inch of you."

"Look at us," she said with a smile, "both getting exactly what we want."

"Almost." He moved his hips against hers again, causing fireworks to shoot off throughout her body. "I promised myself I wouldn't take advantage of you—"

"You're not taking advantage of me!" She was so frustrated at how he kept bringing this up that she nearly yelled, "When will you finally get that through your thick head? I want to have sex with you, and I'm going to be okay when we're done!"

"I was just explaining why I don't have any con-doms on me."

"Oh." She felt a little embarrassed by her outburst. "I keep a box in my bedside table."

She leaned over him to reach for the drawer, but when she felt his tongue slick over the tip of one breast, she completely lost the thread of what she'd been doing. Simply couldn't do anything when such intense waves of pleasure were rolling through her.

She'd never wanted anything as badly as she want-ed to make love to him with no barriers between them. But for all that she trusted Alec, she wasn't stupid. And nothing would make simple pleasure between friends into a forced permanent "relationship" faster than an unplanned pregnancy.

With that thought in the forefront, she finally managed to move far enough away that she could grab the box of condoms from the drawer of her bedside table.

"Thank God," Alec said when she ripped open the brand-new box. "I wanted to kill any guy who'd gotten to use those other condoms. But I'm the only one." He looked extremely pleased with himself.

"Possessive much?"

"Yes." He pulled her down for a kiss. "You're mine, Cordelia. *All mine.*"

Satisfaction shouldn't have shot through her at his words. Not only because she was a liberated, modern woman who could have as many lovers as she wanted—but also because they were just friends. And yet, she couldn't deny that a part of her liked knowing he wanted her to be his, and his alone. For as long as this worked for both of them, anyway.

The truth was, he wasn't the only one feeling possessive right now. Giving silent thanks that he'd broken their kiss for long enough to roll on protection, she put her hands into his, lifted her hips, and said, "And you're mine." Then took him deep in one long, sweet slide.

So.

Much.

Pleasure.

Too much was all she could think as she closed her eyes so that she could focus every ounce of her concentration on how good he was making her feel as he thrust up into her.

Earlier, she'd thought he'd taken her to her highest peak of pleasure. She simply hadn't been able to imagine that there could be more. But over and over again, Alec surprised her. Never more than this moment, when she opened her eyes to find the most gorgeous man in the world staring up at her as though he was thinking the exact same thing—that she'd surprised him too.

Needing to be even closer, she leaned forward to kiss him. But he captured her lips with his before she could get to him. And the way he devoured her told her more than any words could have.

This. Tonight. Being together. She would never forget feeling so close to Alec. Would never regret knowing just how sweet, how good, how powerful lovemaking could be when it was with the right person. Someone who liked her just the way she was. Someone who made her laugh, but also pushed her outside of her comfort zone when she needed that push the most.

The next thing she knew, her back was against the mattress and he was levered over her, her hands in his on either side of her head.

"Come for me, Cordelia. I need to see it. I need to *feel* it."

And then he thrust so high, so deep, so perfectly inside of her that she couldn't do anything but obey. Every part of her shattered, his name falling from her lips as she fell apart in his arms.

She'd never felt so wild, never been so free as she was with her legs wrapped around him and her mouth on his. "Alec." She said his name between kisses, over and over. "Alec. Please." She was as desperate for his release as she'd been for hers, for the moment when he would give her all of himself. "I need you." Because it still wasn't enough. Not yet. *"Please."*

Between one heartbeat and the next, he was on his knees and lifting her hips up off the bed with his big hands to bring her closer. And as he slammed into her again and again and again, every last vestige of his restraint fell away.

She felt possessed.

She felt conquered.

She felt *amazing*.

Especially when, at the exact moment he called out her name, another climax hit her. As if they'd been practicing this dance for years, they moved in perfect rhythm together until they were both finally too spent to do anything but hold on to each other and try to catch their breath.

A while later, she lifted her face from where she'd buried it in the crook of his neck. "Sex with a friend is *awesome.*"

For a moment, he simply stared at her as if he didn't know where he was. As though he couldn't believe what they'd just done. Her breath held, caught, stuttered inside her chest. Until—thank God—his eyes cleared and his laughter came, rolling through from his chest to hers.

"What do you say we find out if sex with a friend is just as good in the shower?"

She was laughing too as he picked her up and carried her into the bathroom. Laughing *and* heating up all over, head to toe. Already desperate for more.

CHAPTER FIFTEEN

The next morning, during Cordelia's press conference in the S&W Aviation building's conference room, Alec sat on her left side, her parents on her right. Flanked by the people who only wanted her happiness, she almost felt ready. Almost felt able to get through it in one solid piece.

Her mother gripped her right hand beneath the table, but Alec made sure the whole world saw her left hand in his on *top* of the table. He'd kissed her, too, before the press conference officially began, but while there were plenty of journalists and photographers there to take note of their intimacy.

His kiss had been both sweet and hungry...and it had instantly taken her back to the previous night they'd shared in her bed, loving each other between her floral sheets. And then in her shower. And then again in the kitchen when he'd finally started to make dinner.

Still, even after all they'd shared, Cordelia knew the kiss was simply part of their plan to make everyone believe they were a couple to keep the fortune hunters at bay. The way her face flushed at his touch, his kiss, his nearness—all of that was real, however.

They hadn't gotten nearly enough sleep, but she wasn't tired. Cordelia couldn't have cared less about rest when the alternative had been so incredible. She wasn't naïve enough to think things couldn't have gone weird this morning when they'd woken up tangled in each other. But it hadn't.

Hot? Yes.

Strange? Thankfully, not in the least.

Especially when Alec had clearly been determined to keep her laughing all morning with one story after another about his and Gordon's customers and the crazy things they'd done over the years. She'd known what he was doing—that he hadn't wanted her stewing about the upcoming press conference. And her heart had grown yet another size bigger at how sweet he was. At how many times he'd gone out of his way to help her through a difficult spot.

A glamorous woman from *The Westchester Times* stood to ask a question, and Cordelia forced her brain back on task. For forty-five minutes she'd answered a rapid string of probing questions about whether she really had been clueless about Gordon all these years, how she was planning to deal with the huge inheritance, if she was going to continue working in her garden store, if she was tempted to buy a chateau in France and cover herself in diamonds and rubies.

Just as she'd planned, she told the truth. But those were the easy questions—about her birth father and her inheritance. Questions about Alec would be much harder to answer, and she couldn't imagine she'd get away today without addressing their relationship. Especially when the two of them had gone out of their way to act like a couple during the press conference.

"Cordelia," the journalist said, taking off her glasses as she spoke, "you've told us you had no knowledge of Gordon until last week and that you're planning on giving the bulk of the money to charity. And yet, you're already in a relationship with Alec Sullivan, Gordon's business partner. I'm sure you can appreciate how that might not add up."

Cordelia's heart was racing as she turned to Alec. "She's right. We don't add up, do we?" She knew she had a role to play, one that made sense on paper. But she needed him to know something too. "And yet, you've already become one of my best friends."

He grinned at her. That beautiful smile he gave only to the people he truly cared about—his sister, his brothers, his cousins. And now, her. Then he turned to the journalists and photographers, who were snapping pictures rapid-fire. He was all handsome confidence and barely leashed power as he told them, "I first saw

Cordelia standing outside this building a week ago, and even from a distance she made me pause. There was something about her. Something that made me want to look a little closer." He lifted her hand to his lips and pressed a kiss to it. "Losing Gordon was a blow. One I'll be recovering from for a long time. But I can't regret that he brought Cordelia into my life."

There were more than a few *aah*'s and *ooh*'s from the members of the press. And they weren't the only ones.

Cordelia would never let her feelings for Alec trap him, and she really did mean everything she'd said to him about not letting sex mess up their friendship. But that didn't mean she would deny the truth inside her heart either.

She'd barely known him a week. But she already loved him. With everything she was, for everything he was.

Not just because of the beautiful things he'd said.

Not just because of the breathtakingly wonderful way he'd made love to her.

Not just because he'd been there for her again and again.

Cordelia loved him because no one had ever been so careful with her heart, so adamant about treating her right, so dedicated to bringing her blue skies and sunshine even on days when that seemed impossible.

"Do you think Gordon would be surprised by how things turned out?" the reporter asked them both.

Cordelia tried not to let the tears that suddenly welled up fall as she replied, "I wish he was still here so that I could ask him." But if Gordon had suddenly appeared, she wouldn't have jumped immediately into asking him questions about his past and why he'd given her up. First and foremost, she would have wanted to thank her birth father for taking such good care of Alec for so long. And for being the father Alec had needed when his own had been too filled with grief to support his son.

It was in that moment that Cordelia suddenly realized that she forgave Gordon for never letting her know who he was. Because Alec had needed Gordon in a way that, honestly, she hadn't. And he'd helped make Alec the incredible man that he was.

More questions were called out from the crowd, but when Alec stood and helped her to her feet, it was clear that everyone else should do the same. "Thank you for coming," Alec said, then deliberately drew Cordelia away from the reporters and photographers, blocking her from them not only with his broad shoulders, but also with the sheer power that radiated from him.

"You did great, honey." Cordelia's mother pulled her into her arms. "You were so strong. So confident. I couldn't be prouder of you."

Her father hugged her too. "Do you want to come and have a cup of tea with us?"

She always loved spending time with her parents, especially when she was feeling a little off kilter. But their lives had already been turned upside down enough by all of this. "I know you're both missing an important district meeting." It would do them good to go back to their normal lives. Plus, she knew they'd worry far less about her if she didn't make a big deal about how drained the press conference had left her. "Thank you for being here for me—" She looked at Alec and amended that. "—for us today. I love you."

The group hug between the three of them should have felt as good as all the other group hugs they'd shared over the years. Only, this time, it didn't seem quite right. Because something was missing.

Someone was missing.

She reached out and grabbed Alec's hand. "Get in here." A surprised laugh rumbled up from his chest as he was all but tackled by a Langley family hug.

* * *

"Thank God that's over." Now that everyone but Alec was gone, Cordelia let herself collapse into her chair. "If I never answer another question about *anything* again, it will be too soon. I should have planned on having somewhere to hide for the rest of the day."

"I thought you might feel that way." He had a glint in his eyes that made her blood heat, even when she felt more wrung out than she could remember ever feeling before. "Do you trust me?"

"Of course I do." She didn't even need to think about it.

He took her hand, led her first to his office, where he grabbed a black leather bag, then outside to the hangars. They walked past one jet after another, finally turning into the last hangar, where there was only one plane.

"This is mine. It's a 1930 Fleet, a two-seat biplane that was used in the military until the end of World War II."

"Alec, it's incredible. Like something straight out of a black-and-white movie." She'd been impressed with the luxurious jets he'd shown her before, but she wanted to run her hands over the biplane's yellow and blue paint.

She wasn't surprised that it was a war plane. Of course that would be the aircraft Alec would love best—strong, handsome, and built to keep flying, to keep moving forward, even through a war. Just like he had.

"Thirty seconds in the air," he said, "and I guarantee you'll forget all about the press conference."

Her heart jumped into her throat so fast she nearly choked on her words. "I told you, I get sick in planes. I'd never forgive myself if I barfed in yours."

He looked utterly unconcerned. "You won't. Remember what I said about Gordon? He never got motion sick when we were flying my plane. It's not like being inside a narrow little tube. Flying in a biplane is what flying was meant to be, Cordelia." He drew her closer and brushed back the hair from her face. "You said you trusted me."

"I didn't think you meant about *this*." But he was right—she did trust him. And if she could find the nerve, it might actually be a brilliant way to reset her memories of today. Flying in Alec's biplane would definitely help her to forget all about the press conference. She took a deep breath. "I might need a kiss for courage."

He didn't need to be asked twice as he gave her a kiss that left her breathless—and made her need more. She put her hands on either side of his jaw and kissed him back as though they were in her bed again, rather than standing in a hangar about to take flight.

No doubt about it, his mouth on hers was better for quelling her nerves than a shot of tequila. Better for filling her senses than a hundred blooming rose bushes. Better for heating her up than a roaring fire.

"Remember this feeling," he told her when they

finally drew back. "And tell me if you feel the same when you're up in the air."

"I won't." She already knew that nothing could make her feel this way. This good. This alive.

When he kissed her again, she knew he liked her answer.

★ ★ ★

The first time Alec had taken the controls of a plane when he was eighteen had been even better than sex. He'd finally felt free.

He had a healthy respect for the elements—rain and wind, thunder and lightning. And every time he lifted off, every time he soared, he felt a deep appreciation for the wonder of the clouds, the endless sky. Hundreds of flights later, he was still awestruck.

Until last night, he'd never felt awe like that outside of a plane. But from the first moment he'd held Cordelia in his arms, from their very first kiss, she'd sent him flying. Higher than he'd known a woman could ever take him. He hadn't realized how jaded all the women he'd been with were until her *amazing* exclamation. And that had been scratching only the surface of her sensuality, from the bed to the shower, and then even the kitchen table.

His entire adult life, he'd held fast to one core rule: Keep everyone at a distance. Gordon had succeeded in getting Alec to trust him after years of constantly proving himself worthy, steady, and sane in every situation.

But for Cordelia? Within minutes of meeting her, he had decided to help her. Within days they were friends. Within a week, lovers.

Introspection had never been high on Alec's priority list. He preferred to leave the past in the past and keep his focus on forward momentum. So he didn't want to probe what it was about Cordelia that kept making him break his own previously unbreakable code of conduct. Not only was he faking a relationship and forgetting to hold his cards firmly against his chest, but for the first time ever, he was more in thrall to his passenger than the joy of soaring through the air.

"Oh...Alec." The wonder in her voice through the headset was big enough to push everything else away. "You were right. This is *incredible*. It's not like any other plane I've been in. Not like anything I could ever have imagined."

When he and Cordelia had been making their plans for the press conference, he'd known they'd need a way to release the tension of a situation that only seemed to cage them more tightly with every hour that passed. More sex was a hell of a temptation—and he wasn't counting that out later today—but only flying had ever worked to completely empty Alec when he was twisted up inside.

He'd also needed to see if he was right, if Cordelia would respond to this flight the same way he did, the same way Gordon always had.

With pure joy.

Her laughter rang beautiful and clear. "I don't even need a barf bag!"

It felt good to laugh, to shake off everything but this flight—and Cordelia. "Ready for some tricks?" When she didn't reply, he teased, "Maybe an air show tumble or a loop-the-loop?"

"No!" Her panicked scream made him laugh harder. Soon, she was laughing again too. "You jerk. I almost thought you were serious."

"Almost?" he teased. "That squeal was pure terror."

"You're going to pay for that later." But he could hear the smile in her voice. And that little hint of wickedness that you wouldn't guess was there unless you knew her the way he did.

"Is that a threat... or a promise?" He loved hearing her swift intake of breath, wished he could see her skin flush, her pulse jump.

"You're making my head spin, Alec."

He was planning on making her head spin a hell of a lot more than this before the day was over. But first, as the airstrip for the Bayport Aerodrome on Long Island came into view, he said, "I'm about to bring us in for our landing." One he planned to make so smooth that she would barely feel the wheels touch down.

Minutes later, he was helping her unbuckle and climb down from her seat. As soon as they were on the ground, she threw her arms around him. Her legs too. And it was perfectly right, holding on to her like that.

"My God, Alec. I loved it! But you know what I love even more?"

He shouldn't have wanted her to say his name. Was stunned that the thought had even crossed his mind when he'd sworn his whole life that he wasn't looking for love. "What?"

Her mouth on his was his answer.

CHAPTER SIXTEEN

Cordelia was on overload. Again.

She'd felt overwhelmed so many times during the past week, but flying with Alec had stirred up something inside her that she hadn't even realized was there. She'd always been happy in her small town, in her small garden, in her small family. But lifting off into a brilliant blue sky, flying over lakes and rivers and cities and parks and people in a historic aircraft suddenly made her see that there was *more*. More to explore, more to experience, more worth taking risks for.

She wanted Alec with a ferocity that blew even her desire from the previous night to smithereens. "I need you," she whispered against his mouth. "I need you to take me. And I need to take you too." She kissed him again, tightening her hold on him with her arms and legs. She couldn't get enough of him. *"Now."*

He began to move, walking with her toward what she prayed was a private space where they could be with each other again. She needed to celebrate with him. Rejoice over how he'd just opened her eyes to so much wonder that she was all but bursting with it.

But instead of taking them inside the small airport, he opened the door to a limousine and slid her into the backseat. "Thanks for picking us up," Alec said to the man behind the wheel. "We're headed to Watch Hill Beach."

Though Westchester County was only two hours by car from Fire Island, Cordelia had never been here with her family. As though she'd been saving it for Alec. She tried to muster up excitement for their journey, but it was difficult when she'd been so hopeful that he'd find them somewhere private to devour each other.

Her thoughts stopped short as a dark divider began to slide up behind the driver. Alec hit a button on the ceiling marked SPEAKER. "My friend and I have a few things to discuss," he told the driver, "so if you arrive before we're done with our discussion, there's no need to come back to open the doors for us. We'll let you know when we're ready to get out of the vehicle." Alec let go of the button and turned to her. "He can't see us now. And unless I hit this button again, he can't hear us either."

Her heart rate sped up as he prowled toward her, pushing her back against the seat so that she was lying flat across it and he was levered over her.

"Won't he—" Her words temporarily deserted her

as Alec began to undo one of the buttons at the front of the dress she'd worn for the press conference. God, she'd never wanted anything so much. Never wanted *anyone* so much. But she'd never had sex outside of a bed before either, except for their glorious romps in her shower and kitchen yesterday. "Won't he still know what we're doing?"

Though Alec lifted his eyes to her face, his fingers continued undoing buttons. "Yes." He pushed aside the silky fabric of her dress so that her bra was fully on display. "How does that make you feel?" He leaned down and pressed a kiss to the flesh that swelled over the cotton. "Does it bother you?" And then a kiss to the other. "Or does it excite you?"

Before Alec, she would have been sure of her answer. She would have been too embarrassed. Nervous about making too much noise or having the driver give her a knowing look when she got out of the vehicle. But with Alec, she could finally admit the truth.

"It excites me."

The whispered words had barely fallen from her lips when he was crushing her mouth against his and all but tearing off her dress.

She'd thought she was desperate for him directly after the flight when she'd jumped into his arms. But that hunger had nothing on how ravenous she felt now. As though the only reason she could breathe, the only reason her heart could still beat, was because Alec's arms were wrapped around her.

Her head was spinning from his kisses by the time he laid her across the seat, completely exposed to his mouth, his hands, his heated gaze. *"Cordelia."* She loved the way he kept saying her name between kisses and fevered strokes of his hands over her curves. *"Mine."*

She arched into his mouth at her breast, his hand between her thighs, pleasure already shooting her so high that she was teetering on the edge. And when he stroked her aroused flesh, then went deep with his fingers, the climax hit her so hard that she forgot they were in a limo with a driver mere feet away. Alec's mouth covered hers and swallowed the sounds of her pleasure.

She'd never felt so wanton. So wicked. Until she came back to earth enough to realize that Alec was kissing his way down her breasts and over her belly, then shifting her so that he could gently push her thighs apart and settle his mouth between them.

As soon as he'd sent the divider window up, she'd known they were going to have sex in the limo. But as his tongue slipped and slid over her, as she gripped his shoulders and bucked her hips up into his mouth, as she begged him for *moremoremore*—she couldn't help but wonder who the woman in the backseat was.

Driven not only by lust, but also by the thrill of new experiences, one after the other. With the only man she could ever imagine trusting to show her this brave new world.

And then, every thought fell away as another climax crashed over her. Even bigger, even more beautiful than the previous one, it was a release unlike any she'd ever had before. Ecstasy that went on and on as he worshipped her body with his mouth, with his hands…and with the care he took to make every second in his arms even better than the blissful moments that had come before.

* * *

Alec tore at his clothes, knowing he was acting like a madman, but unable—unwilling—to stop himself.

He'd never felt this before, as though he were only halfway to whole, and the only way he could get all the way there was with Cordelia. As though he would only barely be holding on until that moment when they were finally together, as close as they could be.

He couldn't get enough of her soft skin, the gorgeous sounds she made when he found just the right spots with his hands and mouth, the way she flushed and heated all over, head to toe, when she came apart beneath his hands and mouth. Satisfaction filled him at just how much she wanted him, but even when she was crying out his name and shattering with pleasure at his touch, it wasn't enough. Didn't come anywhere close to enough.

His heart pounding fast, his hands shook from his desperate need to touch, to possess, to claim, as he tossed away the last of his clothes. Rolling on protection, he knelt on the carpeted floor of the limo, wrapped her legs around his waist, then put his hands on her hips and thrust deep. So deep that both of them lost their breath.

And yet, even as he experienced more pleasure than he ever had before, something told him that even this might not be enough. To sate him. To satisfy him. To make it so that he wasn't always wanting more of Cordelia.

Strong and lithe beneath him, she gave as good as she got, her strong limbs holding him tightly as their tongues danced, their mouths as hot and wet and greedy as the rest of them.

As skin slid against skin, his breath came fast and hard as pleasure rode up his spine. His lovemaking was wild, raw. But Cordelia was not only keeping up with him, she was urging him for more. Begging him to take her over the beautiful edge of bliss one more time.

They fell together, so lost to anything but each other that when the limo took the next corner, they went sliding off the seat and onto the floor. Lying there, their arms and legs tangled, Alec felt his lungs burn as though he'd just sprinted around a track. After a while, he realized the vehicle had not only come to a stop, but the engine appeared to have been shut off as well.

Rolling slightly so that Cordelia's weight rested on him, he stroked her hair. "We made it."

She laughed, her naked breasts bouncing against his chest as she said, "We certainly did." She lifted her face to smile into his eyes. "That was *better* than amazing." She gave a happy little sigh. "Better than the flight, even."

He knew they should get up off the limo's floor and put their clothes on. He'd never been one to linger in bed with a woman after the deed was done to everyone's satisfaction, hating the thought of getting any more entangled with his temporary partner than he absolutely had to be.

But with Cordelia, it was exactly the opposite—the thought of pulling apart grated on him.

In the end, that was what finally had him drawing away. For both their sakes, they needed to keep things fun and friendly.

And nothing more.

CHAPTER SEVENTEEN

"Thank you for bringing me here." Cordelia looked down the long stretch of sand in front of them. "I can't believe we're the only ones on the beach."

"That's because everyone else in New York is stuck in the office," he said with a grin.

Both of them had plenty of work to do, but she couldn't bring herself to care. Not after Alec had sent her soaring in pretty much every way he could. First with his plane and then with his body.

She slid her hand into his, loving how natural it felt to be close to him. Friends to lovers wasn't something she'd ever thought would work for her. She knew better now. "I've been to Long Island before, but never to Fire Island. Now that I'm here, I realize I've been missing out. You're going to have to drag me back to the limo to fly us home."

"You'd miss your garden too much even to stay the night."

She laughed, knowing he was right. "True, but that doesn't mean I won't appreciate every single second we're here today." She kissed him then, just because she felt like it. "How many times have you been here?"

He looked out to sea. "Not much in recent years. But when I was a kid, we used to come a lot."

She was touched that he'd brought her somewhere that obviously held deep meaning, and history, for him. "Your whole family?"

His hand tightened on hers. "My father—" When he paused, she thought he might not continue. "He made a lot of money with his paintings of my mother. Sometimes, if her mood was good, she'd decide out of the blue that she wanted to see the ocean, and he'd hire a plane. Just like that, we'd be here, playing on the sand."

Alec had grown up with private planes and a family fortune. A week ago, she would have assumed all that money and privilege made him untouchable. But now she knew that all the money in the world couldn't have protected Alec from pain.

"My mom loved the water." He'd stopped walking, his gaze reaching beyond the crashing waves, beyond the blue that stretched into the horizon. Almost as though he was looking into the past instead. "She loved to play in the surf, no matter how cold or rough. My father would worry that she'd hurt herself. He'd ask her to come back to the shore. *Beg* her to come back. But she wouldn't. She'd simply laugh and tell him she was happy." Alec swallowed hard. "Finally happy. Until we got in the plane and headed back to the city, where she'd close up into herself again."

Cordelia was glad that Alec was sharing his memories of his parents with her, even if they weren't easy ones. As far as she could tell, he'd kept it bottled up for far too long. "Was she not a city person?"

"The way you love your garden, that's how much she loved the ocean." His deep voice was hushed now, barely audible above the surf. "My father must have known that the city was killing her. I don't know why he didn't just move us out here. Maybe then she wouldn't have died."

"Or maybe," Cordelia said, "it wasn't that clear-cut." From the little Alec had said about his mother, Cordelia visualized a complicated woman with more shades and contours than even a world-class painter like Alec's father could have seen. "Maybe her emotions weren't tied to a place."

"Or to people either." Bitterness swamped his words, and she longed to soothe him. "She was there for us when she wanted to be, then gone the rest of the time. Even when she was in the same room, or at the dinner table, you'd have to fight to get her attention."

Cordelia's heart broke for Alec, for the man who had survived being a little boy who didn't know how to get his mother to see that he needed her. No wonder that as an adult he was so intent on living without a woman's love. She couldn't blame him for closing himself off to ever being in a similar position with a woman again.

"You looked after your brothers and sister, didn't you? When she was there but not there?"

"They'd get too close to a hot stove or be about to fall down the stairs or be hungry or dirty," he said. "Someone had to take care of them. Someone other than a maid or a nanny. Someone who actually cared about them, who wasn't being paid to be there. My father was too busy painting, too busy obsessing over her to step in." Alec's face twisted into an expression of disgust, different from the sadness of talking about his mother. "Hell, I don't even think he noticed us. Because he couldn't see past *her.*"

Alec hadn't needed only his mother's attention, he'd needed his father's too. But he'd had neither. "Have you and your father ever talked about it?"

He dropped her hand, then ran his through his hair. "This is supposed to be a fun afternoon, not a therapy session."

Despite his deflection, his answer was clear. *No,* he and his father hadn't talked about a thing. Cordelia wasn't surprised, given how reluctant Alec had been to get involved in his father's birthday party.

In any case, he was right that this morning's press

conference had been more than enough strain for one day. She wasn't going to give up on helping him repair his relationship with his father, but she could let it rest for the remainder of the day.

She picked up a branch that had washed up on the shore and doodled with it in the sand. "Tell me about your siblings. I realized when we were all in my cottage yesterday that I don't really know anything about them."

Out of the corner of her eye, she could see his shoulders relax. "Harry's fifteen months younger. Like he told your parents, he teaches medieval history at Columbia. He was always a big reader, happy to sit by himself in a room full of dusty books, and learn. He's a hell of a teacher too. His students love him, and I've been to enough of his lectures to get why. He doesn't just tell you about what happened in the past, he brings it to life."

She looked up from her sand drawing. "How does he do that?"

"He's been jousting since he was a teenager—with a horse and armor and everything."

Harry looked so mild-mannered, but somehow that fit. And explained a surprisingly broad and muscular physique for an academic.

"Can you joust?" she asked.

"I couldn't resist the chance to take on my little

brother. One day I hope to best him at it, even though I haven't yet. Harry's a fierce competitor," he said with obvious pride.

"Takes one to know one," she said with a smile. "What about Suzanne?"

"Brilliant doesn't even begin to cover Suz. I swear she understands things about computers and networks and electronic systems that haven't even been invented yet."

"Is that what she does? Invent things?"

"Security is her specialty, but if she sees something else that needs to be done, she'll put her mind to it."

"What about her boyfriend, Roman? He seems like a really nice guy."

"He worked for me a few years back and we became friends. When she got into some trouble last year, we needed someone to watch over her, to make sure no one hurt her. Roman is the first guy I thought of." Alec looked like he was grinding his teeth as he added, "I never thought he'd make a play for her, though. If I had…"

Hiding her smile at what an adorable protective older brother he was, Cordelia said, "I know it wasn't what you planned, but they seem good together."

He blew out a breath before nodding. "They are. He treats her right and she seems really happy. And he knows what would happen to him if he ever took a wrong step."

Cordelia raised her eyebrows. "You'd make him regret it."

He nodded, perfectly serious. "I would. And Harry and Drake would be right there with me."

With brothers like these, she was surprised Suzanne had ever managed to date at all. Speaking of brothers—"My mom practically fainted yesterday when she realized one of her favorite painters was sitting in my living room."

"She's right to be impressed with Drake." Alec looked just as proud of his youngest brother as he was of Suzanne and Harry. "He was always drawing or painting. Right from the start, his talent was obvious. Staggering, really, even as a little kid."

"I'd love to see his work."

"You already have. It's the first painting you see when you walk into the S&W Aviation lobby."

Her eyes went big. "That incredible mountain vista?"

"Drake will be pleased to know your mom isn't the only fan of his work."

She was floored. Not only by Drake's gifts, but by all of the Sullivans she had met. Four extraordinary people who were all so nice, so giving, even to a virtual stranger like her. "You have quite a family, don't you?"

"People always think so, especially when you start

counting my cousin Smith and his Academy Awards and my cousin Ryan and his World Series wins." He shrugged. "But to me, they're just the people I grew up with, people I know will always have my back, just like I'll always have theirs." He pointed at her sand drawing. "Did you mean to draw a flower?"

She hadn't really been paying attention to what she was doing, she'd been so absorbed by what he was telling her. "I guess you're right—I'm never really far from my garden, am I?" She handed him the stick. "It's your turn."

The waves had started to wash away her sand sketch by the time the outline of the plane he was drawing became clear. The best part of it, though, was the stick-figure woman flying the plane with her hair blowing back and a huge grin on her face.

"Not bad," she said, glad to see him relaxed again.

"You think you can do better?"

Laughing, and more than up for the challenge, she took the stick and focused on her second drawing. "How's that?"

He shot her a look when she was done with her fish—scales, gills, fins and all. "You were playing me with your simple flower drawing. You've done this before." The wave lapped at her fish, taking away its tail. "Your fish looks real enough to swim away."

"I've taken a few classes," she admitted. She gave

him the branch. "Though I have to say, your stick figure was brilliant. Do another."

As he took the branch from her, she thought she saw something spark in his eyes. Something that looked like joy. And maybe even pleasure from her compliment.

Soon, she found herself looking at a stick-figure Sullivan family temporarily imprinted in the sand. Suzanne was sitting behind a computer, Harry was astride a horse holding a lance, and Drake was painting.

"Those are fantastic."

She was sad that the waves were already washing his pictures away, although maybe that was part of what made them so special. You knew they weren't going to last forever, so you had to appreciate them in the moment. Just the way she and Alec were appreciating each other. With no worries about the future. Only the sweet time they were able to spend together now.

"Draw yourself too," she suggested. What would he sketch into the sand? The billionaire businessman that the world saw? Or the man she'd been so privileged to get to know behind the dark suit and the cynical expression?

But she was surprised when he said, "You do it. Draw us both."

His eyes were dark now, as intense as that moment when he came into her and watched pleasure explode through every cell in her body from his touch. And yet, somehow this moment felt bigger than that. More important even than when they were making love, skin to skin, mouth to mouth, heart to heart.

Alec wanted to know what she saw when she looked at him. And she wanted to show him. Show him all the ways he was special.

Special not just to her, but to everyone who loved him.

She took a few steps back from the water, wanting a few extra minutes to work on her drawing before the surf washed it away. She bit her lip, concentrating on the press, the slide, of her stick into the sand. Alec stood silently beside her, and she knew his eyes weren't on the sand, but on her. No one had ever looked at her the way he did, with such focus. As though he was endlessly fascinated by her.

She smiled at the thought—what woman wouldn't want Alec Sullivan to be fascinated by her? It was a nice daydream, but she knew better than to dwell on it. She wouldn't have him forever, but that didn't mean she wouldn't appreciate every moment of *now*.

Pieces of both of them came together bit by bit on the sand. She didn't draw one of them first and the other person next—that just didn't make sense. Because when she saw Alec in her mind's eye, she saw herself there too.

"There." She propped the branch in the sand at her side. "The two of us are now immortalized." She grinned at him. "For the next sixty seconds, that is."

But he wasn't grinning as he stared down at her drawing. She'd drawn them both in her garden. He had just picked a carrot from her vegetable bed, only to have it promptly stolen by a bunny. Alec's expression as the bunny took the carrot was her favorite part of the drawing. Because he was clearly happy that the rabbit had gotten such a prize. So happy, in fact, that when you looked at the picture you had to wonder if he'd pulled the carrot for the bunny, rather than for dinner. She'd drawn herself standing nearby, holding a fistful of just-picked flowers, laughing at the scene playing out before her.

"No one else would have drawn me like that." His voice was low, his tone serious. "You're not seeing the real me."

She looked down at her sand-sketch, the surf already beginning to blur its edges. "Of course I am." She turned back to him, needing to touch him as her hands went to either side of his face. "I've never seen anything but the real you, Alec."

His mouth was on hers before she could take her next breath, his kiss so passionate, so full of need, that she knew if there had been a bed nearby, they would already be in it, clothes off, limbs tangled, bodies connected. On and on he kissed her, like he'd never get enough of her. And she felt exactly the same way. As though he was *everything*—the beginning, the middle, and the end all at once.

Finally, he lifted his lips from hers, but he still held her tightly, her cheek to his chest, their breathing ragged, their hearts racing against each other. The sun was starting to fall in the sky now, beginning its slow descent toward the blue water below.

"We should get back to the plane. In case the weather changes."

His words rumbled through from his chest to hers. She didn't want to leave, didn't ever want this day together to end, even though she'd known all along that it would.

★ ★ ★

Alec couldn't remember the last time he'd felt so good.

He'd given Cordelia the joy of flying, pleasure in the limo, and the sand and sun—but she'd given him back even more. With only a broken branch, the sandy beach, and her brilliant eye for everything around her, she'd shown him she understood him in a way that no one else did.

Because he didn't allow anyone close enough to see it. To see *him*.

But Cordelia hadn't needed him to let her in. She'd

found the lock to his heart and opened it without even trying. With every word, every question, every smile, every laugh—even her tears—she'd drawn him deeper, uncovered more.

With more time, what else would she unearth?

And would he be able to live with what she found?

For more than thirty years, Alec had been careful. Deliberate. At first, he'd focused on just getting through. Later, he'd concentrated on making his mark. He'd allowed himself to feel pleasure, both in bed and out, but moments of true joy had been few and far between. His sister's and brothers' successes, the birth of each of his cousin's kids, seeing his siblings and cousins find happiness—those were all things to celebrate.

But for himself, Alec knew better than to ask for too much. Knew how pointless it was, how frustrating, to ask for things you could never have. As a child, he'd made dozens, hundreds, *thousands* of silent wishes, endlessly hoping that his mother would feel better. He'd vowed to be a better son, to be perfect, to do whatever it took, if only she would stop crying. He'd been so angry with his father for not knowing how to make her smile. For not knowing how to make her happy. If his father truly loved his wife, shouldn't he have been able to make everything okay?

When Alec's wishes, his hopes, hadn't come true,

they'd all been replaced with anger. At his father for failing. At his mother for taking her life. And at himself, most of all, for not being able to do more than stand by helplessly while his entire family crashed and burned.

This past week with Cordelia was more than Alec had ever thought to have. He wouldn't ask for more. Couldn't risk asking for more. Not when she'd already given him so much already, so freely.

If they spent too much more time together, he'd hurt her. Hurt the best friend he'd ever had. Hurt her the way he'd been hurt all those years ago—by making her hope, making her wish for things that could never be. By making her think she could change him, change his mind, change his future.

The flight back was smooth. Cordelia had been full of wonder on the way out, vocal with it too. But they were both silent, not only during the flight and landing, but also when he helped her out of the plane and walked her to her car.

"Thank you for the beautiful flight," she said.

He couldn't resist pulling her into his arms, even as he prepared to say good-bye. "I just wanted to make you happy." He hadn't planned on saying anything that honest, but with Cordelia he never seemed to have any choice in the matter. From the start, he'd known she deserved his honesty. Even if it hurt.

"You made me very happy today, Alec." She

reached up to brush his hair away from his forehead. "I hope I made you happy too."

He had to kiss her then. Not only to forestall any more words—he knew he didn't have any of the right ones—but also because kissing Cordelia was the fastest way he knew to get to *happy*. He wanted nothing more than to take her home and make love to her. To listen to the sounds of her pleasure all night long, until she fell asleep, sated, in his arms.

Instead, he made himself give up her mouth and force his hands from her waist. Made himself step back. "I'm sure you've got to check on things at your store."

She didn't reply right away to his obvious brush-off, holding his gaze for a few moments longer than was comfortable. "I do. And I'm sure you've got a lot to deal with at the office too."

He drank in her big, honest eyes. The beautiful flush on her cheeks. Her just-kissed mouth. "Roman texted to let us know he'll have security outside your cottage day and night, all week."

"I don't need bodyguards, Alec."

"With news from the press conference just hitting, I need to know you're safe." Last night he'd made sure of it by staying with her in her cottage. In her bed. But he couldn't do that another night. Not if he wanted to make sure they were clear about only being friends. Clear, most of all, with himself.

He was glad when she didn't argue with his reasoning, even more glad when she put her arms around him and held him tight. But when she let him go, gave him a kiss on the cheek, then got into her car and drove away, he was anything but glad.

And full of more helpless wishes, more foolish hopes, than he'd had in thirty years...

CHAPTER EIGHTEEN

The Langley Garden Center had never been so busy. Partly because of Cordelia's sudden notoriety, but also because the weather was *perfect*. Overnight it seemed every bush, every plant, every tree had burst into bloom.

All of Alec's siblings had been in during the past week to check on her, which was very sweet. Only Alec hadn't been by. He'd texted her a couple of times to make sure she wasn't having trouble with the press or with the security crew assigned to watch over her. But his notes were brief and to the point.

It stung, of course. How could it not? She wasn't expecting a great big love affair, but that didn't mean going from making love one day to barely speaking the next was her favorite thing in the world. At the same time, she understood the way Alec's mind and his heart worked. She couldn't love him and not understand that he wasn't happy with the way he'd opened up to her. With how much he'd shared with her on the beach. There was nothing he hated more than talking about his mother or father and revisiting the past.

She was a good enough friend to give him some space—for now, at least—because he was not only still reeling from losing Gordon, but was also doing the work of two men. But despite his obvious discomfort over opening up to her on the beach, she couldn't help but feel that it was exactly what he needed to do.

Fortunately, in just a few minutes they would come face to face again at Harry's house in Manhattan for a birthday-planning meeting. Though seeing Alec tonight was nowhere close to a date, she'd still taken a few extra minutes after work to clean up, going so far as to put on the white skinny jeans she rarely wore. Dirt was an occupational hazard, so white was rarely a good idea. She'd also found a pretty sea-green top her mother had given her and had even splashed out with some mascara and lip gloss.

Anticipation made her heart beat a little faster as she pulled into the spot Harry had blocked off for her in his small parking area in front of his house. Two weeks ago she hadn't even known Alec Sullivan. Now, a week without seeing him was too long.

She was just getting out of the car when Harry stepped out on his front stoop to greet her. "Cordelia, I'm glad you're here. I hope the drive wasn't too bad."

She smiled at Alec's brother. Harry Sullivan might not make her heart go pitter-patter, but he was still one of the most attractive men she'd ever seen. How, she wondered, had no one snapped him up yet? The brilliant, gorgeous professor, who also happened to know his way around a medieval jousting pole, was going to be quite a catch for someone one day.

Did Harry have the same hang-ups about love as his older brother? Had his parents' marriage—and its end—taken as big a toll on him? Or had Alec taken care of everything so that Harry could escape into his books?

"It was nice to get out of my greenhouses for a little while, actually." She grabbed the potted plants she'd brought for each of Alec's siblings before kicking her door shut and heading up the stairs. "I'm really looking forward to seeing everyone." She handed him a green pot. "This is for you."

"You didn't have to bring me anything." But he looked pleased that she had.

Suzanne and Roman called their names from around the corner. "It's so good to see you again," Suzanne said as she enveloped Cordelia in a warm hug. "Is one of these for me?"

Cordelia laughed, appreciating how direct Suzanne was. "I remembered you were admiring the chenille plant during the garden tour last week," she said as she handed her the blooming plant in the hand-thrown pot.

"You're the best," Suzanne said. "No wonder Alec

is crazy for you."

Cordelia nearly dropped the third pot she was holding for Drake and Rosa. Had Alec said something about his feelings for her to Suzanne? And did his siblings know they'd slept together? She couldn't see Alec as someone who would kiss and tell, though, not even with his family.

"I like your brother a lot too."

Grinning, Suzanne craned her neck to see into the house. "Is he here yet?"

"Not yet," Harry said as they headed in. "Drake and Rosa are on their way from a meeting at her foundation that ran a little long." To Cordelia, he said, "Rosa has recently put together a foundation to fight online bullying."

Cordelia didn't pay much attention to celebrities, but Rosa's story had been so big even she couldn't miss it. "I think that's great."

"We all do," Suzanne agreed. "Oh good, Harry, you've got a bottle of red open already. Just warning you guys, but after the crap day of coding I just had, I may polish off one of these all by myself."

It could have been so easy to be intimidated by Alec's family, to feel as though growing and selling plants couldn't measure up to their huge successes. But they were all so easygoing. Even Alec, when he forgot to brood, she thought with a small smile.

Harry's house wouldn't have looked out of place in England, with comfortable leather chairs and thick rugs and leather-bound books covering every surface. The space fit him really well—it was cozy yet masculine—although Cordelia couldn't help but be struck by the fact that it seemed a bit lonely. It was the perfect bachelor pad. Only, did Harry still want to be a bachelor?

A knock came at the door and Cordelia's heartbeat immediately kicked up in anticipation of seeing Alec's handsome face. When Drake and Rosa appeared instead, she hoped no one could see her deflate.

There were hugs all around, she gave them their potted plant, and soon everyone had a drink in their hand and were relaxing into their seats. Everyone except Cordelia. Alec could just be late. But something told her his absence had nothing to do with losing track of time.

Harry's phone dinged, and he pulled it out of his pocket. She already knew what it said, even before he told them, "Alec just canceled."

"We'll see about that," Suzanne said, her mouth tightening into a flat line as she quickly typed a message into her phone. Within seconds, she got a reply. One that made her curse. "He *doesn't have time for this* right now?" She made quotes in the air. "Does he actually think I'm going to let him get away with this?

That any of us are?" She shoved her phone into her bag and started to get up. "Swear to God, I'm going to drag him here."

"Suz." Harry put his hand on her arm. "You know he didn't want to be a part of putting on this party."

She made another sound of frustration before dropping back to the couch. "Dad is trying so hard. Why can't Alec see it?"

"He does." Drake reached out to put his hand over Suzanne's. "You know his experiences, his childhood, were different from ours, that he was old enough to see it all go down and remember everything that happened. That's why you've got to cut him some slack with this, Suz. We all do."

"I'm not saying he wasn't a hero for keeping us together after Mom died." Suzanne's expression was so sad that if Roman hadn't already put his arm around her, Cordelia would have. "I just don't think it's good for him to keep pushing Dad away forever. Not just Dad, but all of us."

That was when Suzanne suddenly seemed to remember that she wasn't just with her family, shooting Cordelia a look.

But Cordelia had already made a decision. She put down her wine glass and announced, "I'll go see him." She picked up her bag. "I'll talk to him about your father's party. About how important it is. To everyone." *Including* him.

"You don't have to do this," Harry said. "He's our brother and this is our mess."

"Alec bent over backward to help me last week. He was there for me before I even knew I needed him. Now it's my turn to be there for him." She gave Harry a small smile. "Even if *he* doesn't know he needs me, I do."

Harry held her gaze for a long moment, one where she was pretty sure he was taking her measure, weighing whether she was up to the task of turning the tide with his brother. "Okay then, the rest of us will work out the details for everything we can figure out without your or his input." Harry walked her to the door and stood on the front step watching her as she went to her car. She was just getting in when he said, "Cordelia?" She turned to look up at him. "Thank you."

"You don't have anything to thank me for yet."

"You care about Alec." Harry's expression was full of emotion. "That's already enough to be thankful for."

* * *

Alec poured himself a second double shot of whiskey and downed it in one fiery gulp. Soon, he hoped, he'd be drunk. Drunk enough to sleep. Drunk enough to stop the mental playback of his parents when he was a kid, happy times that he'd forgotten ever existed until he was back on the beach at Fire Island last week. Drunk enough to forget about his father's party. Drunk enough to stop thinking about Cordelia.

But no amount of work, no amount of exercise, no amount of alcohol was doing a damn thing to erase her from his system. She was there in every second of every day, in his office talking about his shark smile, on the tarmac marveling at the planes, in the shower with the hot spray dripping down her luscious curves. Most of all, she was there in his head, making him feel like the world's biggest jackass for bailing on his siblings tonight, for not wanting to be a part of his father's big birthday celebration.

Why was he even bothering with the shot glass? He'd need to pour the entire damned bottle down his throat to find even the slightest relief. Which was exactly what he was about to do when his doorbell rang.

He knew. *Knew*. It wasn't his sister. Wasn't one of his brothers. Cordelia was standing out there. Coming to call his bluff. Coming to say to his face what no one else had the nerve to say.

That he was a selfish SOB. That he needed to suck it up for one night and cook a meal for his father and family. That he shouldn't have gone dark on her all week. That he was a coward for hiding in his penthouse apartment with a bottle of whiskey.

Dropping the bottle on the counter, he stalked over to the door and yanked it open. Her eyes went wide for a split second as she took in his state of disarray. He'd ripped off his suit when he got home and couldn't be bothered to put on more than a pair of faded jeans. His feet were bare, his hair was standing on end from running his hands through it, and he was all but breathing fire.

"What part of *I'm busy* didn't you get?"

"The part where I missed you too much to care." She walked past him, put her bag down on his entry table, then turned to him. "It's nice to see you, Alec."

God, she sure knew how to turn him inside out. Especially when seeing her was the best thing that had happened to him in seven days straight.

He followed her into the kitchen. "Want a drink?"

"Thanks, but I have to drive home, so I'd better not."

No. He didn't want her going anywhere. Didn't want her leaving him. Not tonight.

"In that case, I'll drink yours." He poured another shot and threw it back.

"Come sit with me, Alec." She reached out toward him. "Tell me about your week."

He wanted nothing more than to sit with her. But that was a lie. What he really wanted, more than anything in the world, was to drag her onto his lap, tear off her clothes, and bury himself in her.

The only way to stop himself from doing that was to convince her to leave. And the only way to convince her to leave was to be an ass. An even bigger one than he'd already been this week.

He shoved his hands into his pockets. "You're not here to find out about my week. You want to know why I bailed on the meeting tonight."

"Actually, I want to know both things. But if you want to start with tonight, I'm all ears."

She was one cool customer. Tough too. So much tougher than he'd thought on that first day he'd seen her standing on the sidewalk outside his office building.

"I'm still going to cook for the party," he told her. "Harry, Suz, and Drake are perfectly capable of working out the rest of the details without me."

"Of course they are." She looked at him as if he was missing a screw. Which, honestly, was how it felt, with all the whiskey swimming around in his system and her ridiculously delicious floral scent mucking up the brain cells that were still functioning. Her formfitting white jeans and silky top weren't helping any by showcasing every beautiful curve. "That's not why they wanted you at the meeting tonight. They were hoping that this party would help you get closer to your dad."

"They know better than to hope for something that's never going to happen." Alec deliberately turned away from her and walked toward the floor-to-ceiling glass that looked out on the lights of the city.

"Then you should have gone to Harry's house and told them that." He heard her footsteps, knew she was coming closer. Every muscle in his body tensed in an internal struggle to keep from reaching for her. "They might not have liked hearing it, but they would have understood." She was standing beside him at the window now. So close that her shoulder, her hip, were nearly touching his. "Just like you should have told me you needed space, instead of just disappearing this week." He could feel her eyes on his face and was powerless not to meet her gaze. "I would have understood." She licked her lips. "I *do* understand."

Everything crashed down around him in that moment. His pride. His frustration.

His self-control.

"I'm sorry." If only he could draw her against him, feel her heart beating against his one more time. "You deserve better than that." His throat felt raw, but not because of the whiskey. Because of the shame of having hurt her. "Better than me."

The last thing he expected was to see her roll her eyes. "Seriously, you're going to have to work a lot harder than that to get rid of me. I'm your friend. You're my friend. Sometimes friends freak out, screw up, go dark for a while. This time it was you. Next time it might be me. But that's okay, because one blip, one mistake—doesn't mean our friendship is over."

"What does it mean?"

"That's up to both of us." She looked at him with those bright green eyes that never held anything back. "What do you want, Alec?"

He knew he shouldn't allow himself to say it. Knew he should keep his answer locked inside. But he also knew that he might never sleep again or ever manage to sober up if he didn't get out the truth.

"Tonight, all I want is *you*."

CHAPTER NINETEEN

Cordelia knew he would wait for her response, that he wouldn't take anything from her until he was absolutely sure that she wanted to give it. Just as she knew that he'd always been honest with her, even now when lust was tearing through them both.

Tonight. That was what he wanted her for. Not tomorrow. Not next week. Certainly not next year.

Making love again wouldn't mean anything beyond tonight—and she couldn't deny that a part of her ached more than ever at the sure knowledge that he would never be her Prince Charming and that the odds of the two of them ending up at the altar one day, staring into each other's eyes while making vows of forever, were zilch.

Other women might have tried to change him, but Cordelia would never do that. Because the Alec Sullivan standing in front of her right now, the man who had just told her one truth she had desperately wanted to hear—that he wanted her—alongside another she didn't—that it would only be for tonight—

was the man she had fallen for. First as a friend. And then as so much more.

Tonight was all he promised her. Knowing that, she could either walk away—or she could grab at the night with both hands. Revel in it with everything she had. And she could be happy knowing she was finding such wonderful bliss with a friend. One who meant more to her than any other friend had before.

"I want it too," she said softly. "Tonight. *You.*"

"Tell me you're sure." But his hands were already in her hair, his body already pressing against hers. "Tell me you understand."

"I'm sure." She whispered the words against his lips. "And I understand. Tonight only. With no promises of anything more."

"I don't deserve you," he said. And then his mouth came crashing down on hers before she could tell him that he *did*.

Alec deserved so much more than he was willing to take. Or to ask for. But she would give it all to him anyway. Every last piece of her heart, because she wanted to give it to him. *Needed* to give it to him.

"Let me love you, Alec." She was running her hands over his bare chest, following the path of her fingertips with her lips. "Let me make you feel as good as you've always made me feel."

His hands tightened in her hair, the muscles in his

chest jumping beneath her hands and mouth, as he let her taste him, revel in him, tease him, tempt him. She dropped to her knees, put her hands on the button of his jeans, popped it open, and began to work the zipper—and all the while, she could feel his dark, intense gaze on her. She licked her lips, held her breath in glorious anticipation, then finally dropped his jeans to the floor.

She'd guessed he would be naked beneath the well-worn denim. She'd known he'd be magnificent. But she hadn't realized just how much she'd want to kiss his naked flesh, to run her lips, her tongue over his hard length. Until it wasn't enough, and she had to take him inside her mouth, one hard, beautiful inch at a time.

Her name was a groan of pleasure from his lips as she took him deep, humming with joy at his delicious taste. He was so hot, so powerful, so alive. She'd never wanted anything more than she wanted to take him over the edge. To feel him lose control with her, inside of her.

But before she could make the fantasy real, he was pulling himself from her mouth and lifting her into his arms.

"You're a goddess," he said as he strode with her out of his living room and up the stairs. "But I need more tonight, Cordelia. I need to feel you coming beneath me, need to hear you calling my name, need to know I'm the only man who can make you feel this good."

"You are." She had never learned to be coy, and wouldn't have bothered playing that game with Alec even if she had. "You do."

"I want to believe it." They were in his bedroom now, and he was lowering her to her feet. "I *need* to believe it."

"Touch me," she said. "Kiss me," she begged. "Love me," she urged. "And you will."

She expected him to throw her onto the bed. To tear off her clothes. To ravish her. Instead, he carefully put his hands on either side of her face and kissed her.

Gently.

Sweetly.

Reverently.

Her heart swelled. Bigger and bigger until she was sure it would burst through her chest.

No one had ever kissed her like this. No one had ever touched her as though she was the most precious thing in the world to him.

And he was just as precious to her.

She wanted to be skin to skin. Wanted there to be nothing between them. She drew back from his mouth to tell him, "I started taking the Pill. Last week."

The heat in his eyes leaped another hundred degrees. "I'm clean."

"Good." She couldn't contain her smile. Or the desire that raced through her, hotter, faster than ever. "I want to feel you, Alec. *All* of you."

"You will." His words were more than a promise. Stronger than a vow. "But first…" His touch was light as he reached for her top and drew it over her head. "I'm going to kiss you." He lowered his lips to her breastbone and pressed his mouth to it. "Everywhere."

The word was muffled against her skin, but she heard it in his kiss. In the way he slowly ran his lips over every inch of the skin he'd just bared. Her shoulders, her arms, her wrists, the swell of her breasts, and then lower down over her stomach, before turning her so that he could rain kisses over the nape of her neck, and then her back, her waist.

He didn't spin her around before reaching for the snap of her jeans. And when he remained on his knees behind her as he peeled away the white denim, the feel of his warm breath over her bare skin was impossibly erotic. Especially when he bent just a little lower to kiss the curve of her hip where it peeked out from her panties.

She'd done something crazy earlier this week. She'd gone to a store in town that she'd never visited before, one that sold frilly things. In the back, she'd found some lingerie in delicate pink silk. It was something she'd never considered wearing before now, but she'd wanted to feel like one of her bright, pretty flowers tonight. Wanted Alec to peel away her clothes just the way he was now and see that she had bloomed. Only for him.

"Look at you." His voice was low. Sensuous as it caressed her skin the same way his hands and his mouth did. "My beautiful Cordelia."

He held her hips in his hands as he ran his tongue up the back of her leg from her ankle to the curve of her hip. She shivered with delight as he did the same to her other leg, knowing she would have fallen if he hadn't been holding her so firmly.

Everything inside of her ached for him. "Please," she begged, just the way he'd said he wanted her to. "*Please*, Alec."

He finally turned her then, so that his mouth was level with her sex. She ached, throbbed, burned for him. For his touch. And he knew. Because—*thank God*—he pressed his mouth to her. Over silk. And she moaned.

"Tell me," he said.

"It feels so good." She all but panted the words. "*You* feel so good."

"Mmmm. So good."

The sound vibrated between her thighs. And then he was sliding silk off her hips, down her thighs, until it landed as a small pink scrap of fabric on the plush rug.

"Here." He blew lightly against her slick flesh. "I dream about kissing you here, Cordelia."

At first his lips touched her bare skin with soft, nearly chaste kisses. Until, suddenly, he swirled his tongue in such a sinful way that she saw stars behind her eyelids. And when his tongue dipped hot and fast against her, then slid deep, she came completely apart, one beautiful shock of pleasure after another.

She hadn't yet begun to recover from the breathless orgasm when he picked her up again and laid her on the bed. Her bra was still on, but he didn't seem in any rush to take it off. Not when he seemed to be having such fun running his tongue along the edges where silk met skin.

After her explosive climax, she should have been sated. At least a little bit, for a little while. But she already knew that one taste of ecstasy with Alec was never enough. Especially when he was teasing her like this with little kisses on sensitive flesh, slow swipes of his tongue, sinful nips of his teeth.

She would have begged again, but she couldn't find any more words. Could only arch into his mouth, into his hands, in a silent plea for him to do more than tease.

Alec Sullivan wasn't a man who could be easily swayed, however, and when he covered the taut tip of one breast with his mouth and she felt wet silk slide between his tongue and her shockingly aroused skin, she realized he was right to show her all the different shades of pleasure. All the different ways he could make her feel good.

And *oh,* was he ever making her feel good as he moved his mouth to her other breast, utterly focused on her pleasure. She couldn't stay still on the bed, even with his thigh between hers, her hands in his on either side of her head. She writhed against him, desperate to find the next peak, knowing it was close, knowing it would be *amazing.*

"Look at me, Cordelia."

She opened her eyes just in time to watch as he flipped open the clasp on her bra. Her breasts sprang free, and he slid the pad of one thumb over the sensitive flesh.

"No matter what I do," he said, "no matter what you feel, promise me you won't look away."

Her breath caught in her throat at his deeply sensual request. "I promise."

His lips turned up at the corners, even as his gaze went almost black. "All day, all night, I fantasize about you." As he spoke, he ran his hand over her naked curves. From breast to hip, finally stopping with his fingers splayed over her pelvis. "Touching you." He moved his hand lower, so that he was nearly touching her sex. "Kissing you." He lowered his mouth to hers for the briefest moment. "Telling you how good you feel. How good you make *me* feel."

"Tell me now," she urged.

"So damned good, Cordelia." He slid his hand to cup her between her thighs. "And getting better every single second."

She knew what was going to happen, yet the plunge of his fingers still took her breath away. Pleasure sparked along every inch of her skin, especially where he was moving inside of her. She rocked her hips against him to try to get closer, and when she did, he didn't just give her what she needed, he gave her something she hadn't even realized existed before him. A connection so strong, so deep, that she felt it in more than just her body, more than just her heart, but her soul too.

She was on the verge of climax when he suddenly shifted, drew his hand from between her thighs, grasped her hand in his again, then plunged deep.

They moved together in a beautiful dance that was at once instinctive and passionate. She nearly closed her eyes at the exquisite joy of their lovemaking, but she'd made him a promise. And she would never, ever break her promises to him. Not one made on a night of lovemaking that she'd remember forever. And not her promise to let him be free after the night was over either.

He didn't say a word as he took them both higher and higher until they couldn't hold back the tidal wave of pleasure another moment. But his gaze told her he'd never experienced anything so sweet. So real. So *perfect*.

And it was.

Absolutely perfect.

CHAPTER TWENTY

Alec woke with Cordelia in his arms. With her soft warmth pressed along the length of his body, as he listened to her deep, even breathing and took in the smile on her lips even as she slept, he realized he'd never felt so happy, so content, so at peace.

But when she stirred, he forced himself to let go and slide out of bed.

It wasn't what he wanted. Hell no, it wasn't. For the first time in his life, Alec was tempted to chuck in everything he knew to be true about love and try to give his heart to Cordelia. He wished he could pretend that he was capable of a happily-ever-after, that he could believe a real relationship with her wouldn't be a house of cards that would come blowing down at the first storm.

Alec made himself step into a freezing cold shower, standing beneath the icy spray just long enough to soap up and wash off. His movements felt robotic as he dried off, then dressed in a suit. But he had to do it, had to make sure he'd shifted one hundred percent back into real life before Cordelia got out of bed and her gorgeous curves, her sleepy eyes, her radiant smile, tempted him back down a road he knew he shouldn't keep traveling.

He'd never cared this much about anyone. Never thought he was *capable* of caring this much about a woman. All his life, he'd proved to everyone that he was happy being alone. Now, he had to prove it with Cordelia. Even if it was killing him to pull away from her like this.

He was in the kitchen drinking his first cup of coffee when she walked in, hair wet from a shower. She was wearing her pretty shirt and jeans from the night before.

"Good morning." There were no shadows in her eyes. No awkwardness in her movements as she went to the coffee machine and poured herself a cup. "The view from here is positively amazing on a clear morning. Do you ever get used to it?"

For a moment—more than one actually—he was speechless. Despite her having said that she understood last night wouldn't mean they were in a relationship, a part of him had thought that the intensity, the brilliance, of their lovemaking might have changed her mind. Changed her the same way it felt like she changed him every time they were together.

But she seemed totally fine on this morning after.

Perfectly happy to move on from their sizzling hot night and embrace the day ahead just as friends.

He was glad, of course. The last thing either of them needed was some big scene about how she wanted more than just friendship and why he couldn't give that to her. He worked to shove away a foolish feeling of disappointment as he said, "Honestly, I like the view from your cottage better."

She looked surprised, but also pleased, by his comment. "Really?"

How could I not, when it means you're there? He bumped the heel of his hand into his forehead as if to knock out the forbidden thought. "I've looked at city buildings for most of my life," he explained. "Your garden is something new."

When she remained silent, he tried to think of something else to say to keep things from getting awkward. He'd never felt tongue-tied around a woman before. The morning after had always been easy, smooth. But today everything felt different. As though last night they'd crossed some sort of emotional boundary, some invisible heart-shaped barrier. And now he didn't know how to get back to where they'd started.

Finally, he said, "What do you have on tap today?" Hell, in a minute he was going to be asking her about the freaking weather.

Thankfully, she didn't look like she thought anything was out of the ordinary as she said, "Just another day in paradise. What about you?"

He couldn't push away a feeling of dismay that it had already come to this—talking about the view from his apartment and their daily office schedules. Then again, this was where things needed to be between them, wasn't it? Even, steady ground. No big emotional highs meant no big emotional lows. After all, Alec's entire life had been about avoiding the emotional swings his mother and father had seemed to thrive on.

"Our quarterly staff meeting starts at ten," he told her. "It's always a good chance to get feedback from everyone. Especially now that I'm going to be making some major changes."

"Because Gordon's gone?"

"S&W Aviation was his dream." Alec hadn't been willing to admit this to anyone. Even himself. But he suddenly needed Cordelia to know. "Don't get me wrong, I loved the power, the thrill, the chase, the wins."

"Past tense," she noted. *"Loved."*

He blew out a breath. "Gordon and I brought in the best people from around the globe to work with us. Women and men who know exactly how the business should run, where it should go, what makes people want to book with us. Most important, they come to the office excited every day. This past week I've realized that's who should be running S&W—someone who's excited about it. And that just isn't me any-more."

"You're going to step down as CEO?"

"Not right away. But soon. Honestly, it's not the same without Gordon. I've realized this week that it was never about the planes, it was about our friend-ship. And without that, there doesn't seem to be much point."

He waited for her to push him on embarking on a cooking career now that his aviation business wasn't going to be taking up all of his time. Instead, she simply said, "I'm proud of you. For knowing you're ready for a change." It had been the perfect opening for her to try to convince him to open a restaurant. But she wasn't at all predictable this morning.

He wished he could tell her to take a seat at the kitchen island while he whipped up something for them to eat. Chopping, using his frying pan, watching her enjoy his food—all of those things would help to settle him down.

But his meetings this morning meant they couldn't share a long, cozy breakfast together. They'd had a good night, and now they had to say good-bye, two friends who, thankfully, had managed not to screw things up with each other.

She took her cup over to the sink and rinsed it out. "I'll be around at the nursery all week if you want to discuss the menu for your father's party."

"Thanks. I already texted Harry, Suz, and Drake to let them know not to worry."

She gave him a big smile. "I'm sure they were happy to hear that."

It was the *hope* in her smile that worried him. Clearly, she understood that their relationship could never go any further than it already had. Somehow, he needed to make her understand that his relationship with his father was at the end of its line too. "I know you mean well, but—"

"Butt out?"

"In a nutshell, yeah."

Clearly frustrated with him, she inhaled deeply, then blew her breath out slowly. He could almost hear her counting to ten inside her head before she spoke. "Your father's ring tone—I hear it a lot on your phone." She held up a hand before he could reply. "It's not that I'm stalking your phone or anything, it's just that he calls a lot. He wants to make amends, doesn't he?"

Alec shrugged. "I gave up trying to figure him out a long time ago."

"Why?"

"When someone disappoints you enough times,

you get to a point where you stop caring."

"But what if you can't stop?"

For a moment, he almost thought she had jumped from talking about his father to talking about *them*. About the fact that it was nearly impossible to stop himself from caring more and more about her every day.

When he didn't reply, she came closer. It amazed him how she was never afraid to come toe to toe, face to face with him, even during difficult discussions—whereas he had spent a lifetime doing whatever it took to avoid that kind of situation.

"I know things were bad when you were a kid," she said softly. "Really bad. But all I can think is that if you already don't have a relationship with your father, then what do you really have to lose if you give him another chance now?"

"There's nothing left to lose. She's already gone."

He didn't realize he'd spoken the words out loud until he saw the shock on Cordelia's face. "Your mom." Her words came at him as if through a thick, soupy fog. "You blame him for what your mom did." He could almost see the lightbulb go on over her head. She stared at him in horror as she asked, "Do you think he had a part in her suicide?"

"Of course he did." His words were crisp, ice cold. As cold as he suddenly felt, head to toe. "He should have known she wasn't happy. He should have done something about it, something more than just painting more and more canvases of her. He should have figured out how to make her smile. He should have reminded her that there were reasons to keep living. Four kids who were counting on her not to leave us."

"*Alec.*" She'd whispered his name last night, but never in this anguished tone. "I'm sorry. I'm so sorry that your parents hurt you so badly. That they hurt all of you."

Ever since the day his mother died, Alec had never allowed a chink in his armor. But then Gordon had thrown Cordelia into his life and he'd forgotten that keeping everyone out meant keeping her out too.

Finally, he remembered.

"I need to head into the office now."

"Alec, please don't shut me out."

But they both knew that if he didn't, there would be hell to pay. "I'll walk you to your car."

She stood where she was for a few moments longer, and he guessed she was trying to decide whether she should press the issue. At last, she took her bag from the counter where she'd left it last night, and followed him out the door in silence.

★ ★ ★

Cordelia was shaking as she drove out of the city.

It had taken every ounce of self-control to be *only* his friend this morning. But as soon as she'd awakened and realized he'd taken a shower, was already dressed and brewing coffee, she'd known their night was officially over.

It had been a perfect, sexy, fantasy night, start to finish. A night she refused to regret, even though she was going to need a little time to come back down to earth. It would help to be surrounded by her flowers, her vegetables, her lovely customers. To know that she was back in a life that had always fulfilled her before.

Only, she couldn't stand the thought of going back to a life without Alec. And from the way he'd shut her out this morning after she'd gone too deep with her questions about his father, she was all but certain that was what he intended. Perhaps even without that intense conversation, he would have tried to shut her out, simply to ensure that she didn't start getting the wrong idea about their lovemaking actually leading to *love*.

Coming to a stop in the bumper-to-bumper traffic, she blew out a frustrated breath. Alec Sullivan was the most complicated man she'd ever known. He was also the most caring, helpful, brilliant, and beautiful man on the planet. One she refused to give up on, no matter how much he clearly wished that she would.

The little boy he'd once been who had unconditionally loved his father—and his mother—was still there. She was sure of it. Hopefully cooking for William Sullivan's birthday party would help Alec remember some of the good things.

But she couldn't stand the thought of just waiting and hoping. She needed to do something, needed to be proactive. The traffic was at a complete standstill as she pulled out her phone and dialed Information.

CHAPTER TWENTY-ONE

Alec wasn't surprised when Harry walked into his office that afternoon. "I already told you, just because I didn't make it to your place last night doesn't mean I've bailed on cooking for Dad's party. I'm still holding up my end of the bargain."

"I'm not here about the party," Harry said.

Now Alec *was* surprised. "What's up, then?"

"You tell me." People often mistook Harry for a soft touch. But beneath that brilliant academic exterior, Alec knew his brother could be hard as nails.

"Just business as usual," Alec replied, though it was as far from the truth as things got. Not only was he working on an exit plan from his company, but Cordelia was never far from his thoughts.

"What about Cordelia? Was she just business?"

How could his brother think that? A rush of fury had him answering before he could stop himself. "You know she wasn't." No, he wouldn't let her be past tense. Not yet. "She isn't."

"If I knew," Harry said, "I wouldn't be here asking

you to explain what the hell you're playing at with her."

Alec got up from his desk, walked over to the drinks cabinet, poured himself a double shot, and threw it back. He almost never drank in the middle of the day, but at this point he didn't give a damn about normal. All he wanted was to make it through. Without baring his soul to his brother. And without breaking down and calling Cordelia, begging her to forgive him for being an ass *again*. Because he knew what she'd expect if he called—she'd want to talk more about his father, want to dig deeper into a mess that was better left untouched.

He put down the glass, then turned to face his brother. "Gordon's death—it changed everything. Especially when I found out about Cordelia. Even more when I met her."

"Because you liked her?" Harry asked in his typically insightful way.

"What's not to like?" Alec knew there was no point in lying about that—not liking Cordelia would be akin to not liking butterflies or rainbows. "That first week, we were both just trying to figure things out. I helped her, she helped me. But now that we're over the hurdles, we're getting our normal lives back on track." He shot his brother a look. "I know you were all wondering what was wrong with me these past couple of weeks, what had happened to the brother you've known all these years. Well, those two weeks were a weird blip that's over now. It's time to get back to reality."

"A reality that doesn't include Cordelia?"

Harry's words were like a jousting lance straight to Alec's heart. Just the way he'd won that time Alec had gone up against him in the field. "We're friends."

"Friends is good. Although," Harry had to add, "I've never seen you look at a friend the way you look at her."

"She's beautiful." Another thing Alec wouldn't try to pretend wasn't true. "Of course I look."

"You've got your pick of beautiful women. Women you couldn't care less about." Harry wouldn't let it go. "But Cordelia means something to you. And I know you must mean something to her, or she wouldn't have gone to you last night."

"She's got a misguided notion that Dad and I are going to make up after all these years," Alec told his brother. "That's why she came last night, to try to hammer a heart into me where there isn't one."

"She knows about what happened when we were kids?"

"She knows. And she still thinks things can change for me and Dad."

Harry finally sat, as though the wind had just been

taken out of his sails. He took off his glasses and rubbed a hand over his eyes. "You know what drives me crazy about studying history? Everyone always thinks they can look back at the past and say how they would have done things better. How they would have avoided making mistakes. When the truth is, everyone in the past was doing the best they could in the circumstances they were dealing with. Even the people who totally blew it." He put on his glasses. "I'm not going to say that what Dad did, or how he behaved, was okay. I'm not even going to say that you should forgive him. Neither of those things is up to me. But I can't leave here until I say something about Cordelia."

Few people could command Alec's attention the way his brother could, so he didn't look away, didn't move behind his desk. He simply waited.

"She has nothing to do with the past. She didn't know our mom and dad. She didn't know you as a child. And yet I still think Cordelia has seen more of the real you than any of us have since you were a kid. Suz and Drake might have been too young to remember what you were like before Mom died, but I remember who you were before everything went dark. Somehow, Cordelia sees that. She sees *you*. And she's not someone you can scare away." With that, Harry got up and headed for the door, but before he left he turned, as though he had one more thing to say. "From where

I'm sitting, the past looks a hell of a lot less interesting than the future. Especially if you're lucky enough to share that future with a woman as great as Cordelia."

★ ★ ★

Cordelia had all of the five-hour drive to the Adirondacks to figure out what she was going to say to William Sullivan. And yet, here she was, standing on his front porch, ringing the doorbell, and she *still* hadn't figured it out. She had to stop herself from wiping her sweaty palms on her jeans.

When William opened the door, she was instantly struck by the resemblance between Alec and his father. She hadn't been with it enough at Gordon's service to take in very many details about William when Suzanne had pointed him out in the crowd, so she felt as though she were meeting him for the first time.

"Cordelia, I'm glad you called." He gave her a smile, one tinged with obvious concern. "Come on inside. Or, if you'd like, we can sit on the porch." He gestured at the vista before them. "It's a perfect Summer Lake day."

"The porch would be great."

"Iced tea work for you?"

She nodded gratefully, her throat feeling parched. God, she was nervous. Nervous about butting into Alec's life. Nervous about saying the wrong thing.

Nervous that she'd read things wrong and that William would end up being just as resistant as Alec to fixing things between them.

He brought out a pitcher and two glasses, and they sat in two Adirondack-style rockers. She decided not to beat around the bush. "You must be wondering why I came."

"I'm glad you did. I was sorry about what happened to Gordon. And I can only imagine the shock it must have been to find out he was your birth father after all these years."

She took a large gulp of iced tea. "It was sad. Surprising. But if he hadn't named me in his will, I wouldn't have met your son."

"Alec is the reason you're here, isn't he?"

She nodded. "We've become friends."

"Just friends? I know you can't always trust the press, but from everything I've read, it sounds like the two of you are a couple."

She realized William didn't know about the plan they'd made for the press conference. He was the only family member who hadn't been at her cottage the morning the news of her inheritance had hit Page Six. "Alec wanted to pose as my boyfriend to scare off the fortune hunters. I wasn't sure we should do that, but everyone agreed."

"Everyone?"

Ugh, she was already putting her foot in it. "Your other kids." Just as she'd expected, he looked hurt at being left out. "They were all nearby when the news broke that Gordon had left me everything. I'm sure that if you'd been there—"

"You don't have to pretend for my benefit, Cordelia. I'm left out for a reason."

She sighed, knowing he was right—there was no point in her having come all the way to Summer Lake if she was going to paint a picture that didn't exist. "Honestly, I'm not totally sure why I'm here. More than anything, I just wanted to meet you."

"I wanted to meet you too. Any woman who can claim my eldest son's heart must be special. Less than five minutes with you and I can see that you are."

"I haven't claimed his heart," she clarified again. "That's just for the press."

He didn't argue with her, but said instead, "He's claimed yours, hasn't he?"

She felt her cheeks go hot. "I'm not good at lying, and something tells me you could see through me even if I were, so I won't try to tell you that he hasn't." But she needed him to know the truth. "We're just going to remain friends. He doesn't want more, and I would never ask him for it."

"You drove five hours to meet with me. So why wouldn't you apply the same determination to winning my son's heart?"

She knew she had to pick her words carefully. It was one thing to admit that she'd fallen for Alec—and that she would give anything to win his heart. But she didn't want to hurt William any more than he already was by telling him that *he* was the reason Alec didn't believe in happily-ever-afters.

"Some people expect love to be waiting at the end of the rainbow. But for others..." She shook her head, not knowing how to put it any other way. "Others can't see the rainbow, so they don't believe there's a prize waiting for them."

"It's my fault," William said in a grim, guilty voice.

Darn it, this was exactly what she hadn't wanted him to take away from what she'd just said. "I'm not saying that."

"You don't have to. I already know it. I've known it for a long time. After my wife died, it took me far too long to climb out of my grief, my shame, to see how big my kids had grown. That they weren't kids any-more, but adults. And by then, I was so far to the outside of their lives that it seemed impossible to get back in. So I didn't try. Not really. Not the way I should have."

"Grief does strange things to people," she said, wanting to comfort him. "My behavior at Gordon's service attests to that firsthand. I can't imagine how difficult it must have been to lose your wife, the mother of your children."

"I couldn't keep her here," William told her in a voice made raw with emotion. "I couldn't keep her with them. I swear I tried, but no matter what I did or said, no matter how much I pleaded with her, she just kept drifting farther and farther away from us all." From the look on his face, it was as though time had rewound thirty years and he was back with a wife whose sadness pervaded everything. "For three decades, I've tried to wrap my head around what happened. But I still can't."

"I'm so sorry, William. I didn't mean to drag up painful emotions. Forgive me." She stood. "You've been so nice to meet with me. I should go."

"Please, at least stay for lunch." She watched as he worked to shake off his grief. "We don't have to dredge anything else up. But we could still get to know each other better, I hope." He gave her another one of those smiles that reminded her of Alec's.

She was never able to resist Alec when he turned on the charm. It turned out she didn't have much luck resisting his father either. "Okay, that would be nice."

They went inside and made sandwiches, and though they didn't talk about anything serious again, the stories William told her about Alec and his siblings playing on the lake, goofing off at school, and clowning around with their cousins, were enough to tell her everything she needed to know.

William Sullivan wanted the very best for Alec. Happiness. Success.

And, most of all, *love*.

CHAPTER TWENTY-TWO

Alec couldn't believe how slowly the past seven days had dragged by. He'd find himself staring at the clock wondering why everything seemed to be stuck in slow motion.

Seven mornings ago, Cordelia had left his city penthouse. Seven days had passed in which they had barely spoken—as far as he was concerned, a handful of short phone calls and texts didn't count. Seven nights had gone by in which they'd slept apart.

He'd done everything he could to get back to normal, to live his life the same way he had for decades. He'd worked from sunup to sundown, getting his transition team in place at S&W Aviation. In the spare time he had left, his trainer at the gym had put him through some serious paces *and* he'd gone for long runs. He'd also kept his promise to his siblings and had been looking through recipes for his father's birthday dinner.

But none of his usual tricks was working.

His energy and focus flagging from lack of sleep—

and worse, lack of Cordelia—Alec dragged his attention back to his meeting with one of his best customers. Randy had built an organic food company from the ground up in the United States and was now taking it abroad.

"Thanks again for getting me and my VP onto a plane tonight," Randy said. "Making this spur-of-the-moment meeting in Paris could be the difference between getting into the big chains or not."

"I'm glad we could make it work." Alec had to juggle the schedule for a couple of jets later in the week, but that was one of the things S&W Aviation did best. If the customer had a problem, they went out of their way to solve it.

"Any chance I could get you to take these as thanks?"

Alec looked down at the concert tickets Randy had just put on the table—and his chest clenched tight. *James Taylor*. First row. Tonight at Tanglewood.

"She'll love them." He spoke without thinking. "One of my friends is a huge James Taylor fan," he explained.

"If that's the case, Tanglewood is the venue for her. The concert area is intimate, with only five thousand people under the covered top. And it's just a couple of hours' drive from here. I've also got reservations for tonight at one of the local B&Bs if she doesn't want to make the drive back after the show."

"That's great." Alec stood. He'd need to pick up Cordelia right away if they were going to have any chance of getting to the concert on time. "Have a great flight to Paris."

"I will. And if you can convince your friend to take you along with her, you shouldn't miss JT. His show will blow you away, especially if you know the songs."

Randy had no idea just how well Alec knew the songs. So well that he would never have considered going to a James Taylor show.

Until Cordelia.

* * *

Cordelia's first shock had been seeing Alec Sullivan walk into her nursery, commanding and gorgeous in jeans and a dark T-shirt. Her second had been when he told her he had a special surprise for her tonight.

"You want me to put Brian in charge, pack an overnight bag, and then get in your car with you—but you won't tell me where we're going?"

"I promise, Cordelia—you're going to love it."

After a week of short and somewhat stilted phone conversations, maybe she shouldn't still trust him. But she did. And she couldn't help wanting to be with him. Even if it was just for a few hours.

Besides, he wasn't the only one who hadn't called

or texted much this week. She hadn't either. Partly because she felt guilty about going to see his father behind his back. But also because she was still trying to figure everything out.

Despite meeting William, she hadn't yet hit on a brilliant idea to help Alec and his father reconnect. She hoped the surprise birthday dinner would be a step in the right direction, but the only thing she was sure of at this point was that she wanted to be Alec's friend. And friends did things like cutting out of work early for spur-of-the-moment road trips, didn't they?

"Okay, you're on." She loved seeing his smile. "Let me throw some things into a bag and we can go."

"I'll nose around the garden while you get ready," he said. "I've been looking at recipes for the birthday dinner, and I should make sure we'll have enough of what I need."

She gave him a huge smile of her own, glad that he was still one hundred percent on board—with that, at least. Fifteen minutes later, they were on the road. The weather was clear and sunny…and they were in a cherry-red 1953 Buick Skylark convertible.

"This is such a beautiful car," she said. "Do you collect cars as well as planes?"

"If you want to see an amazing car collection, you need to visit my cousin Zach in San Francisco. I don't have many, but this one is my favorite. I rarely get a chance to drive it, but it seemed perfect for our trip today."

"Perfect because we're headed to…?"

"You'll know in a couple of hours." She tried to think of every possible destination within a two-hour radius of Westchester County. "I can feel your brain hurting from here," he teased.

She tried to relax into her seat. "I'm such a planner. I don't do spontaneous things like this very often. You're the only one who ever succeeds at convincing me to blow things off and be a little crazy."

"Is that good or bad?"

She was surprised that he looked nervous about her answer. "It's great." She reached over, put her hand on his for a brief moment. "Really great."

★ ★ ★

"Tanglewood?" Cordelia saw the sign at the side of the road and turned to Alec in surprise. "I've always wanted to come here and see a show. And I always meant to visit Fire Island too. It's like you're reading my bucket list."

Her enthusiasm made him grin. "If you've actually got a bucket list, I want to see it."

"No way," she said with a shake of her head. "Some of the things on it are really embarrassing."

"Like what?"

"I started making the list when I was pretty young—it was my parents' idea, so we all did it together. Needless to say, some of the things I dreamed of doing when I was ten don't hold up all that well over time."

"Like…"

"I *really* wanted to go to a candy store and buy one of everything."

"So the fruit and veg girl has a sweet tooth, huh?" She flushed and he thought, for the millionth time, how beautiful she was. "What else did ten-year-old Cordelia Langley want to do?"

"Have you heard of American Girl dolls? From what I know of Suzanne, I'm guessing your sister might not have been much of a doll person."

"She wasn't, but plenty of our customers have daughters. S&W Aviation spends a great deal of money in the American Girl doll store every Christmas."

"I always dreamed of getting to spend the afternoon in the flagship New York City store picking out the full set—the doll, her home, her clothes, all that." Even now, she looked pretty dreamy about it. "But the dolls are so expensive that I would never have actually asked my parents to take me there. They would have felt compelled to buy me one, and I would have felt guilty about them spending so much money."

While Alec wished Cordelia could have had the

dolls she'd longed for, he was glad that candy and dolls were the things she'd wanted most. It was further proof that she'd had a good childhood. Gordon would have been very happy to know it.

"How come I can pester you for two hours about where we're going and you stay locked up like a vault?" she asked as they were directed into the parking lot. "Whereas you work on me for thirty seconds and I'm spilling all my secrets?"

"Because of my Sullivan charm?"

"No kidding. And now I know exactly where you got it."

He parked and turned off the ignition. "What do you mean, you know where I got it?"

Her eyes grew big. And, if he wasn't mistaken, guilty. "I was going to tell you soon. I meant to tell you before now, but it never felt right over the phone this week."

His gut tightened. She never usually looked nervous. And she'd never kept anything from him either, partly because she was honest to the core, but also because she wasn't afraid of him. Which meant that whatever she'd kept from him this week, he wasn't going to like it.

"I spoke to your father." Her words came out barely above a whisper. "Actually, I went to see him. At Summer Lake."

"When?" Alec's voice boomed out so loudly that several people walking past his convertible in the parking lot turned to see what the problem was.

"The day after we talked in your kitchen."

"We did a hell of a lot more than talk."

Her skin flushed again. "I know. But then that morning when you told me more about your mother and father—"

"That was a mistake. I shouldn't have laid any of that on you."

"I'm your friend," she said passionately. "You can lay *anything* on me."

"Is that what you've been telling yourself? That it's okay to butt into my life, into my father's life, because you and I are *friends?*"

Her eyes were glassy with tears about to fall at any second. And then one did, sliding down her cheek. Proving that he was a Grade-A jerk.

"Damn it." He reached out and wiped it away. "I didn't bring you here to make you cry."

"I know." But another tear fell. "And I didn't want to make you angry by butting into your personal life, but I needed to meet him, Alec. After everything you've told me, I couldn't just let him be this shadowy figure inside my head."

"And now that you have?"

"Promise you won't get upset?"

He gritted his teeth. "I won't get upset."

"You will." She paused, then hit him with, "I think you and your father share a lot of similarities."

"I'm nothing like him!" Passersby turned to look at them again to see why he was yelling. Alec worked to modulate his tone as he added, "I'm not angry, I just don't agree with you." He ran a hand through his hair. "Look, can we not talk about my father and just head in and enjoy the show?"

She looked torn, and he knew there was more she wanted to say. Probably a list of all the ways she believed that he and his father were similar. Which was the last thing he wanted to hear.

Fortunately, she simply nodded. "Of course we can."

They got out of the car and were walking toward the venue when she noted, "I can't believe so many people have on James Taylor concert shirts. I heard he lives in the Berkshires, so he must be really popular around here."

"That's who we're seeing."

She stopped dead. "Wait...you've brought me here to see *James Taylor* play?"

"And you're going to love every second of it!" a stranger who had overheard the last part of their conversation called out.

"You told me he's one of your favorite musicians.

So I'm assuming you must want to see him play live."

"Of course I do. It's right at the top of my bucket list. But...how are you going to sit there and listen to his songs?"

"I'll be fine." He had to give her this, had to give her something in return for all the unexpected joy she'd brought into his life—and also to make up for being such a grouch a minute ago. He refused to let a few old folk songs scare him.

"That's why you didn't tell me where we were going," she said softly. "Because I wouldn't have let us come if I knew what you were going to put yourself through."

"Cordelia." He made her stop walking and turn to look at him. "All I care about tonight is that one of your wishes is coming true. And it's all I want you to care about too."

"But—"

"Promise me." She'd asked him for a promise earlier. Now it was his turn. "Promise me you'll relax and enjoy the show."

She didn't answer for several moments as she tried to read his expression, which he kept carefully neutral. Finally, she said, "Okay, I promise."

He reached for her hand and held it as they walked into the venue. The lawns all around the covered concert building they called the Shed were packed with couples and families having picnics on blankets.

"I can't believe I'm here," she exclaimed with excitement. "Did you know Tanglewood concerts began in 1937 and that the Shed was once a horse arena? I read a really fascinating article about it recently."

He'd taken other women to concerts, but no one that he enjoyed being with the way he enjoyed Cordelia's company. She was happy to share a beer and a hot dog in the onsite beer garden, was fascinated by the old concert programs and historic documents in the museum, and wanted to explore every inch of the gardens and vistas on the vast Berkshire property. A couple of hours later, the sun sank and the lights flashed, letting everyone know it was time to find their seats.

Alec showed their tickets to the usher. "Wow, these are great seats! Do you need help finding them?"

"Thanks, we've got it covered." Alec put his hand on the small of Cordelia's back and guided her toward the stage.

"We're going to be really close to him, aren't we?" she said when they were still about twenty rows back.

"We are." Way closer than he'd ever thought he'd come to James Taylor, that was for sure. "That's us." He pointed to the two open seats in the middle of the front row.

"No way."

Cordelia wasn't into clothes. She didn't care about jewelry. And though she'd enjoyed being in a top-of-the-line private jet, it hadn't rocked her world. At last, he'd found something to make her truly happy.

And it was worth any price he had to pay for her to have it.

CHAPTER TWENTY-THREE

Cordelia felt as though she'd walked into a dream. Not only had she gotten to spend an entire afternoon and evening with Alec, but any second now James Taylor was going to walk out on stage and start singing her favorite songs. From only five feet away!

She was bouncing with excitement in her seat as the lights inside the Shed went down and the stage lights came up. Everyone jumped to their feet, and then there he was. Her favorite musician, playing the first chords to "Carolina in My Mind."

Tears sprang to her eyes, she was so overwhelmed, so grateful that Alec had done this for her. She threw her arms around him, laughing as she hugged him. "It's like he's sitting in my living room playing just for me." She was so relieved to see him smile back. Maybe he really would be okay with this. "Thank you."

"You're welcome." He nodded up toward the stage. "Now enjoy the show, just like you promised."

And, oh, did she ever enjoy it. She'd seen JT's PBS special, of course, and watched snippets of his other shows online. But actually getting to listen to him live as he sang "Sweet Baby James" and "Country Road" and "Shower the People"...

It was the most wonderful gift anyone had ever given her.

She felt full to the brim, as happy as she could ever remember being. And then, the lights dimmed even further and the band left the stage, leaving James alone to sing one of his biggest hits of all. "Fire and Rain." The song William Sullivan had played on repeat when his wife died.

Cordelia turned away from the stage, needing to make sure Alec was okay.

But he was gone.

Jumping out of her seat, she headed toward the exit, berating herself with every step for allowing herself to get lost in the music. She shouldn't even have let them come inside, should have insisted that they leave as soon as she realized what Alec had planned.

He was tall and broad, so she could make out his shape as he strode past the crowds of people on the lawns. But it was dark enough that she was afraid she'd lose him. She picked up the pace, running now, not caring that people probably thought she was nuts.

Out on the lawn there were speakers so that people picnicking could hear the music. Which meant that even after leaving their seats, there was no way to escape the lyrics as James Taylor sang about how he couldn't believe the woman he loved was gone and that he wouldn't get to see her again.

Alec finally stopped at the far edge of the grass, and she sprinted over to him. He was facing away from her, and when she gently put a hand on his back, she could feel his heart beating wildly through her palm.

He didn't turn around right away, and when he did, the bleak expression in his eyes nearly dropped her to her knees. *"Alec."* She felt tears well up again, but it wasn't her turn to cry right now, damn it. "I'm so sorry. I shouldn't have let us stay for this show. Shouldn't have made you listen to these songs."

He didn't speak for several long moments. Finally, he said, "I had to bring you here." He reached for her, brushing a lock of hair back behind her ear, his touch sending sensation zinging through her. "I knew you'd love it."

"I do, of course I do. But nothing that hurts you this much is worth it, Alec. Can't you see—all I want is for you to be happy?"

The way he looked at her then...she'd never seen that look in his eyes. Never seen that look in *any* man's eyes. Not for her. "I didn't just bring you here because I knew you'd love the show," he said in a rough voice. "I brought you here because—"

He paused then, and in that brief silent space, she

couldn't help but hope desperately for the four-letter word he'd told her, more than once, would never come out of his mouth.

"Because?" she prompted in a breathless voice.

"You make me happy." He put his arm around her waist, drawing her close. "Happier than anyone or anything ever has."

Disappointment she had no right to feel choked her. Of course he wasn't going to say he loved her. He'd made it clear from the start that he wasn't looking for love. Until now, she'd pretended to heed his warning, had felt so tough sleeping with him and then going on with her day unaffected—when the truth was that no one, and nothing, had ever affected her the way Alec Sullivan did.

"You make me happy too." She forced herself to smile for him, even if the barest upturn of her lips was all she could manage. "No matter what happens, Alec, I'm going to be your friend. Through thick and thin. Good times and bad. Rain, sleet, or snow." Her vows of friendship to him were as important to her as any marriage vows would one day be to someone else. The thought of anyone else being this important to her, though, made her stomach churn.

He lowered his forehead to hers. "Through thick and thin, Cordelia. Good times and bad. Rain, sleet, or snow. I'll always take care of you." A rogue tear fell down her cheek as he gave her vows of his own. "Always."

She shouldn't want to seal their promises of friendship with a kiss. Especially when she knew sleeping together was a really bad idea. They'd thought they could blur the lines without paying a price for it, but they couldn't. *She* couldn't. Her heart ached to think they'd had their last time together and hadn't even known it.

"We should go," she said, forcing herself to move out of his arms.

"The show's not over yet."

"I loved it, Alec. Absolutely every second of it." She took his hand and headed for the exit. "But I'm ready to go now. Especially since it's late and we've got a long drive back."

"Actually, we've got reservations at a local B&B. But it's up to you whether or not you'd like to use them."

"For one last night together?" She didn't want there to be any gray areas. Couldn't let there be, for both their sakes.

"For one last night together," he agreed in a low tone that reverberated with desire *and* emotion. "I want to memorize every one of your curves, Cordelia. I want to capture the sweet little sounds you make when I touch, kiss, just the right patch of skin, so that I can hold on to them forever. If you'll let me, I'll make sure tonight is one neither of us will ever forget."

He hadn't even touched her yet beyond holding her hand, had simply told her what he wanted, but it was more than enough to make her insides spark, sizzle, melt for him. "I don't need tonight to keep from forgetting you," she said, "but I want it anyway."

And then their mouths crashed together in the kiss she'd been longing for all week.

* * *

Alec couldn't believe it. Couldn't believe the word that had nearly fallen from his lips.

Love.

He'd almost told Cordelia he *loved* her.

It had to have been his rioting emotions from hearing "Fire and Rain." From the crazy two weeks they'd had. From the mind-blowing sex.

Whatever the reason for the insanity that had gripped him out on the lawn at Tanglewood, he'd stopped before he could blurt it out. Cordelia deserved so much more than a man who had no idea what love meant for him. Especially when he knew *exactly* what love meant for her—and he was positive he could never live up to what she wanted, what she needed.

Suggesting the B&B was his last-ditch effort to hold on to her, just a little while longer. He'd assumed she'd say no, but just as she'd surprised him so many times before, she surprised him yet again with a *yes*.

Together, they walked up the curving stairwell of the century-old home that had been converted into a B&B. The furniture was antique, the wood floor gleamed beneath their feet, and Alec's heart had never pounded so fast. Cordelia had done this to him from the first moment he'd met her—she'd thrown him off his game by making him want to protect her, laugh with her, adore her.

She had the key and when she put it in the lock, he exhaled the breath he'd been holding. She could still change her mind—and of course he'd respect her wishes if she did—but he prayed she wouldn't. There were only eight hours until the sun rose again. Eight hours he wished he could spin into eight million.

But there was more waiting out there for Cordelia than a cynical businessman who felt like he'd only just learned what it felt like to be happy. After tonight, he'd force himself to turn her loose to find true happiness with someone else.

These next eight hours, however, were all theirs. Together, for one final night of bliss.

CHAPTER TWENTY-FOUR

"You're trembling," Alec said after they'd closed the door behind them and were standing together in the middle of the bedroom.

How, she wondered, could someone become as necessary as breathing? As precious as the sun rising? As magical as the first bloom in spring? Her knees already felt weak just from being this close to him. "It's because I want you so badly."

"I want you more." He teased her first with his sexy words, and then by brushing her hair back over her shoulder and lowering his mouth to the curve of her neck. One feather-light kiss that made her knees even weaker.

She had to brace herself with her hands on his broad shoulders as he slowly ran his lips along her neck until he found her earlobe. He bit down gently and her entire body melted into his arms. "Alec..."

"I love the way you say my name," he murmured into her hair. "Say it again."

The way he was pressing kisses all across her collarbone had her purring it instead. *"Alec."*

"That's how I'll remember it." He lifted his head so that they were face to face again. "Sweet." A dark heat lit his gaze. "And desperate."

Oh God, was she ever desperate for him as she put her hands on either side of his jaw and dragged his mouth down to hers. He'd promised her a night of unforgettable lovemaking, but she couldn't wait another second to be his. And to know that he was hers, one last time.

"Please," she said as she yanked at his shirt, his jeans, trying to get them off. "I need you."

Thankfully, her words seemed to flip a switch inside of him, from slow to fast. He was pulling her dress off and down her body as he said, "I need you too." Her bra came off next and then her panties, until she was completely bared to him. "You take my breath away, Cordelia." And then he was taking hers away too as he cupped her breasts so that he could lave both at once.

It would have been so easy to get lost in blissful sensation. But even this wasn't enough to sate her hunger for him. Tearing at his clothes the same way he'd torn at hers, she stripped away his shirt and jeans until he stood gloriously naked, his barely leashed power evident in every rippling muscle and sinew.

He lifted her so that her legs came around his

waist. "Hold on to me. And don't let go."

Before she could tell him that she never, ever wanted to let him go, he was filling her, one broad stroke of his body into hers that had her crying out in pleasure. He tightened his hold on her hips, the muscles in his arms bulging as he lowered, then raised her, in a breathtakingly sensual rhythm of unbridled passion. And then they were falling onto the bed, rolling in a tangle of limbs and heat, until she was straddling him.

"Let go for me, Cordelia. Don't hold back."

She couldn't have held back, even if she'd wanted to. Because nothing had ever felt so good. Or so bittersweet as he crushed his mouth to hers at the exact moment that release shot through her. Every part of her lit with fire as she shook from the explosions that Alec was setting off with his hands, his mouth, his strong body all around hers.

And then he was calling out her name, sounding awed. And, for a moment, at peace.

★ ★ ★

Alec lay in the oversized clawfoot tub in the corner by the window with Cordelia against his chest. He was greatly enjoying running his hands over the bubbles on her soft skin.

"This is so nice," she murmured. "Just to be lazy

for a little while."

"The birthday party must be taking up all of your free time."

"That's been really fun to work on," she told him. "It's figuring out what to do with all of Gordon's money that has my brain spinning."

"Were the advisors I recommended not helpful?"

"They were. But there's actually something else that I've been chewing on for a while, but since I didn't think I'd have the capital anytime soon, I just let the idea go."

"Gordon didn't leave his money to you so that you could give it all away." Alec threaded his fingers through hers and watched them float together on the water. "I guarantee he'd be pleased to know he was able to help you make a great new business move." He nudged the side of her neck with his nose. "So what's the idea?"

"You know how I've been thinking about expanding the garden center with more parties and events in the barn? Well, in England, garden centers often have restaurants on site." He could hear the excitement in her voice. "I've read a lot about them, especially one just outside of London called Petersham Nursery that sounds amazing."

"I've been there for lunch a couple of times." At her incredulous look, he explained, "I have a cousin who lives near the nursery, in Richmond."

"There really are Sullivans everywhere, aren't there?" she said with a laugh.

"You can't throw a rock without hitting one of us," he joked. "Petersham is a great place. Your customers would love something like that at your garden center. I'll bet people would even make the trek out from the city for it." For the first time in a long time, he had that excited feeling in his gut. The one he used to have when he and Gordon were building S&W Aviation from nothing. "You could easily put up a greenhouse-type space for the seating area, one with a retractable glass roof so that you could open it up on warm sunny days, then build on a kitchen in the back. And menus based on your produce would not only wow people's taste buds, they'd also all be running to your cash registers after lunch to buy up seeds and starts. You've got to do it, Cordelia."

"That's what I keep thinking," she agreed. "Only, I've got one big problem."

"I'm sure it's nothing we can't figure out together. What's the problem?"

"I only know one chef I want to hire. But I'm not sure he'll be interested in my small garden center."

"If he isn't, he's an idiot. Tell me his name and I'll convince him to do it."

She shifted slightly in the tub so that she could look

directly at him. "His name is Alec Sullivan."

For a long moment, his brain couldn't process the words. "I'm not a chef."

"We both know you are." She let the water float her back against him. Taking his hands in hers, she wrapped his arms over her chest and yawned. "You're a lovely bath pillow too."

Other people who wanted something from him would have kept pressing their case. But Cordelia knew that planting the seed was enough to start him thinking, planning, dreaming about having a restaurant in the middle of her garden.

She pressed her cheek to his shoulder and closed her eyes. The moonlight streamed in, lighting up her beautiful face. He wanted to memorize every feature—the thick sweep of her eyelashes over her cheekbones, her full rose-colored lips, the curve of her ear.

She yawned again, her eyes still closed as she said, "I haven't slept well this week."

"Neither have I." Because his bed had felt too big. Too lonely. And every time he got into it and closed his eyes, thoughts and visions of Cordelia crept in before he could stop them.

He'd planned to make love to her all night long, not wanting to waste so much as a minute of their remaining time together on sleep. But the dark smudges under her eyes, and the fact that she clearly couldn't keep them open, made Alec change his mind. When the water began to cool, he lifted her out of the bathtub, wrapped her in a thick white towel, and carried her the short distance to the bed.

Making love with Cordelia was mind-blowing, but amazingly, getting to hold her all night while she slept in his arms was even better.

He laid her down on the crisp, lavender-scented sheets, and though her eyes were still closed, she reached for him, saying his name in a sleepy tone. He quickly dried himself off, then climbed in, pulling her close, relishing the feel of her strong yet curvaceous body against his.

Words he wished he could say, promises he'd give anything to offer her, crowded the tip of his tongue.

But love and marriage had only ever meant one thing to Alec—pain. And he couldn't stand the thought of causing Cordelia the kind of pain his parents had given each other. She stirred in his arms as though she couldn't get close enough. When he drew her more tightly to him, she made a happy sound in her sleep. One that made his chest ache with emotion.

Thankfully, tomorrow morning wasn't good-bye. They might end up working together in the future after all, in her garden center rather than his aviation company. And he planned on being her friend forever.

It would have to be enough.

CHAPTER TWENTY-FIVE

If someone had told Cordelia that she'd be walking on clouds *and* racked with heartache simultaneously, she never would have believed it possible. But even a full week after her afternoon and evening with Alec at Tanglewood and then in the B&B, the sweet bliss, the pure joy, the breathtaking pleasure still lingered. She would find herself in the midst of her flowers day-dreaming about his kisses, his hands roaming over her skin. Standing in full sun, thrill bumps would break out across her skin at the sensual memories.

Their final night in each other's arms had been about so much more than sex, however. For a handful of precious hours in the dark, she'd felt as though Alec had dropped his walls and let her inside his heart.

Yes, she missed his touch, missed his kisses. But most of all, she missed being close to him.

Thus, the heartache.

She knew she'd gotten closer to him than anyone else ever had. And she felt lucky to have vaulted so many of his walls. If only that felt like enough…

Catching herself daydreaming again, she silently told herself to snap out of it. William Sullivan's birthday party was tonight, and she needed every ounce of focus. Mooning over Alec Sullivan was definitely not in her job description.

Suzanne had invited William to stay with her and Roman for the weekend, the ruse being that they wanted a small family dinner in his honor. Cordelia was certain William was happy that his kids wanted to celebrate his birthday with him. She couldn't wait to see how thrilled he'd be about the big surprise party.

Cordelia had thought she understood what Suzanne meant when she'd said the Sullivans were a huge family. But she honestly couldn't have conceptualized anything like this—of the one hundred and fifty guests, more than half were Sullivans who had come from all over the world to celebrate with William and his children.

Beautiful. Accomplished. *Nice.* Those were the top three words that came to mind when she thought about the family members she'd met so far today. Cordelia's head was spinning as she worked to keep straight the Sullivans who fought fires and took photographs and raced cars and built sailboats and restored historic homes.

She already knew about Smith Sullivan, the movie star, and Ryan Sullivan, the pro baseball player. Another movie star, Tatiana Landon, was engaged to billionaire Ian Sullivan. Marcus Sullivan owned the Sullivan Winery in Napa and was married to Nicola, a pop star whose songs Cordelia had been listening to for years. Ford Vincent was yet another rock star at the party, married to a pretty and very fun cousin of Alec's named Mia. They lived in Seattle. And then there were Alec's cousins Sophie and Lori Sullivan, twins from San Francisco, each of whom had bagged seriously gorgeous husbands. Lori looked about to pop any day now with her first child, while Sophie had twins of her own.

But she was getting the biggest kick of all from the Sullivan kids, who ranged in age from nearly one to ten. They'd been running through her gardens for hours, and every time one of their parents started to apologize or tried to rein them in, she made sure they knew that not only did she love kids, but also that she definitely didn't mind things getting a little messy.

Most of the little Sullivans were currently focused on a new garden bed she'd suggested they put together—shoveling soil, planting seeds, watering the dirt until it turned to thick mud, and then playing gleefully it. She was glad that she wasn't the only one covered in dirt stains. All of them would have to be hosed off before the party, she thought with a laugh.

"Chips off the old block, each and every one of them."

Alec's sudden appearance at her side sent an instant shot of joy coursing through her veins. "Oh, hi!" Her voice sounded a little too chirpy, but she was doing the best she could. Hopefully in a few months—or years—she'd be able to act normal around him. As though she wasn't head over heels in unrequited love. "I was just about to check with you in the kitchen to see if you needed any help."

"Aunt Mary has taken over for a few minutes," he told her. "She sent me out here to see if *you* needed any help."

"Mary is just wonderful," Cordelia said. "Although I can't imagine what it must have been like to raise eight kids. Not to mention giving birth to them."

A surprised laugh shot from his throat. "People are rarely brave enough to mention *that* part."

"I think *crude enough* is a better way of putting it."

She loved it when they teased each other like this, with easy, friendly banter. They hadn't avoided each other this week, thankfully, but that didn't mean Cordelia wasn't having a hard time getting used to their new dynamic.

Friends meant she could touch him with her hand on his arm, or even over his. It meant she could hug him. But anything beyond that was out of bounds. Especially sizzling-hot, naked kisses. Feeling her cheeks flame, she hoped he'd think it was the sun she was reacting to, rather than him.

"What can I help with?"

"Everything's under control, although I probably should stop the mud-slinging before it gets even more out of hand." One of the kids was currently holding down a smaller one and spreading mud on the top of his head, while a toddler was spinning in a circle, hurling hunks of mud at anyone who wasn't fast enough to get out of the way.

"Are you kidding me?" Alec looked like he thought her suggestion was nuts. "Sullivan kids are raised on this. You can't hold your own in a field of mud, you deserve to go down."

While he was enjoying watching the kids play, she let herself look at him. Really look, the way she'd only gotten to look at the B&B when she'd woken up a few minutes before he did. He truly was a shockingly handsome man. But it was more than his perfect features that had stolen her heart—it was how sweet, how kind, how giving he was on the inside.

"Your family is great," she said, her heart feeling even softer and mushier than it usually did.

"I know." He looked over to where her mother and father were pitching in by arranging vases of flowers for each of the dining tables. "I'm glad your parents could be here today. I like knowing they're always there for you. Although I thought I made it clear that we'd like them to be guests, not unpaid staff."

"Trust me, they're happier helping than standing around with a drink."

"Just like you." His eyes were warm as he turned to her, reaching out to brush some hair back from her face and making her knees go weak the way he always had before—and surely always would. "Suz texted. They're heading out and should be here soon."

"I can't wait for your father to see everything you've done for his birthday, all the people you've brought here to celebrate, and then to top it all off, the amazing dinner you're putting together. He's going to be so touched."

Unfortunately, talking about his father's feelings was all it took for Alec's face to shutter. "If you're sure everything's good on your end, I'd better get back to the kitchen."

"I'll do one final check of the grounds, send the kids off to their parents to get cleaned up, and then go clean up myself." She looked down at her clothes. "I swear I wasn't rolling around in the mud with the kids, it just looks that way."

"You wanted to play with them, didn't you?"

"Who wouldn't?"

He didn't disagree, and she suddenly had a picture of what Alec had been like when he was three or four years old. Before the weight of the world had landed on his shoulders. Before he'd lost the two people who meant everything to him—one from suicide, one from grief. He'd probably been just as goofy, just as silly, just as happy as Smith Jr., who was currently smearing mud all over his twin sister's cheeks. Jackie, to her credit, was beaming as though she were getting a top-flight spa treatment.

Alec and Cordelia both had places they needed to be, but neither of them moved away for several long moments. Finally, Cordelia forced herself to pick up her feet and say, "See you in the barn in a little bit."

★ ★ ★

Cordelia had no idea how close Alec had been to grabbing her hand and skidding into the mud with the kids. Three weeks ago, he would never even have considered it. Then again, until Cordelia showed up in his life, it was unlikely he would have spent this much time working out and perfecting the menu for his father's birthday party either.

Or even attending it.

Now that he'd given his executive staff more responsibility, he'd been able to cut way back on his hours this week at S&W Aviation so that he could spend the bulk of his time in the kitchen. The employees at the local farmer's co-op in the city not only knew him by name now, they also understood precisely how high his standards were for the produce he was buying to test his recipes.

Still, the ingredients that he could get near his city apartment were nowhere near the quality of what Cordelia grew. Her fruit and vegetables were extraordinary. No wonder her garden center was always busy. She sold only the best. Just like her birth father—even if he was selling rides on planes instead of greens.

Yet again, Alec found himself wishing Gordon could be here to see Cordelia glowing in her element. His friend would have been so proud.

Pride. It was a word Alec had been chewing on all week. Especially after Cordelia's visit to his father in Summer Lake, when she'd come back saying she thought the two of them were similar.

He hadn't wanted to hear it, even though the truth was that it was part of the reason he'd never allowed himself to fall in love. Because he couldn't fail a woman the way his father had failed his mother.

Fortunately, just because a romantic relationship couldn't work, that didn't mean a business relationship was out of the question. He'd been giving her onsite restaurant suggestion a ton of thought this week. Any way he turned it over in his head, it looked good. Especially the part where it meant he'd get to see and work with Cordelia every day.

"William's driving into the parking lot!" Alec's

Aunt Mary untied the apron she'd put on to protect her dress. "The appetizers are ready to go out with the waitstaff, Alec, so we should be fine for the next half hour at least." She reached out a hand. "Come, let's say hello to your father together."

Mary Sullivan was one of the wisest, nicest people Alec had ever known. Once a world-famous model, she'd married her true love, Jack Sullivan, then ended up raising their eight kids alone after he'd died of an aneurysm at only forty-two. Alec had never heard her complain, but he sometimes saw flashes of sadness in her eyes when it seemed clear she was wishing she could share something with Jack.

Alec guessed she'd seen the same in him more than once over the years, when he was wishing his mom was still around to be a part of his life, his achievements, even his struggles. Perhaps that was why he felt closer to Mary than to his uncles Max and Ethan—Alec and Mary were kindred spirits in loss. And he was glad for the steady warmth of her hand in his as they headed out of the kitchen and into the main seating area of the barn.

His brothers, Suzanne, and Cordelia had done a great job with the decorations. The barn looked both festive and masculine, with plenty of the blues and deep greens his father preferred mixed in with the floral arrangements and colorful electronic paper lanterns hung from the ceiling. Marcus Sullivan had donated several cases of wine and bubbly, and Jake McCann had done the same with his popular artisan beers. Alec's cousin Cassie had carefully transported the birthday cake from her bakery in Maine. Her cake-making talent was such that Alec had been working on her for years to let him invest in a chain of Cassie Sullivan-branded products. Hopefully after everyone tasted her cake tonight, they'd join him in pestering her to expand her business.

On each plate lay a handwritten menu. Cordelia had insisted on writing each one personally, and though he'd tried to talk her out of the gargantuan job, she'd been right. It was the extra touches like the handwritten menu, and the large baby-gated play area in the back corner of the barn, that made all the difference.

Mary walked with Alec until they were standing with Harry, Drake, and Rosa. "Thirty seconds, every-one," Drake said when Suzanne texted him to say they were walking up the gravel path.

Alec's heart was pounding faster than it should. After all, he was simply standing there waiting for his dad to show up to his party. Taking a covert deep breath, he worked to unclench his teeth. Especially since, as the eldest, he knew everyone would be expecting him to take the lead in the celebrations.

The door opened and William walked into the barn. "Surprise!" A hundred and fifty voices rang out, reverberating against the wooden rafters.

William was clearly stunned as he looked around the large space. "You've thrown me a surprise party?" The way he said it, it sounded as though he didn't think he deserved such a big celebration in his honor.

Alec knew it was time to step up to the plate. "Happy birthday, Dad," he said as he moved toward his father. "We figured eighty-five was a pretty big deal, so—"

"Eighty-five!" his father sputtered as everyone laughed.

"Seventy-five is a pretty big deal too," Alec said with a grin. "And the perfect excuse for another family reunion." With that, he handed his father the ice-cold Adirondack Brewery beer he preferred and let well-wishers surround him.

As he headed back toward the kitchen, Harry waylaid him. "Well done."

Alec shrugged off the compliment, knowing how low his brother's expectations were. "Dad looked happy to see everyone, so it's already a win." Alec grabbed a beer from a passing waiter, then pushed through the swinging door to the kitchen.

Cordelia had insisted on setting a place for Alec at his father's table, along with his brothers, sister, and their significant others. But he wasn't planning on using it. He needed to be here in the kitchen all night.

Currently, the waiters were circulating with trays of roasted sunchokes with smoked paprika aioli, daikon summer rolls, and pickled French breakfast radishes. Alec's cousin Mia had already come in to exclaim in raptures over the appetizers, which he appreciated, even knowing she tended to have that over-the-top reaction about things. He'd long wondered if there was any man who could keep up with her—but as soon as he met her husband, Ford Vincent, he'd known they were the perfect fit. The rock star had happily given up touring to settle down in Seattle, and Mia had never looked happier.

Alec plated the roasted rutabaga salad with pistachios and charred onion, thinking back to the many family weddings and birthdays he'd been to during the past several years. One by one, his cousins and siblings were finding true happiness. Even Lori, his San Francisco cousin, whom everyone had been sure would remain footloose and free forever, was about to have a baby. Alec still couldn't quite get over the fact that she lived on a farm with her husband, Grayson—not to mention the chickens and pigs and goats. When Alec had visited them earlier that year at the tail end of a business trip, he'd been surprised by how much he liked their place out in the wilds of Pescadero. Alec had always assumed city penthouses were more his style.

Then again, no place had ever felt quite so much like home as Cordelia's cottage and garden.

As if he'd conjured her up, she came through the door, all smiles...with his father in tow. "I told the birthday boy you would be back here."

"Son, you've gone above and beyond tonight." His father sounded a little choked up, which put Alec on instant alert. "I had no idea you were throwing me this party. None at all. And Cordelia said you're single-handedly cooking a farm-to-table dinner from her garden."

Just then, Cordelia was grabbed by one of the servers who needed help in the seating area, which left the two men alone. "It's no big deal," Alec said.

"Putting on dinner for a dozen people is hard enough," his father countered as he walked up to the large stainless-steel worktop. "Feeding more than a hundred of us is a marvel."

"Cordelia has great produce. And plenty of people have helped." Even to his own ears, Alec could hear how terse, and grudging, his responses were. "But yeah, I came up with the menu."

"Even as a tiny kid, you were a hell of a cook." His father picked up one of the edible nasturtium flowers and twirled it around in his fingers as he spoke, as though he had nervous energy to expend. "I remember the first time your mom and I found you standing at the stove, cooking scrambled eggs. You couldn't have been more than four. I ran over to yank you back from the stove, but she told me you knew what you were doing. She made me see that you were perfectly capable, even though you looked so small. It wasn't long before you were moving beyond scrambled eggs—my amazing kid who already knew his way backward and forward around a kitchen. And later..."

As the flower dropped from William's hand, it suddenly struck Alec that his father's skin looked a little strange. Gray and sort of shiny. "Later, all I could think was thank God you knew how to cook, so your brothers and Suzanne wouldn't go hungry."

"Not tonight, Dad." Alec's voice was borderline curt. "Everyone's here to have a good time, get a little drunk, eat some birthday cake. Not to hash out old family dramas."

"When?" His father's voice was so quiet that Alec barely heard the word. "If not tonight, then when are you going to be willing to sit down with me and work things out?"

"There's nothing to work out." Alec's words sounded as hollow as they felt.

William's color looked even more off as he said, "You can't really believe that."

"How the hell do you know what I believe?" Alec's

CHAPTER TWENTY-SIX

Alec cooked and plated the main course with total focus. Plenty of relatives popped their heads into the kitchen at one point or another during dinner, but he didn't encourage anyone's help, not even Cordelia's. Five minutes with her and she'd get out of him that his father had come begging for reconciliation—and that Alec had stomped those wishes into the ground.

For the past hour, the words she'd said to him at his apartment two weeks ago had been playing over and over inside his head: *I never even had a chance to know Gordon, but your dad is still right here. Don't you want to at least try to make things better while you still can?*

And the truth was, Alec wasn't exactly proud of himself as he whipped up another batch of the cashew-based bell pepper sauce. Once dinner was over, once they'd served the cake and the band started playing, maybe he should do something crazy like force himself to find his father and open the door. Not all the way, but wide enough that William would know he was finally prepared to give listening a shot.

Suddenly, a scream sounded from the dining room. One that had Alec dropping the spatula and running into the barn.

His father was no longer at his seat of honor. Instead, he was lying on the ground with Suzanne ripping open his shirt and tie. She had already started CPR by the time Alec dropped to his knees beside them.

"Dad." Alec grabbed his father's hand, hating himself. What the hell had he been thinking? How could he have ignored the signs in the kitchen, William's gray pallor, the sweaty sheen of his skin? "Can you hear me?"

"He's unconscious." Harry was on his knees on the other side of their father, along with Drake. "He had a heart attack. We've called 911."

Soon, sirens sounded outside the barn and the local paramedics were running in and strapping William onto the gurney and starting an IV. He came to just long enough to swallow some aspirin, and to see Alec standing beside him, and then the paramedics were hurrying him into the ambulance.

"I need to go with him to the hospital," Alec insisted. "He needs to know I'm with him at all times." No one argued as Alec got into the back of the emergency vehicle, while Harry, Suzanne, and Drake said they'd follow in their cars.

As he sat beside the gurney and took his father's hand, Alec noticed just how similar their hands were, with large palms and long fingers. But there were dark spots and wrinkles on his father's skin. In Alec's mind, his father was still the same man he'd been thirty years ago when tragedy struck their family. But somewhere along the way, William Sullivan had aged.

Alec hadn't been able to stop time, but he'd been hell-bent on keeping forgiveness and understanding at bay as if time actually had stopped. For three decades, he'd let anger and blame fester. Inside himself *and* between the two of them.

To what end? he suddenly had to ask himself. So that he could lose his father before they'd ever really had a chance to know each other?

No. His father couldn't die. Couldn't disappear on him like Gordon had. Like his mother had.

Not when there was so much unfinished business between them.

Not when Alec had been such an ass to him for so long.

Not when he'd never given his father another chance to be a father.

Not when he'd never given himself a chance to be a son.

Shock. Fear. Frustration. Myriad emotions swirled within Alec. But to his surprise, one emotion rose above all the rest.

Hope.

Alec had never hoped so hard for anything. Never wished, never prayed, never bargained so intently for an outcome before. For his father to make it through this and come out the other side. Better. Stronger.

Alec would trade anything, give up every penny, to get his father through this.

He thought he'd learned long ago that hoping, wishing, was pointless. But he couldn't believe that anymore. *Refused* to believe that. Hopes and prayers were all he had right now, and by God, he was going to give them everything he had.

"You're going to be okay." Alec's voice was rough, raw. "You have to be. I won't leave your side, Dad." His voice broke on *Dad.*

The ambulance stopped in front of the Emergency Room, and the doors were flung open by hospital personnel. One of his siblings had already called in William's information, and the doctor was planning to take him immediately into the cath lab for surgery to inflate a balloon that would clear the blockage in his heart.

They had to pry Alec's hand away from his father's. He didn't know how long he stood there after they'd gone, fear clamping down on his chest so hard he could barely breathe.

He felt a hand on his arm. "Alec." Cordelia's gentle voice was the only thing that could have soothed him even the slightest bit. "The paramedics got your father here in record time and he's in great hands. The surgeon worked on a colleague of my parents, who couldn't sing her praises enough."

"He tried to talk to me in the kitchen," Alec confessed, needing her to know everything, needing to admit what he'd done out loud. "But I wouldn't listen to him. Wouldn't even let him say thank you for tonight. I should have stopped plating the damned salads and let him talk. You were right, I should have given him a chance. But I never did." Alec had never felt so bleak, so lost in the dark. "If he dies, I'm to blame."

★ ★ ★

"Alec, no."

Cordelia took his hand and drew him into a small meditation garden to the side of the waiting room. There were big windows along the outer wall, so the doctors would be able to find Alec easily if they needed him. So would his siblings, who would be walking in any second. But before they arrived, they needed to speak privately.

"Your father is a very strong man," she said in a firm voice. "He'll pull through this. And when he does, the last thing he's going to want to hear is that you blame yourself for anything that just happened. I know you're stunned right now, and scared. But I won't let you take the blame for this. None of us will."

The steel in her words finally made him look at her. "He doesn't know, Cordelia." Her heart broke at the grief in his voice. "He doesn't know I love him."

"He does."

"How could he? When he told us Mom died, I yelled *I hate you* over and over at him. That's the last thing he knows. That I hated him. Because I haven't let anything change since I was five years old."

"I guarantee there's no possible way he believes you hate him. He would have understood why you said it, because you'd just lost your mother in the most horrific way possible. And he wouldn't have blamed you for it. No father would."

"I've spent the past thirty years making sure he couldn't forget."

"*No,*" she said again, even more forcefully this time. "You've spent the past thirty years doing the best you can, the same way he has. I may have only spent a couple of hours with your dad at Summer Lake, but it only took a matter of seconds for me to know how much he loves you. And that he's never given up hope that the two of you can find your way back to each other."

The tears that fell from Alec's eyes as she spoke told her how much he wanted that.

She put her arms around him and held on tight. Soon, she knew his family would need him with them in the waiting room, their big brother who always held them together. Through thick and thin. Good times and bad. Alec was the one they could count on to keep them whole.

"Stay," he said, and she was holding him so tightly that his request reverberated from his chest to hers. "Please."

"I'm not going anywhere," she promised him. "Whatever you need, I'll take care of. You can count on me, no matter what."

★ ★ ★

Alec and Cordelia sat with Harry, Suzanne, Roman, Drake, and Rosa in the waiting room. After discussing the details of the surgery, they'd all been sitting silently. Waiting for news. Waiting for the doctor to come out and tell them everything would be okay.

Aunt Mary was still back at the barn corralling and comforting one hundred-plus worried Sullivans and family friends. If anyone was up to the task, though, it was Mary.

Just as Cordelia was clearly up to the task of making sure he and his siblings had whatever they needed as they kept vigil in the waiting room, having gotten coffee and soda and water for everyone during the past few hours. But when she went to refill Harry's coffee cup, Alec grabbed her hand and pulled her down into her seat. He wanted her to stay right there beside him. Her hand in his. Her gentle voice soothing him. "We don't need anything."

Except her. He needed her. Because she was his lifeline, his rock, the one person who would get him through tonight.

She curled her fingers through his, then laid her head against his shoulder. And for the briefest moment, a tiny ray of light shone through the darkness. Just from knowing that he didn't have to do this alone.

His brothers, his sister, his cousins—all of them were there for him too. But Cordelia wasn't at his side because they shared the same bloodline, or family history. She'd *chosen* to be with him, to be his friend, to stand beside him even when the chips were down.

He'd almost blurted out that he loved her at Tanglewood, while James Taylor was still singing "Fire and Rain." But he'd been so stunned by what he felt that he'd forced himself to come up with a million rationalizations for why love couldn't ever make sense for him. That he was destined to hurt her the way his father had hurt his mother. That he couldn't stand to give her false hope for a forever after that might never come.

That since he was incapable of changing his bleak past, it meant a bleak future was also set in stone.

Now, suddenly, he realized that in the same way he'd screwed things up with his father, he was blowing it with Cordelia.

What would it take for him to accept the truth of what he felt for her? A horrible accident? Another hospital waiting room? Or would it be the day she finally gave up on him and found a man who wasn't afraid to love her the way she deserved to be loved?

Gordon had given Alec the ultimate gift in bringing Cordelia into his life. Finally, he could see that no matter how bad his past, only a total idiot wouldn't grab at a future with her with both hands. And not let go even when his dark memories, the nightmares from his childhood, tried to wrench her from him.

"Cordelia." He didn't care that they were sitting in the waiting room with his family all around them. In fact, he was glad Harry and Suz and Drake were there. Glad they would all hear what he had to say. "I need to tell you something. Here. Now."

She lifted her head from his shoulder and shifted to face him. "What is it?"

"I—"

"William Sullivan's family?" The doctor who had been operating on their father stepped into the waiting room, and all of them jumped out of their seats.

"Yes," Harry replied. "We're William Sullivan's family."

The doctor smiled at them. "I'm very happy to let all of you know that the procedure was a success. Your father is going to have to take it easy for a while, and lay off the hamburgers," she said with a grin, "but I know a fighter when I see one. And no wonder, with his kids all here waiting for him to be a hundred percent again. I'm sure you have questions and I'll be happy to answer them all. I'd like to get William settled into recovery first, and then I'll come back out to chat."

"When can we see him?" Alec asked.

"Let's give him a few hours to sleep off the anesthesia, and then we'll see if he's up to a short visit."

People liked to say money could buy happiness—but Alec would happily give every single penny he had just to be able to sit at his father's bedside and watch over him until he woke.

"I promised him that I'd be at his side when he woke up," Alec implored. The doctor had to understand how important this was. "I need to be there with him in recovery, not in a few hours, but now."

She looked like she was going to refuse his request, but then at the last second she nodded. "Just you. And only if you remain quiet and stay out of our way."

People very rarely gave Alec Sullivan orders, not when he was always the most powerful man in any room. But he was more than happy to obey the doctor.

The kiss he gave Cordelia before he left the waiting room was one of new hope. And, though he hadn't yet had a chance to say the word, *love*.

* * *

Cordelia lifted her fingertips to her lips, which were tingling from Alec's surprise kiss. Everyone was doing their best not to make her uncomfortable by staring at her, but she could tell they were all more than a little surprised by Alec's behavior.

"I'm so glad your father is going to be okay." Cordelia hugged Suzanne, and then Harry and Drake. When everyone sat down again, they were all much more relaxed now that the doctor had given them good news.

"Dad will be glad to see Alec in the room with him when he wakes up," Harry said. "He'll know what it means, that it's the olive branch he's been waiting for."

"Hopefully it's more than just that," Drake said. "Hopefully Alec will not only listen to him, finally, but also talk to him."

"For the first time, Alec seems to *want* to talk." Suzanne looked at Cordelia. "About more than just Dad."

Cordelia was still flushed from the kiss Alec had given her—and from the anticipation of whatever he had been about to say before the doctor walked in.

He'd looked so serious. So determined. And yet, at the same time he'd seemed totally vulnerable, as though he'd finally stripped away his armor.

Alec's siblings knew Cordelia and Alec were friends. But she was pretty sure none of them had guessed they had also been lovers. Not until he'd kissed her in front of them all.

"I care about Alec," she said softly. "Very much." Maybe it would have been easier to stay silent, but they'd welcomed her into their family circle, and she wanted to be as honest with them as she'd always been with their brother. "I know you won't be surprised to hear that he's become my best friend. He's always there for me and I always want to be there for him too." She made herself look Alec's siblings in the eye. "But if you're hoping that he's changed his mind about…" God, she was really wading into the deep end, wasn't she? "About relationships or falling in love, I don't think he has." Her stomach was clenched and her throat was tight. "I know other women have tried to change Alec, but I could never do that to him. He's never tried to change me—he's simply accepted me for who I am and what I believe. And I feel the same way about him. Whatever changes he wants to make, whether it's with his father or his job or even his haircut, I'll be right there supporting him in any way I can. But those changes will always be up to him, not me."

Suzanne took Cordelia's hand, one woman in love comforting another. "From the first moment we met, I knew you were special. And it's obvious my brother feels the same way, regardless of what he has or hasn't said to you about his feelings." She squeezed Cordelia's hand. "No matter what happens from here, if you and Alec stay just friends—or if he finally pulls his head out of his you-know-what and realizes how good the two of you are together—as far as I'm concerned, you're already one of us. You're part of our family, Cordelia."

"Just like Gordon." Cordelia's words were thick with the overwhelming joy of belonging to such a wonderful group of people who would always have her back, no matter what.

"No one understood Alec better than Gordon," Harry told her. "Not even the three of us." He smiled as he added, "But you, Cordelia, seem to understand Alec best of all."

That's because I love him, she thought. And though she didn't speak the words aloud, something told her she didn't need to.

Because Alec's family already knew.

CHAPTER TWENTY-SEVEN

"Son…you're here."

William Sullivan woke up two hours after Alec took his seat at his bedside. His father's voice was weaker than usual, but still stronger than most people's. William had always been larger than life, and it was beyond strange to see him lying in a hospital bed with tubes sticking out of him.

The nurses had made it clear that Alec shouldn't upset his father in any way once he woke up, and he'd promised to take the utmost care. But he couldn't let another second go without saying what he should have said a long time ago.

"I'm so glad you're okay, Dad. And I'm sorry. So damned sorry that I kept pushing you away, that I shut you out every time you tried to talk. When you were lying on the floor of the barn, all I could think was that I'd lost my chance to know my own father." He gripped William's hand, not shoving away his painful emotions for once. "I want that chance, Dad."

His father's eyes were damp as he said, "I do too."

"You don't need to try to talk," Alec said, even as relief flooded him that it wasn't too late for the two of them. "You need to save your strength to get well."

"I already feel a million times better. Just because you're here."

"I'm not going anywhere, Dad. Not without you."

William's eyes closed and he fell asleep again. Alec didn't let go of his hand, not even for a second. An hour later, when a nurse came in to check his blood pressure and IV, his father woke with a smile. And a request.

"Talk to me. Tell me about Cordelia."

"*Subtle* and *Sullivan* might start with the same letter," Alec said with a smile, "but that's as far as the connection goes."

"I really like her," William said, undaunted.

"Me too." The only reason Alec didn't use a stronger word for his feelings was because he wanted to say it to Cordelia first. Wanted her to know before anyone else that he loved her. "I know it might not seem like it from the outside, but Gordon loved her and wanted the best for her." Alec thought again about the note Gordon had left for Cordelia's adoptive parents—asking them to give her everything he couldn't, and trusting them with her life, her happiness. "He was wrong to think that meant staying out of her life, but he was right to bring us together. She makes me want to be a better man, makes me think it might even be possible."

"You don't need to be a better man, Alec."

"Yes, I do. And I will be. Starting here, now, by fixing things with you, no matter what it takes."

But his father simply shook his head on his pillow. "You've always carried so much weight on your shoulders, son. Carried the entire family since you were a child. It's time to stop taking care of everyone else, Alec, and start taking care of yourself. And this time, let all of us help *you*."

"Harry, Suz, and Drake—they've already been trying to help," Alec told his father. "Mostly by pointing out that I'm going to lose the best thing that has ever happened to me if I don't wake up and get my act together."

"They're right."

Alec hated being wrong about anything. But the thing he hated most was screwing up something with someone he loved. That was why it had always been easier to keep his distance. But he couldn't do that anymore, couldn't make sure a wide gulf always lay between him and everyone else.

"The past few weeks," he said, "you kept asking me if you could help."

"Anything," William said. "Anything you need, I'll make it happen for you."

Even lying in a hospital bed, his father still radiated power, and Alec believed he truly would move heaven and earth for him. If only he'd understood this sooner.

"Help me convince Cordelia to marry me." Maybe he should ask her to consider dating him first, but Alec had never been a patient man. Once he knew what he wanted, he moved heaven and earth to have it. Three weeks of knowing Cordelia was more than enough for him to know that he wanted her by his side forever. Not just as his friend, not just as his co-worker, but as his *everything*.

"You're not going to need my help with that, Alec. I may not know Cordelia well, but I'm damned positive about how she feels about you."

"You also know how great I am at shutting out the people who matter most," Alec reminded him.

"Fortunately," his father said, "those also happen to be the people who love you the most. When Cordelia came to me, I nearly begged her to sit for me, nearly dragged my paints and canvases out of retirement just so I could paint the love in her eyes when she talked about you, when she said your name. Nothing could be more beautiful for a father than knowing that someone else loves his child as much as he does."

Alec's throat tightened up. "If she's willing to give me a chance, will you do me the honor of officiating at the wedding?"

His father nodded solemnly. "It would be the greatest joy of my life, son. The greatest one of all. Only..."

"What is it, Dad?" Alec looked at the numbers on the machines and the drip to see if anything seemed off. "Should I call the nurse? The doctor?"

He was about to press the call button when his father put a hand on his arm. "No, don't call anyone. I don't want them to make you leave before I finally get the chance to say something to you that I haven't been brave enough to say before."

After so many wasted years, Alec hated to waste another second. But his father had just come out of major surgery. "The nurses told me not to do or say anything that would upset you—"

"Forget the machines. My heart is strong enough for me to say this. It's time," his father said. "Now that you're finally here. Now that *I'm* finally here with you."

Alec took a deep breath. "I'm listening."

"I don't know if you remember, but your mother loved flying. Once we got in the air, she would always be so happy. Free from everything that weighed her down on the ground." When Alec shook his head, William said, "She loved to cook too. Do you remember that?"

Even if Alec had blocked out other things, how

could he forget that? "Of course I do. She's the one who taught me."

"She always marveled at what a quick learner you were. She said you not only made every dish better than she did, but that you had a knack for knowing exactly what was missing from a meal and what might overpower it." William squeezed his hand. "I know she hurt you, Alec, but I hope you know how much she loved you."

"I loved her too." But while Lynn Sullivan would never be able to hear Alec say the words, this was his chance to make sure his father did. "I love you, Dad."

"And I love you, Alec. I've always loved you. Even when I didn't show you. Even when I wasn't there for you."

"Dad—" This was everything Alec needed to hear, but he couldn't let his father make himself sick again. "You don't have to do this now."

William continued as if he hadn't spoken. "It's no excuse, but I saw so much of her in you. Only the good, beautiful parts of her. And yet, it was still too much for me. Every time I looked in your eyes, I saw Lynn. And I grieved all over again. So I disappeared." Tears rolled down William's cheeks. "I know you blamed me for her death. And you were right. I didn't know how to love anyone enough. Not her. Not you. I have so much to make up for, and I will. I promise you,

I will."

Alec instinctively put his arms around his father and hugged him in a way he hadn't since he was a little kid. "We both screwed up, Dad. But it doesn't matter what happened in the past, because we're both going to work like hell not to keep making the same mistakes in the future."

His father smiled through his tears. "I'm proud of you, son. So damned proud." He squeezed Alec's hands. "Tell your brothers and sister I'm ready for them to come in now. It's time for you to go and get the girl of your dreams."

CHAPTER TWENTY-EIGHT

Alec Sullivan was a changed man.

Cordelia knew it the moment he walked out of his father's hospital room. Whatever decision he'd made was so powerful, so big, that it almost felt as though it had caused a seismic shift in the earth's plates.

She smiled at the thought as she finished slicing a perfectly ripe tomato. She'd driven Alec back to her cottage and convinced him to sit in the garden with a glass of wine while she made him something to eat. Though it was morning now, heat was already rising up from the ground, and the air was scented with flowers. After so many hours inside the hospital, he needed to listen to the sounds of the ducks calling to each other in the nearby pond and to enjoy the light breeze rustling through the leaves of the maple tree beside her cottage.

She knew they had a lot to talk about, but she wanted to wait until both of them were able to think clearly again. Her mother had taught her that fresh food always helped, and she smiled at the sight of Alec in her garden as she walked out with a lantern and a plate of tomatoes drizzled with olive oil.

He speared a bite, then groaned with pleasure as he swallowed—the sound close enough to the ones he made in bed for her skin to heat up. "Swear to God, you must sprinkle some sort of magic potion over your plants, Cordelia. No tomato ever tasted this sweet. Here."

He held out the fork for her, and when their eyes locked as she bit into the tomato flesh, she wished it were his skin she was tasting instead. "It's good."

"Better than good." But he put the plate down and took her hands in his. "I don't know what I would have done without you. Thank you for being here. For being with me."

"You don't have to thank me for anything." Still, his appreciation made her warm all over. "I'm just glad William is going to be okay."

"When he woke up, we talked." She loved seeing the smile on Alec's face as he told her, "We talked about forgiving each other. About letting go of the past and starting over with each other. And we talked about you too."

"Me?" She was stunned. "Why?"

"He likes you. A lot." Alec grinned. "In fact, when you were at his house at Summer Lake, he was tempted to drag out his paints for the first time in thirty years, because he wanted to paint you."

"Me?" she said again, unable to get out more than that, even though she sounded like a broken record.

"He said he wanted to paint the look in your eyes."

"Which look?"

"*Love.*"

She felt her skin flush, knew her eyes had widened, knew she was giving everything away. But she couldn't stop herself, couldn't pretend to be just his friend. Not this morning, not after everything that had happened. But before she could say anything, Alec spoke again.

"That morning when the press were outside your cottage door and I suggested that we make the world think we were together to keep the fortune hunters away, you said you didn't want me to lie about my feelings for you. But the only person I was lying to was myself, Cordelia. Because I was already in love with you." He lifted his hands to her face and held her so gently, so sweetly. "I fell in love with you the first time I ever set eyes on you, standing outside my office building, so beautiful and brave." He lowered his forehead to hers. "You're the most magnificent, loving, sweet, *and* sexy woman I've ever known. And I love you. With all my heart."

She was so stunned, so choked up, so over-whelmed, that she couldn't do anything but press her lips to his in a kiss of pure, raw emotion. Finally, she found her voice. "I love you too. I fell in love with you when you were so kind, and then I fell even more in love with you when you took care of me in a way no one else could have. And when you touch me, when you kiss me, when you make love to me…" She had to kiss him again. "I never knew such pleasure was possible. Or that it can get even better and better every time."

"I don't know if I'll ever feel like I deserve your love," he confessed in a hoarse voice. "But I'm going to work like hell to earn it, every second of every day that we're together."

"You don't have to earn anything, Alec. I love you for all the things that you are—dark and light. Rough and gentle. And most of all, because you're a man who would do anything for his family, for his friends, even for a stranger who showed up in his office owning half of his company." She laughed softly. "Gordon must have known you were my other half. That's why he sent me to you."

"He almost told me about you, I realize that now." She was stunned silent as Alec told her, "We were drunk one night after a deal had gone bad, and he said he didn't regret losing the business. He said losing a few dollars was nothing compared to his biggest regret. Compared to his wasted chances. Compared to dreams and hopes that were lost forever. He asked me what my dreams were then, if planes were what I really wanted to do, if there was anything I was hiding from. Anything I was afraid of. I thought he was trying to get me to talk about my father, so I shut him down. Laughed off his talk of dreams and hopes and happiness, even though those were the very things I'd been hiding from for so long. But I don't want to hide anymore. When I'm with you, I know I don't have to."

And then, before she realized what was happening, he was down on one knee in the middle of her garden.

"I love you, Cordelia. I want to share all of your hopes, your dreams, your happiness—and I want to share all of mine with you too. With the family we're going to make together." He plucked a pink cosmos from the bed beside them and held it out to her. "Marry me and I promise I'll make you the happiest woman alive."

She dropped to her knees in the dirt and threw herself into his arms. "I already am."

EPILOGUE

It hadn't been easy for so many Sullivans to carve time out of their busy schedules to travel to New York for William's birthday party, but they'd all found a way to make it happen. Everyone's return to Cordelia's garden only a week later should have been impossible, but Alec's wedding was an event so epic that no one would have dreamed of missing it.

"The harder they resist," Cassie said so that only Harry could hear, "the harder they fall."

Harry couldn't deny his cousin's assessment. Alec was standing in front of the rose arbor, waiting for Cordelia to walk down the aisle, looking happier—and more in love—than Harry could ever have hoped for.

"They were meant to be together," he said to Cassie. "Cordelia is Alec's perfect match."

Everyone stood as "The Wedding March" began and Cordelia appeared on her father's arm in the garden looking radiant in a flowing, pale yellow gown, carrying a bouquet of pink cosmos, with an enormous smile on her face. No bride had ever looked more certain about the man she was marrying, and no groom had ever looked so grateful that she was his. As a bonus, last night at their rehearsal dinner, they'd told everyone that they would now be working together on the new restaurant at Langley Garden Center.

Cordelia was only two-thirds of the way up the aisle when Alec headed down to grab her and kiss her as though he'd wouldn't survive if he didn't have her in his arms that very second. The crowd whistled and clapped with obvious approval.

When Alec finally let her go, Cordelia's smile was even bigger than it had been walking down the aisle. Clasping each other's hands, they made their way to their spot in front of Harry's father. Walter, still grinning, kissed his daughter and took his seat in the front row beside his wife.

"Family, friends," William began, "we're gathered here today to celebrate the love between two very special people. Cordelia Langley is the woman every father dreams of for a daughter-in-law. And Alec..." Harry's father looked too choked up to speak for a moment. "You'll never know how much I respect you, son. How much I cherish you. How much I love you."

Alec reached out to put his hand on his father's shoulder and William's shook slightly as he covered it, holding on for a long moment. Alec had shared with Harry, Suzanne, and Drake some of his discussion with their father in the hospital room, enough for Harry to know that major bridges had been built—and were getting stronger every day.

William cleared his throat. "Cordelia and Alec have prepared their vows. Please," he said, "whenever you're ready." He took the flowers from Cordelia, then moved a step back to give them the full spotlight.

Cordelia turned to face Alec, putting both of her hands in his. "The day we met," she said in a clear and steady voice, "the last thing on my mind was love. I felt lost and confused, hurt and angry. But every moment—every single day and every night—you were kind. Sweet. Helpful. Caring. The knight in shining armor I swore I didn't want, one I was convinced my birth father had foisted on me against my will. But it turns out Gordon Whitley was a very wise man, because he must have known all along that I couldn't live without you and that we belonged together." She moved closer so that she could hold Alec's hands against her heart. "All my life, I've waited patiently for things to grow. But my love for you bloomed in an instant...and I know it will keep growing bigger and bigger forever."

All around Harry, people were sniffling. He was more than a little choked up himself, although what really got him was realizing that his father was crying tears of joy. For so long, all of them had wanted the dark clouds around Alec to disappear. Thankfully, just as Cordelia had said in her vows, Gordon must have known she would be able to reach him in a way that no one else could have.

"You say I'm your knight in shining armor," Alec said in a deep voice that brimmed with emotion, "but don't you know? You're *my* knight in shining armor, Cordelia. You're the only woman in the world who could have reached in and touched my heart. You're the only woman who has ever made my palms sweat, my heart race. Every time I look at you—every time I so much as think about you—I can't keep from smiling. I want to thank your parents—Amy, Walter, *and* Gordon too—for trusting me with your life. With your happiness. And you most of all, Cordelia, for seeing something in me that I wasn't able to see in myself until you loved me. I'll forever be amazed that you believe I'm worthy of you. I swear I'm going to prove to you every single day for the rest of our lives that you chose the right man to love."

There wasn't a dry eye in the house as William stepped forward. "It is the greatest honor of my life to pronounce you husband and wife. Alec, Cordelia, you may now seal your vows with a kiss."

The way they looked at each other as they moved into each other's arms was so intimate that Harry almost felt as though he were intruding by watching.

And when Alec lowered his mouth to Cordelia's, Harry knew their kiss was as much a vow of forever as the words they had spoken.

Everyone was on their feet applauding as Cordelia and Alec made their way back down the aisle. Baskets of flower petals had been placed at the end of each row, and the very happy couple laughed as the fragrant, colorful petals rained down upon them.

"Do you really think that?" Cassie asked Harry as they headed over to congratulate the happy couple.

"Think what?"

"What you said before they said their vows—that everyone has a perfect match?"

A picture instantly came to Harry's mind. One he shook away. This was a day to celebrate, not to get lost in thoughts about the past.

"Sure, don't you?"

"The way my luck in love has gone," Cassie said, "I'm honestly not sure anymore."

Harry put his arm around her shoulders. "Maybe we can fix that today," he suggested. "Any wedding guests catch your eye?"

"One happy ending at a time, Harry. And given the way this family does things," she said as she grabbed two champagne glasses from a passing waiter and handed him one, "we all know yours is next."

Before he could reply, she clinked her glass against

his, then headed off to congratulate the bride and groom. Leaving Harry thinking about happy endings...and whether Cassie was right and his actually *was* next.

Anything was possible, he supposed. After all, Alec and Cordelia had just proved that in spades. From across the garden, he raised his glass to the happy couple in a silent toast to true love prevailing yet again.

★ ★ ★ ★ ★

For news on Bella Andre's upcoming books, sign up for Bella Andre's New Release Newsletter:

BellaAndre.com / Newsletter

ABOUT THE AUTHOR

Having sold more than 6 million books, Bella Andre's novels have been #1 bestsellers around the world and have appeared on the *New York Times* and *USA Today* bestseller lists 62 times. She has been the #1 Ranked Author on a top 10 list that included Nora Roberts, JK Rowling, James Patterson and Steven King, and Publishers Weekly named Oak Press (the publishing company she created to publish her own books) the Fastest-Growing Independent Publisher in the US. After signing a groundbreaking 7-figure print-only deal with Harlequin MIRA, Bella's "The Sullivans" series has been released in paperback in the US, Canada, and Australia.

Known for "sensual, empowered stories enveloped in heady romance" (Publishers Weekly), her books have been Cosmopolitan Magazine "Red Hot Reads" twice and have been translated into ten languages. Winner of the Award of Excellence, The Washington Post called her "One of the top writers in America" and she has been featured by Entertainment Weekly, NPR, USA Today, Forbes, The Wall Street Journal, and TIME Magazine. A graduate of Stanford University, she has given keynote speeches at publishing conferences from Copenhagen to Berlin to San Francisco, including a standing-room-only keynote at Book Expo America in New York City.

Bella also writes the *New York Times* bestselling "Four Weddings and a Fiasco" series as Lucy Kevin. Her sweet contemporary romances also include the USA Today bestselling Walker Island series written as Lucy Kevin.

If not behind her computer, you can find her reading her favorite authors, hiking, swimming or laughing. Married with two children, Bella splits her time between the Northern California wine country and a 100 year old log cabin in the Adirondacks.

For a complete listing of books, as well as excerpts and contests, and to connect with Bella:

Sign up for Bella's newsletter:
BellaAndre.com/Newsletter

Visit Bella's website at:
www.BellaAndre.com

Follow Bella on Twitter at:
twitter.com/bellaandre

Join Bella on Facebook at:
facebook.com/bellaandrefans

Follow Bella on Instagram:
instagram.com/bellaandrebooks

49318400R00208

Made in the USA
Middletown, DE
13 October 2017